CITY OF BLOOD AND FIRE

A WAR OF BANES AND DEMONS
BOOK FIVE

KEVIN HARKNESS

SHOUTING ROOM BOOKS

CITY OF BLOOD AND FIRE

To my family for putting up with my obsession. To my friends for humouring me. To my editor, Sophie Playle of Liminal Pages, for her patience. To imaginary worlds. To ideas that come out of nowhere. To all the old stories, and to all the new ones.

Also by Kevin Harkness

A War of Banes and Demons Series:

City of Demons (Book 1)

City of Masks (Book 2)

City of Sand (Book 3)

City of Shadows (Book 4)

DRAGON ISLANDS
Shakin Bay
THE FAR NORTH
Ice Harbour
Lakeside
Forest Edge
Itaalk Valley
THE NORTH
North Ar
Bangt
Three Roads
THE MIDLANDS
Hilly's Farm
Solantor
Terrich
Shirath
Akalit
River Ar
Old Torrick
Illick
South Ar
THE SOUTH
Ruins
Old Carving Well
THE FINGERS
THE FAR SOUTH
City of Fountains
Mother of Waters
BAY OF TEARS
THE FAR FAR SOUTH

CONTENTS

CHAPTER I

HEROES AND VILLAINS

The demonbane crept forward, one hand playing out the length of his weapon, a rope weighted on one end by a pick-hammer and on the other by a spiked ball. He scowled at his prey, a wavering, dancing image, a creature more shadow than substance. It hissed, and long claws reached out. A short beak split open to show rows of nail-like teeth. The man scowled and swung the heavy ball, slowly at first but picking up speed until the weight was a blur and the air sung as the weapon spun above his head. Suddenly, he flung it at the shadow creature. There was a ripping sound, and the terrifying image disappeared.

The audience cheered. Some stood up from their benches and applauded the scene. The bane came to the front of the stage and spoke, one hand laid upon his chest.

"Now the beast, with blinded eye, its servant killed, must flee or die. Yet in those shadows did I spy, a fire in that other eye? I fear the beast will soon return, for in that orb, a rage did burn."

"Marick!" a girl of perhaps sixteen years shouted over

the renewed applause. She ran off-stage, crouching down to hide behind the painted wood scenery. In one hand, she dragged a ruined paper demon.

A young man came over to pull her to the back of the platform. The prop fluttered behind her, and he used his walking stick to knock it down.

"Shhh!" he said. "They'll hear you, Son-neen. What's wrong this time? You're much better at playing the monster. I saw a man in the front row almost faint when you waved it around."

The girl glared at Marick and pointed to where her thick black hair was somewhat mussed.

"He almost hit me. Again! I told you to make him practise more."

The offending actor came around the back of the stage from the other side, hidden by curtains that hung from temporary supports. Those backdrops and all the rest were fragile things; torn by the wind, soaked – as much as the audience – in a rain, even subject to fire from the lamps and torches that provided light; but this was the traditional way a play was presented in the city of Shirath, at night, out in the open, and in the middle of the Palace Plaza.

The curtains survived the actor's careless passage. This young man was older than the other two, much taller, and very handsome, even with the thick coating of blue and white paint on his face.

"That went well," he said. "But Son-neen, you have to make that demon jiggle more or they'll never see me as a hero."

Marick sighed and straightened the strip of gold cloth that lay across the actor's chest.

"This sash, Toonan, the paint on your face, and my excellent writing says you're a hero. And please watch Son-neen's head or you'll be fighting thin air in the next perfor-mance and I'll have you made up like a clown! Now go, get ready. The next scene needs to start."

The younger man walked over to a stool, limping slightly, and sat down. Son-neen handed him a cup of tea, poured from a pot over a brazier kept as far as possible from the curtains. The winter was almost over but the evenings were still cold, so a hot drink was very welcome. Marick sipped and looked up at his business partner.

"What was the profit tonight?" he asked and smiled when Son-neen's eyes lit up.

"We took donations after the clowns and dances. That, plus the king's subsidy, minus salaries and the cost of props." Here she used a toe to nudge the paper demon, a painted image stretched on a reed frame that moved at the joints. It fell over the side of the platform to lie upon a pile of such pretend monsters. "We cleared six silvers and twenty-three coppers, by Shirath count. Slightly more in real coin."

By this, she meant by the counting of her own home, the City of Fountains far to the south, against which she measured all success, culture, manners, and common sense. She offered the account book to Marick, who shook his head.

"That's your job, not mine. I write the plays, serve as ambassador to the audience, and choose the actors. You calculate and wave pretend demons – and dodge Toonan's enthusiastic acting! Just be glad that rope-hammer is painted wood, not Garet's iron monstrosity."

"Garet the Hero," Son-neen said. "You'd think no one would come and see such a stupid story when they could be doing something useful, but the seats are full every night."

"Those seats were a good idea, weren't they? People

used to stand for hours to watch a play. Now they have benches to rest on while we fill their eyes and ears."

Son-neen nodded. "The other change you made, they seem to like that too."

Marick laughed, quietly, for the scenery was almost changed. He stood up, and the girl draped a long silver cloak over his shoulders. "Toonan and the other actors didn't like it much," he said. "Talking in a play? You think I'd asked them to fight a real demon! Well, I agreed with Dorict on this, Heaven shield me! We needed more than just jumping around and pantomime to tell these stories. Besides, I let them keep the makeup."

On a Shirath stage, heroes, villains, and clowns each wore special colours on their face, so the audience always knew who to cheer and who to hate.

Son-neen snorted. "Ha! Their faces look as silly as their clothes."

The girl had a long-standing complaint about the colourful way people dressed in this city. Her own town used bright colours for their houses and wore dull shades themselves, more fitting to a people both fiercely proud of their town and numbingly serious about their work. The only reason she had volunteered to wave the demon model was because she could wear all black and hide behind the fake shrubbery.

Marick settled the shiny cloak more comfortably around his shoulders. "Since you only take the money and they give it, I'd say the audience's opinion matters more than yours."

He limped out upon the stage, and the crowd erupted into applause again, slapping one hand on the back of the other. The young man held up his walking stick, and several people nearest to the stage *oohed* and *aahed*. The head of the stick was not the common ball of wood or curved handle, but a demon's head, carved in silver, the crests sweeping back to form the grip and the mouth opened in a snarl.

"Good people of Shirath," Marick shouted, his voice deeper than it had been a season ago. This last year had been full of changes for the one-time demonbane. He had lost friends and regained them, made new ones, learned to walk on a wood-and-brass leg, and written several plays that his fellow citizens seemed to like. He had also grown an inch; a fact he was prouder of than anything else.

"Brothers and sisters of this great city, we now go forward in time, to when the heroes, Garet and Salick, fight the Duellists upon the Centre Bridge, defending that symbol of our united city against those who wished to tear it apart. I give you, the Duellists!"

Two actors slunk onto the stage, rapiers in hand and shaking their fists at the rising hiss from the crowd. Several people threw stale buns and wrinkled apples at them, and the two made a great show of knocking them aside with their swords. Marick raised his stick again, and the audience's cries subsided.

One of the two actors, a thin man with a pointed beard jutting from his red and black makeup, swished his sword about and spoke.

"Salick's my cousin, but I'll not stay my blade. The banes must all pay for the mess that they made. We'll deal with them first, and next with the king. Now see what sweet chaos our efforts will bring."

The actors pulled scarves up over their faces and retreated to the side of the stage.

Marick moved forward, pushing aside half apples and pieces of bread with the tip of his stick.

"Such villainy! But our heroes faced them, arm for arm, steel for steel."

He bowed and retreated to the shadow of the curtains. As he left the stage, two more actors entered opposite. One was Toonan with his rope-hammer, the other a woman bearing a trident. Both wore the uniform of Shirath's demonbanes: black boots and trousers, a grey long-sleeved shirt, and a purple vest – and each had a coloured sash draped across their chest.

The crowd cheered again then quieted as the two made ready to speak. The woman spoke first.

"I fear for the banehall after seeing that show. Now let us return, for our master must know, how the king and the Duellists muddy our names, with rumours and plays and Shoronict's foul games."

Toonan laid a dramatic hand on her shoulder and answered in big, round tones.

"Salick, my love, do not weep for our fate. The master will save us from the sword-wielder's hate. The king must be warned their ambitions are bold, but who can get near him so he can be told?"

The two villains jumped out, and, after poetic insults, a grand fight began among the four. All the actors were agile, and the ringing of swords against trident and pick-hammer made a harsh music. Near misses brought gasps, and a hero's desperate counter raised cheers from the watchers.

Two such observers lingered at the back of the crowd, standing with those too late to find seats. They wore leather coats, hooded and fur-lined, almost too warm for the night. This earned them a few odd looks when they had joined the audience, but not for long, for the play was wonderful and there were many strangers in the city these days.

The two looked at each other. One, a young woman,

said to the other, a young man, "I don't remember Draneck being so well-spoken, do you?"

The other shook his head. "No, he wasn't. There was a lot more spitting and grunting than words, if I recall the scene as it really happened, and the sashes are all wrong. Shall we have a word with the writer?"

"Yes," the woman said. "Let's, but watch to the end first."

The other rolled his eyes but stayed by her side. In the finale, when an older actor, using a shield on one arm and letting the other hang by his side, killed a paper demon and then collapsed in his own theatrical death on the stage, the young man put his arm around the trembling shoulders of the woman.

"Claw him," she said. "He should know better than to make Master Mandarack's death into cheap entertainment."

The two skirted the audience while Marick and the actors took their bows. They were waiting for him when he came back to his stool with Son-neen trailing behind, carrying the last tattered monster.

"Sorry," the girl said, dumping the prop over the side to join the other. Several children grabbed it and ran off, yelling and waving it in an enthusiastic retelling of the scene just played. "We don't need more actors, or investors, or anything. Go away."

Toonan came up, glowing from the approval of the audience.

The young man in the fur cloak pointed at the actor and said, "I just have a question about him."

He pulled back his hood, and the young woman did the same. The man was dark-skinned, his black hair grown below his shoulders and a patchy beard covering his cheeks and chin. The woman was blond, with piercing eyes, which now drilled into Marick.

"Salick! Garet!" the boy said and grabbed them both in an embrace. "You're back! This is wonderful, but why such looks? Don't be mad, the king approved this and all my other plays. Branet did too, though he wasn't happy about it, so stop glaring at me."

Son-neen came closer to peer at the two.

"These two are the ones you and Dorict talk about so much? They don't look very heroic."

Garet frowned at the girl. "That's my point! How could you think *he* even looks like *me*?"

Son-neen looked from Garet to Toonan and back again. She scratched an ear before answering. "I see what you mean. You're too short."

The explosion that followed came mainly from Salick, and it took some time for Marick to calm them all, explain who Son-neen was, shoo away the curious actors, and get the others cups of tea. They sat on bits of scenery while labourers stacked the benches and cleaned up.

"When did you come back?" Marick asked. "I'm not a bane anymore, in case you missed that, so I don't get the news as quickly as I used to."

Garet snorted. "I doubt that, but we just came in as night fell, so we're ahead of the news. No doubt everyone will know by dawn. We went to the hall and spoke to Master Chovan. She fed us and sent us on to the palace since Branet is already there."

Salick nodded. "We were on our way to report when we were . . . distracted by this horrible display of lies and exaggeration," she said, eyeing the guilty party.

Marick waved the comment away. "Oh, Salick! The same stiff bane I remember from my youth. Listen, my skill is in the proper telling of a story, and each tale needs a dash of, well, lies to tell the truth at its centre. Besides, as the best playwriter in the city, why should I limit my talent to dull reality?"

"You were a better bane then you are a writer," she said.

At that, Marick reddened. "Not always, but that's another tale." He leaned forward. "Salick, the city needs these stories. If you talked to Chovan, you know we're expecting the demons to attack from the north within a few ten-days. Our people need courage and sacrifice poured into their hearts so they can spit it out again when that happens. To lie in that cause is an honour, isn't it?"

Garet smiled. "The same scheming Marick I remember so fondly from my youth! What happened to your leg? Was it that old arrow wound the Masks gave you? I suppose you have to wear a brace like Master Tarix now."

Marick smiled and hit the limb with his stick. This produced a dull, hollow sound, not of struck flesh but of wood and brass.

"Oh, I left it somewhere in the desert," he said, waving the matter away with his other hand. "Now, are you two married yet? I'm sure you have stories to tell."

"No!" Salick said, reddening, but with her eyes fixed on his leg. Hidden by trousers and boot, she could not have guessed the nature of his wound. She began to speak but was stopped by the return of the Marick's energetic partner.

"Go!" Son-neen said, waving her arms at all three of them. "Tell your tales somewhere else, for we still have work to do here. Marick, you go to the palace with them. You're no good for ordinary work anyway, and there's still a lot to be done before we're ready for tomorrow's play. What is it, anyhow?"

"*The Battle of the Bridge*," Marick said, and stood up. "You two are heroes in that as well. If you want to see it, I can promise you good seats."

Salick started and looked up from his leg. "Claw you, Marick," she began, then gathered him in a hug. Garet threw arms around them both. The boy wriggled free and almost fell, save for Son-neen's help.

Salick's cheeks were wet. She glared, but the tears kept coming.

"Your leg! But Marick, how could you? You put Master Mandarack's death up there for everyone to gawk at? He was your master too!"

Son-neen steadied Marick then turned on the banes. "Why not? That's the best part of the play. Did you see how many people wept when Mandarack dies? Everyone! Marick even cried when he wrote it!"

She walked over to stand in front of Salick and grasp her hand.

"Look, if he made a play about when the slavers attacked my city and it showed my father dying – because he did – I'd cry too, and if I saw it a hundred times, I'd cry a hundred times. But I'd be glad too, because everyone who watched would know what he did for his neighbours, and they'd know his name was part of the City of Fountains forever. That's what these people see about your Mandarack."

"*Master* Mandarack," Salick said. "And they should have known it already."

"Master Mandarack," Son-neen said, nodding her head and briskly patting Salick's hand.

Garet looked from the girl to the boy.

"Maybe you should have come north with us, Marick. It would have kept you out of this trouble, at least."

Son-neen scoffed. "Hah!" She bent over to pick up his walking stick. "Then he would never have met me, and I've done him more good than that leg ever did. Here, take this and go with them so I can work in peace. Toonan, don't sneak off. There're props to store, and we have to make a lot of demons for tomorrow."

The three others climbed down from the platform, Marick rejecting any help in the matter. He lowered himself carefully and straightened his coat.

"Let's go then. I haven't seen the king in some time; he's very busy these days and doesn't watch many plays, though the people love it when he does attend with the queen. He's become more of a hero than you two, despite my best efforts."

"Well, you can end those efforts now," Garet said. "I'm not happy you've made me into a paper hero."

"It's the demons that are paper," Marick said. "The actors are just good looking and loud. What did you think of Meesa, the one who plays you, Salick?"

"She's too old and too . . . rounded in the front," the bane said. She pulled the coat tighter around her frame as if to emphasize a slim, athletic build that a season and more of travel in the North had only made stronger.

The last of the crowds passed, many stopping to congratulate Marick and look briefly at the shadowed faces of his companions. Now the Palace Plaza was almost empty, save for two guard patrols that marched in opposite directions around the great open space. Beyond the semicircle of the plaza's walls was another set of walls, magnified, that enclosed the wards of the north side of the city, and all that was mirrored across the River Ar by the other eight of Shirath's sixteen wards. Together, those two halves made one grand city, river-split but joined by three bridges and a looming threat of war.

"Looks like Trax is keeping everybody up tonight," Marick said. He pointed across the plaza to the windows of the palace shining in the dark. Another squad of guards stood by the front door, and more stood at the magnificent building's corners.

"That's good," Salick said. "Better to give our news to many people once than over and over to a few."

Marick shook his head. "It will be bad news, I'll bet. We've had no good news about the demons since Kaela and Shula caught all of Lord, sorry, *ex*-Lord Tiralsh's spies. The ones she didn't take with her, anyway."

Garet looked at him, puzzled. "What does Lord Tiralsh – she's from the Trader's ward, isn't she? – what does she have to do with demons?"

Marick blew out a long breath. "Walk slowly, and I'll tell you all I know," he said and smiled slyly. "So at least you won't look like some ignorant farm boy just come from the Midlands."

Garet smiled, having been that boy only a couple of years before. He tousled the blond hair on Marick's head, surprised to find it higher than when they'd last seen each other.

"Tell us quickly," he said. "Or we'll have to walk back and forth like those guards to make up the time."

Marick gathered his thoughts.

"Well first, it turns out that Lord Tiralsh had something to do with Gost's rebellion and the formation of the Masks. Her son, Tarock, was following her orders while she kept her own dainty hands clean. Did you know she bought his freedom after he was caught?"

Salick nodded. "Word reached us in Solantor before they let us leave the city to go north."

"A bad idea, to let coin pay for treason," Marick said. "And we bled for it. After you two left, the demons started making very specific attacks, ones meant to weaken the city as a whole. They even attacked the bridges."

Salick shook her head. "Losing them would have hurt us badly. How could the banehall respond to an attack on the palace side if we couldn't cross the Ar?"

Marick rang the tip of his stick on the plaza's paving stones. "Too true! And, to add to the misery, Tiralsh and her followers poisoned food meant for the banes in a ward's small hall, wrecked arrow-throwers, even tried to kill Allifur and Corfin. Don't worry. They're both all right – and Blue Sashes, Heaven shield us! They got caught up in the mess when Dalesta found a fancy handkerchief of all things and asked the two of them to return it while she went with Tarix into the forest. The pair of them wheedled me into helping find out who it belonged to. Well, no good deed goes unpunished, they say. That scrap of silk belonged to Tiralsh and was proof she had conspired with Lord Sacourat of the Fifth Ward to help the demon masters damage the city's defences." He took a deep breath and grinned at the travellers.

"And that," he added, "is not a tenth of what's happened since you left!"

Garet frowned. "I don't know Tiralsh at all, but I've met Lord Sacourat. I hope she's in a cold dark cell by now!"

Marick shrugged. "You'd have to ask Heaven that, since Tiralsh killed her before she escaped. Cutting off a loose thread, no doubt. We think the traitor's gone to join her masters in the northern forest."

He tilted his head and regarded his friends. "I don't suppose you ran into her, did you?"

Salick flicked him a look. "We'll tell our stories later. What else do we need to know before we see the king? Go on, unless you need a good shaking to continue."

Marick sighed. "I missed your gentle spirit, Salick. Let's see, Tiralsh had more than just brutes wielding bows and poison. She had demons hidden in a silkstone room beneath her house, and powders that could put them to sleep and wake them to do whatever mischief she wanted."

"Claws! This is true, not one of your exaggerations?" Salick demanded, stopping to grasp Marick by the arm.

"I swear it by Heaven's dome," Marick said. "I saw it firsthand, along with Allifur. Tiralsh threw us inside that room to be eaten by the demons when they woke. Luckily, we managed to escape."

"How?" Garet asked, rather suspiciously.

One of the passing guards called out to Marick, and he waved in return.

"That's Cirta, one of Bixa's lieutenants. I should put him in a new play I'm writing. It's about Tiralsh's treachery. As to how we escaped, talk to Allifur. It was her brilliant plan that saved us. For myself, I will only say that being inside a demon is not as final as we were led to believe."

He pulled his arm free and tapped his cane again on the stone paving.

"Now, we're almost there, so here's what you really need to know: that little toad Tarock was captured again by Master Tarix and her team. They went into the forest and found a hidden road that went north, and he was on it, along with some truly horrific beasts and at least one of their masters. That one died – accidently killed by Dalesta in defence of Tarix. Bad luck that, though she caught Tarock to make up for it. By clever questioning, Trax got Tarock to tell how his mother was supposed to keep using demons and other tricks to weaken the city until the spring equinox, which fast approaches."

Garet tried to take this all in and match it to what they had found even farther north.

"And what happens then?" he asked, more to himself than to Marick, but the other answered.

"Trax thinks they will attack in force, another army but bigger than the one we fought before. Hallmaster Branet and Captain Bixa have doubts, since we beat the first army. They think the demon masters would not be so foolish as to try the same trick twice."

"What do you think?" Salick asked.

Marick grinned and looked up to appreciate the glory of the palace, its fine windows, gilt accents, and decorative guards.

"Me? I think foolishness is more common than fear, and more dangerous, at least to us," he said, and waved the two ahead.

They stepped into the pool of light cast by the lamps above the palace door. The guards all wore silkstone helmets – protection from the aura of fear that was a demon's nature – and held out levelled pikes.

"Who's that with you, Marick?" one asked. She stepped forward to get a better look.

"It seems you're famous, playwriter," Salick said, pulling back her hood, "but we appear to be forgotten. Maybe we should have painted our faces! Guard, we come to see Hallmaster Branet and the king. And though I don't look like the prancing wench who plays me, I am Salick and this is Garet."

"Heaven shield us!" the guard said.

THE KING LOOKED TIRED. Dark shadows lay under his eyes, and his welcome was not as enthusiastic, or even as polite, as Garet had expected.

"You're back then," Trax said. He waved them to chairs and left the more animated greetings to others in the room.

"It's good to see you safe and returned to us," Master Tarix said. She hugged Salick and then Garet.

Branet clapped a large hand on their shoulders. "It is good, very good, especially if you bring us better news than we've had all winter."

Bixa, the captain of the guards, added her own greetings. "News or not, king's agent, I'm glad to have you back, and Shula will be too," she added, naming the head of Trax's spies.

"Sit down," the captain added. "We'll bring more food, if you're hungry, and wine in any case." She signalled the nearest steward, and the man left to get more plates.

"We ate a bit at the hall," Salick said, "but a season of travel keeps you hungry. Your arm, Bixa, is it at all improved?"

The guard captain took her left arm out of its sling and carefully moved it in a circle, flexing her fingers and rotating the wrist. "As you can see, much painful work by the physicians has helped, but I'll never bear a shield or bow again. Enough of that. You two seem unharmed, though by your looks, something weighs heavily on you."

"Aside from Marick's wretched play, you mean?" Garet said and gave the writer a mocking glance. The target of his jibe smiled and took a chair against the wall. Garet turned back to Bixa. "But yes, we have seen much, and have much to tell."

He looked to Trax, but the king was studying a model of the city that sat upon the great table in the centre of the room. It was made of wood and plaster, and as far as Garet could see, was accurate down to the last block of tenements and the number of gates that pierced the outer walls.

"Your Majesty," Garet said, and Trax looked up, frowning.

"Yes?" he said, clearly annoyed, then his features cleared, and he managed a smile. "Sorry, Garet, I'm occupied by the dire possibilities of the next days. It would be helpful if you could narrow them down to a single calamity."

Garet and Salick looked at each other, then at the hall-master, who nodded for them to speak. It was Salick who broke the silence.

"We have seen the place where the demons are made by a people called the Itaalk. It was very . . . disturbing."

Bixa nodded. "Claws!" she said. "So, some of what Tarock told us is proven true. Demons aren't natural horrors but formed out of . . . what? He was not clear on that point, no matter how much he gibbered."

"Animals," Garet said. "At first, and probably for the last six hundred years. That is why they vary so much in size and shape, we think."

"At first?" Trax asked. He poured wine for himself and sipped at it steadily. The steward returned with laden plates and put them within reach of the banes. For now, the two let them be.

Salick shuddered. "We found something, in caves hidden within a valley in the northern forest," she said. "Many stone boxes that held human bodies, not dead, and not really human anymore. A demon jewel had been cut

into their foreheads. It was changing them, making them
... demon-like."

Bixa looked at Trax. "The 'new type' of beast Tarock
spoke of. Human demons! Heaven shield us, you saw this
with your own eyes or just heard tell of it?"

"Saw it," Garet said. "We snuck into one of the cham-
bers and opened a coffin – that's what they call boxes like
that in places where they bury their dead instead of burn
them. There was a woman in it, or at least she had been a
woman. We'd met her in a place called Lakeside Town."

The guard captain looked from Garet to Salick and back
again. "And she was turning into a demon?"

Salick nodded. "Yes," she said. "She already had a
demon's beak and teeth, as well as the beginnings of skull
crests and the blue and red colour of the beasts. Even her
eyes ..." She shuddered.

"How many?" Trax demanded, his eyes fixed on Salick.

Branet leaned forward, fists upon his knees and staring
just as intently as the king.

Master Tarix laid a hand on Salick's arm and said, "Go
ahead, tell us."

The bane swallowed. "Hundreds," she said. "At the
least. Maybe a thousand or more. We used the distance
viewer Lord Andarack gave us to look into the other caves
from the safety of the valley's rim. There were many cham-
bers, and most held at least two hundred boxes. We
couldn't tell if all of them were full, occupied, I mean, but if
they were ..."

There was silence for some time, and the two banes
took the opportunity to eat some of the food on their plates.
They had travelled far in difficult conditions and had
missed many meals in their rush back to tell their dreadful
news. The king stared at the model in front of him, and

then suddenly stood. He swept away a pile of papers, and the others watched the pages fly across the Shouting Room to pile like leaves at the feet of the unmoving stewards.

"Not sneak attacks then, Bixa! Nor a blockade to starve us out, Branet! Claws, we've wasted too much time on those chances. It's to be a war, like in the old days before there were cities, when petty lords who styled themselves kings would fight to survive – and destroy their neighbours."

He picked up the remaining papers, crumpling them in a clenched fist.

"Now all our plans are useless, unless we can come up with a plan to defend the city against, what did you call them, 'Human demons?' If we can't find a way to defend the entire wall from thousands of them at once, we'll die, each and every one of us."

He dropped the papers to the floor and glared at his guests. "Please excuse me, for the queen wished to see me before this night turns to day."

He walked from the room, followed by half the stewards. The rest began to pick up papers and stack them neatly back on the table.

Branet sighed. "Don't blame him for his nerves. I have them myself, and now you two have stretched them to the breaking point with your news! How do these Itaalk, these forest dwellers Tarock told us of, get their clawed hands on demon jewels in the first place? Is it some magic they have to make them out of nothing?"

Garet swallowed before answering. "Not magic, unless you count dragons as magical creatures to begin with."

Branet's brow furrowed, and he growled, "Dragons? Don't we have enough to deal with already? Must we fight dragons too?"

Salick looked down at the plate of food in front of her. "No, the dragons aren't our enemies," she said. "Though they are a danger in the North. I . . . talked to one. It spoke in my mind, with images that led us to that Itaalk valley. Hallmaster, this is the strangest truth we found in our travels: demon jewels aren't a natural part of a demon, or even things made by the Itaalk. The jewels are dragon eggs."

Tarix breathed out, a whoosh of sound. "Whew!" she said and leaned back in her chair. "Eggs? But there have been thousands, no, tens of thousands of demons attacking us over the centuries, and that's just for Shirath! Dragons must breed like flies to make so many jewels. I mean eggs!"

Garet smiled. "Not really. One dragon does lay many clutches, but that's because they have to. Believe it or not, it takes the hundreds of eggs in a single nest to make up one dragon." The incomprehension on the faces of his listeners made him hurry on. "Listen, when we first saw a dragon, coming to burn a town in the North because its eggs had been stolen, it seemed like a flock of birds, all moving together but made up of individual fliers. Then it came together. It formed into a huge winged beast and began to burn the town. It didn't breathe out fire like the songs say but gave off heat the way demons give off fear. When the parts merged, Salick and I both saw that its head looked like a demon's."

Salick looked up at the hallmaster and said, "Demon bodies might be different, but we all know they have the same type of head. The leathery beak, the skull crests, and those dead eyes – the dragon had them all."

Garet took up the tale again. "We lived through the attack by hiding in a stone building with the townsfolk and getting half drowned in buckets of water. That refuge survived, but the rest of the town was destroyed. We followed the dragon north to where the sea Itaalk live, then came upon, well . . . came upon my father."

"Your father?" Tarix said, her mouth dropping open. "That must have been hard! You've spoken of him as a violent brute, and so did Mandarack. Claws! Well, how did that reunion go?"

Since Garet seemed unlikely to answer, Salick spoke instead.

"As well as could be expected, I suppose. He'd changed from what he once was, and he had found some peace living by the Northern Ocean, with an Itaalk woman named Barla." She held up a hand at Branet's frown. "I know the forest Itaalk are our enemy, but the sea Itaalk are very different from their cousins. The ones who live farther north think of dragons as we think of Heaven, maybe, and hate the Dragon Brigades that hunt them and steal their eggs. Some of the sea Itaalk can see visions in the lights the dragons make in the northern sky, like how our astrologers see the future in Heaven's dome. There's something to it, maybe. Barla said she saw us coming a long time before we arrived."

"Did you see these lights?" Bixa asked. "It would be useful if we knew what was going to happen."

Salick shook her head. "We did watch them, but I think without training you are . . . overwhelmed by a torrent of images. It's not always the future you see. I saw a picture of Marick, wounded."

She turned to where the young man sat uncharacteristically silent against the wall. His eyes were wide.

"You saw?" he asked.

Salick nodded. "I did, though the nature of the wound was not clear. Barla was better at it; she could make some meaning out of what she saw. She was the one who took us to see the lights, and then to meet a dragon. The brigades had hunted down most of the ones on the mainland shore, so we had to travel to an island to find it. Like I said, I talked to the dragon, more with images and emotions than with words, and it showed me that valley. It was very angry about the place."

Tarix looked at her. "It must have been strange to converse that way. And you found the valley after that?"

"Claws, after that vision, I was like an arrow aimed straight at it! The journey there wasn't easy though. We found a lot of evil on the way. Lakeside Town was empty, the people taken by the Dragon Brigades to be made into demons. We even saw children taken!"

Tarix looked at Branet. "Now Vinir's tale of slavers coming north through the desert makes more sense."

Marick leaned forward and said, "They weren't just tales, Master. Remember, I was captured by those slavers and brought north. Those pieces of scum brought humans and animals to trade to these Itaalk, more raw material for their demon-making!"

"Claws and teeth!" Tarix said. "So much news and all of it bad. I wish Relict was here to hear this. It would give strength to his arguments in the other cities."

The hallmaster shrugged. "Only for those willing to listen. Some would be deaf to any truth we tell them!"

"Where is Master Relict?" Salick asked, looking around the Room of Harmonious Discussion, better known as the Shouting Room. She remembered Tarix's husband was the city's travelling diplomat of late, going twice to Solantor on fruitless missions to get help in this demon war.

"He's looking for allies," Branet said, and then waved the topic away. "Maybe it's just as well he doesn't have this bit of news. Who would believe that demon jewels come from dragons?" He held up a hand at their protests. "Don't mistake me. I believe you. It's just that, well, I suppose I'd always thought that the jewels were some kind of Heaven-cursed magic that the demons made themselves."

Salick nodded. "So did we, Hallmaster," she said, and grimaced. "But we saw what we saw in those stone boxes."

Garet searched in his pockets until he found something, a small stone carving of a winged creature. He put it on the table.

"This is a dragon," he said. "My father told me to show it to you."

"It's fine work," Tarix said. And it was, a delicate silk-stone statue no bigger than her palm that seemed ready to jump off the table and fly away.

Branet bent over to peer at it, and Marick came forward for a better look. Even the stewards, whose impassivity had been sorely tried, stole glances.

"A strange creature," the hallmaster said. "Especially if it is so many creatures at once! And I see what you mean about the head. No bane could ever mistake that."

He straightened and Marick pushed past to gently pick up the carving and turn it about. "This would be hard to show on stage! But it is fine work. I'd never have thought that big brute we met on your farm could make something so wonderful. Though I suppose he had a hand in making you."

Garet bristled at that, but Salick put a hand on his shoulder. "Still a fool, I see," she said, but Bixa shook her head.

"Marick's no fool," she said. "Or not *all* fool. His plays have kept the spirits of the people from breaking. When you know something terrible is coming, the weight of that knowledge can be overwhelming." She looked at the door through which the king had but lately left.

"Don't worry about our king, Bixa," Marick said, handing the dragon statue back to Garet. He looked down at the model of the city, the high walls, the palace and the banehall in opposite halves, the great open plazas, and the crowded buildings. "Trax doesn't want to give up, but he can't see how to strike a useful blow. So he's driving himself – and you – crazy with his fears. I think worrying about Lysere and his daughter make it even worse. I hate to admit it, but fine words and a brave painted face can't banish all these terrors!"

Bixa stood. "You're right. Once he settles on a plan, he'll be good again. He's trapped for now. We're all trapped inside these stone walls, waiting for the blow to fall. That's enough to drive anyone mad."

Master Tarix stood and looked down at the half-finished plates on the table. The returned banes were sitting beside them, looking off into some unknown distance. "Salick? Garet? Come, where are your thoughts? Still in that cold northern land?"

Garet shook his head. "I wish they were. You're right, it was cold, bitterly so, but I was thinking of that valley. Marick's right that we're trapped, but the people in those stone boxes are too. I wonder what they've become?"

CHAPTER 2

HOMECOMING

Standing by the Centre Bridge gate, Garet, Salick, and Marick could hear the awnings of the Palace Plaza market flap in a freshening breeze. Marick cast a critical glance at the stage set up nearer the three domes of the temple. All the scenery was stored under the platform, and the curtains were tied back against their posts. After a moment, he shrugged and turned to the others.

"I'll walk over with you," Marick said. He seemed to move easily enough, using his demon-headed walking stick as a support.

"Are you sure you're not shirking work?" Salick said. She smothered a yawn. "Oh, I'm tired! Shouldn't you help your friend? She seems to have so much to do."

The younger man shrugged again. "Son-neen always has so much to do. She frets when there's time on her hands, so I let her handle as many chores as possible."

"So considerate!" Garet said. "Have you set a date at the temple?"

Marick stuck out his tongue, looking for a moment like the impish Black Sash he had been when they first met.

"No. I'm too young, too busy, and too smart to get married, thank you. What of you two? I thought a season in the North would see you wed and carrying a baby by now."

Salick looked back at the palace. "You say Lysere has a daughter?"

Marick laughed. "Yes, Noella, a very serious little girl who thinks before she howls. Now, Master Mechanical Dasanat's son, Mandoran, is newborn and just the opposite – he cries without any thought at all."

They greeted the guards who stood on the bridge masked in silkstone and armed with bows and swords. Two of the guards walked with them across the curved span.

There was a splash below, and their escort put arrows to their strings in a flash. More guards rushed out of both gates and lowered lamps on long chains to search the water.

"Marick?" Salick said and turned to see their companion twitch the head of his walking stick free, pulling out a foot-long stiletto, braced for strength and sharp as a spear point.

She pulled her own knife from her belt, and Garet loosened his rope-hammer. "Where did you get that stick?" he asked. Salick eyed the silver demon head and frowned.

"Not to your taste, Salick?" Marick said, swishing the blade back and forth. "It was a gift, if you must know. A reminder of shared troubles and continued friendship."

The guards found nothing and returned to their posts. Marick joined the two parts of his cane again, and they went through the gate into the Banehall Plaza. It too was empty, save for more patrols. On this side, the guards were joined by black-clad fighters who, like them, wore silkstone helmets.

"I see the Masks are still with us," Garet said. "And there

are many more guards in the plazas and even on the bridges, or at least two of them. I saw lights on the West Bridge, but none on the East when we crossed earlier tonight."

Marick shrugged. "That's because there's nothing left to light up. I told you the bridges were attacked? Well, that one isn't fully repaired. You'd have to jump a Stalker demon's length to get from one side to the other. As for the number of guards, the beast that tore it down had silkstone plates nailed to its skull – I'm not making this up! It dulled the fear it cast to nothing, and since we can't rely on a warning, any noise must be checked."

"What kind of demon was it?" Salick asked. "A Basher?"

Their friend turned to look at them. "No, a new beast, though not one of your Human demons. Listen you two, Branet and Tarix didn't say it, but other things have changed since you left, and not for the better. The demons that attack are not the same as before."

"How?" Garet asked. "Bigger, stronger?"

Marick shrugged. "Some. This Breaker demon that smashed the bridge was big enough, but no stronger than a Tunneller demon. It had arms longer than its body. It must have used them to swim here from up the river. Claws! Ask Vinir to show you her drawings of it, you'll see the back feet were curled and useless, like they were an afterthought. You said demons were made from animals. What animal has legs like that? And it wasn't the only demon that was strange. Tarix and her group killed a big beast with two heads."

"No!" Salick said. She stopped in mid-stride to protest such an aberration. "How could it live?"

"It didn't, not after that other beast, Ratal, was through with it," he said and shrugged, a look of frustration crossing his face. "He wants me to write a whole play about his victory. I'm trying to convince him that Tarix, Kesla, and Dalesta should be in it too, but the man is as stubborn as a stone. Anyway, there have been other weird creatures since then, misshapen things, meant to terrify with their looks as well as the fear they cast. It makes me wonder if the Itaalk people you spoke of have given up on demon fear as a weapon."

Garet frowned. "Why would they? They must know how effective it is. If you're not a bane or protected by silkstone, all you can do is tremble and wait for the demon to kill you."

"True, but you've already seen the number of guards with silkstone helmets. We found lots of it in the Far South, and Tiralsh and her spies must know that we have more masks than trained fighters to wear them."

Garet paused to rub the scruffy beard he'd grown in his travels. "And so they change tactics again," he said. "Just like they did by sending the Caller demon and then having demons attack in numbers. It's like a game; we make a move with silkstone to counter demon fear, and they counter with bizarre demons and surprise attacks."

Marick smiled and pushed the young man back into motion. "I see you didn't leave your wits in the North! Yes, I think they're still experimenting, like Dasanat does with her machines. Your Itaalk are still trying to see what hurts us most."

"They're not mine," Garet replied, with some heat. His dark skin spoke of a relationship with the sea Itaalk through his mother, whose people lived on the northern shore, but he loathed the forest Itaalk for the terrible things they had done, and for what they still planned.

Marick held up a hand, his face serious for once. "Sorry,

sorry," he said. "I meant that you're the ones who found them. I heard the horror in your voices when you talked about that valley. I'm sure it was even worse than I can imagine; horrors usually are, and I don't think of you as an Itaalk, no more than I do Yala and the other sandwalkers. Well, the sandwalkers are a tale for another time. I'm just glad that you two made it back in better shape than I did."

"And I'm glad you found silkstone in the Far South," Garet said, relaxing a bit under Salick's watchful eye. "Very glad. We saw some in the North, but not enough for trade. The sea Itaalk use a bit for lamps and carving, and dragons line their nests with it, but the brigades snatch up the rest of it and give it to the forest Itaalk for those clawed coffins."

"Hmm," Marick said. "Now I know where Tiralsh got enough to build her little cell."

Garet looked up to the great double doors of the bane-hall. Marick tilted his head and asked, "Are you going back to the palace?"

Garet looked at Salick, who was looking at her feet. He turned to Marick and shook his head. "I have to wait here and talk to someone," he said. "You two go on."

Salick left without a word, closing the door with a noticeable thump.

"She's still Salick," Marick said. "That same fire, unfrozen by the north wind. Do you want me to wait with you?"

Garet smiled, put a hand on Marick's shoulder, and pulled him into a one-armed hug. "No, I don't, imp. I'm probably going to embarrass myself, and I don't want you writing that into a play."

Marick chuckled and drew away. "Well, if you don't care for my company, I'll leave you and just make up my own story about your humiliation."

"Go!" Garet said, and the boy left, limping but walking at a good speed with his stick. He saw him pause to exchange words with Branet as the hallmaster came through the gardens. Garet was standing ready when the big man approached.

"Garet? Is there something you needed to add to your report?" Branet asked, frowning in some concern.

"Yes, Hallmaster," Garet said. "I want to come home."

In the record room of the hall, Branet pushed aside piles of paper, looking for a particular ledger.

"Ah! Here it is. Master Arict kept these records in better order than I, may Heaven welcome her! Hmm, I'm not sure, but I think with all the turmoil of that time, your name was never struck off the list of banes. Yes, as I thought. I'll make a note that you are returning, though that might confuse people since no one ever noted you left."

Garet reddened. "I thought you might have struck it off yourself, Hallmaster. I was quite . . . definite when I left."

Branet nodded. "Definite! So you were, and yet you spoke no more than the truth to me, I'm sorry to say. That woman who led the Masks, Shirin, wouldn't have died if I hadn't been so stone-headed about exiling her. No, Garet, you were right enough to leave. My question is, why do you want to come back?"

The younger man took the chair Branet indicated and waited while the hallmaster seated himself across from him.

"I've thought about it during the trip north, and especially after seeing those clawed caves in the forest. Part of it is about Salick, of course. She's been . . . definite in her wish for me to return to the hall."

"Definite," Branet said. "There's a lot of that around these days, it seems. What else?"

Garet looked down at his interlaced fingers. "You heard what Trax said. Maybe I feel a bit of that too, that this could be the end. If it is, I want to finish as a bane. That's all."

"Then that's enough for me," Branet said, and leaned back in his chair. He looked up at the ceiling. "You'd be a fool if you didn't consider the worst. Believe me, I do."

He suddenly stood, displaying the strength and energy Garet remembered. "But we may yet win, or at least survive the coming battle to wait for the next. In hope of that, I'll make one more notation next to your name. 'In late winter of the second year of Hallmaster Branet, Garet, once of the Midlands, is promoted to the level of master.'"

Garet stumbled upright, with very little evidence of energy or strength. He gripped the arm of the chair for support. "Hallmaster, I didn't mean for this, I don't deserve it. I'm too young!"

Branet scowled at him. "No younger than Salick was when she received the Red. Garet, we are sadly short of experienced banes in the upper ranks. Our Reds and Golds have faced the first claws of every battle. Many are wounded beyond recovery, and some have died. You may think me rash, but, Heaven shield the hall, if we keep losing such men and women, I'll have to promote every Black Sash to a Gold and every Blue to a Red! We live in mad times, Master Garet."

"We must," Garet said, "if this is happening!" He swallowed and continued in a quieter voice, "Hallmaster, I wanted to ask a question, if I may?"

Branet put down the pen and nodded for him to continue.

"What is wrong with the king?"

Branet was silent for many moments. At last, he placed both hands on the table and answered. "He cannot change what the world is and what he is. That is what's wrong with him. Claws! Please keep this in confidence, Garet. Trax trained for over a season, nearly two in fact, to make himself a bane. I know! I know how mad that is, but he is my king and was very confident of success. Well, every morning, we met in a cave near the depository of demon jewels. After training with his mask, he would take it off and try to walk ten paces towards an open silkstone box. He kept getting closer until the box was only two steps away, and that was the end of it. No matter what he tried, or how hard his efforts, he couldn't make those last two steps. It nearly broke my heart to see the man fail again and again."

"Banes aren't made by such methods!" Garet said, shocked by this news, for everyone in the hall knew that past generations had tried to fashion banes by exposing people, even children, to demon fear, and it hadn't worked. The only sure way to produce a demonbane was to find a child who had already learned to live with some terrible fear and then train them to fight. Most recruits were not very heroic, at least at the beginning of their careers as banes, but they became heroes nonetheless.

Branet let out a deep sigh. "No, they aren't, and he knows it now. I shouldn't have let him try, but as I said, he was so sure, and he is my king. I think that failing broke the hope inside him, and now he sees his city, including his wife and child, ready for destruction."

Garet stood to take his leave, but the older man stopped him by the door. He looked him up and down, noting the leather and fur coat, the short boots, and the wool pants tucked inside them.

"You look quite odd in those clothes, Master Garet," he said. "We need something to tell the hall you have returned – and have been promoted for your brave service!"

After his mistakes with the Masks, Branet wore only a master's red sash, not one bordered in black and reserved for a hallmaster. He took off this strip of cloth and laid it over the shoulder and chest of Garet's coat. With a broad smile, he propelled the younger man out the door.

The newly made master stumbled before caching himself. Branet was a giant, and the master's sash lay long across his body, almost reaching his knees. Tomorrow he would have to return it and get a new one from the stores. A new sash, new uniform, and new boots.

And maybe a bigger head to take in all these changes!

He shook himself and yawned. Tomorrow then, but what of tonight? He had to find a bed, and soon, for he was nearly asleep on his feet.

He paused at the foot of the stairs leading up to the rooms of the lower ranks. Should he stay on this floor and find a room among the masters? He frowned at that thought. Too many changes for one night. He climbed the steps and knocked on a familiar door.

After some time, a much taller Dorict than Garet remembered opened it, rubbed his eyes, and blinked at the traveller.

"You're back," he said, and started to yawn, then stopped, mouth open at the sight of the red sash. He scratched his head, finished the yawn and waved his friend in.

"Tell me tomorrow," he said, and fell back onto his bed.

CHAPTER 3
A CANDLE OF HOPE

Marick's room in the Thirteenth Ward was nothing so big or comfortable as his old one in the banehall, the same one he had shared with Garet and Dorict, but this space was his own, paid for by the money he made from writing plays. He pushed aside a page of poetic dialogue, put his elbows on the table, and looked out through the window's single pane of glass.

Lady Kaela, Lord Kirel's wife, had found this room for him as a thank you for the trust he had shown in her. Marick lived in it alone. His business partner, Son-neen, stayed in the Stewards School, trading her knowledge of the Far South and its ways for room and board, at least when she wasn't engaged in one of her many other trading schemes. The night's play had been just one of them, and the profit had been quite satisfying.

He smiled and held his hands near the candle flame to warm them. No doubt Garet and Salick's return would set the city buzzing, and some would come to see if they turned up to watch another play. He shook his head and pulled the pages back under the light's small circle.

Trax wants all the news about demons put into a play. Claws, unless he wants it to last a whole season, I don't see how it can all fit together. And why now? It would frighten people more than prepare them, not like the Battle of the Bridge where at least we had a victory. I bet he's up to something. He must want people frightened enough to follow him in some mad plan. Hmm, no matter how nice the man seems when you meet him, there's always the schemer beneath. It makes me quite jealous! But enough of that. How do I write the cursed thing in the first place?

He leaned back and considered. Shudan, the playwriter who had taught him the most, had drummed into the ex-bane what made a story work.

"The points, no matter how strange, must be connected, young scamp," the old woman told him, over and over again.

"Leave a big gap between two events and the audience loses the thread as sure as a weaver does when her attention wanders. Link each event. Show how one causes the next until the ending is as satisfying as a well-baked meal."

The problem, from Marick's point of view, was that real events didn't always show these links. Not at first, and maybe not for years after. After all, for six hundred years, demons had plagued Shirath, and people had known those terrible results without any clue as to what really caused them. Trax was now demanding something even worse: a play all about causes with no results, only terrifying possibilities.

Garet sighed and looked at the false leg Dasanat had made for him. It leaned against the wall within easy reach of the desk and the narrow cot beside it.

That leg, for example, I know its cause and its effect. But that doesn't make it a satisfying story, at least, not to me.

He stood up on his good foot and lifted the candle from the desk. Hopping carefully, he went to his bed and lay down, putting the candle on a stool set on the other side. He blew out the flame and darkness flooded in. He would write Trax's play – he really had no choice in the matter – but he would give the audience some hope, even if he couldn't prove it logically. There were some things the audience wanted more than sense – no matter what Shudan preached.

The darkness brought sleep, and dreams of his time in the Far South. He was floating along a buried river. The water glowed with a subtle green sheen, and the curved roof high overhead was a heaven without stars.

When he awoke, he would know what to write. He always did.

CHAPTER 4

FEAR IN THE FIELDS

"I still don't understand that part about dragons being both one big thing and many little things," Dorict said.

Garet picked up a rock from the edge of the track. "Look over there at those feeding birds," he said.

While his friend watched, the bane skipped the stone over the flattened furrows, not at the flock but near it. The birds rose all at once, a netting of wings that moved together until they settled again one field over.

"Hey," called a man working nearby. "We're trying to get the stones out of the fields, not put more in!"

Garet reddened and called out an apology. He turned to the smiling Dorict. "There, did you see that? How they all rose up at the same time, flew to the next field, and then landed together like they shared a single thought? That's what a dragon looks like when it forms."

They were waiting in the fields by the outer gate of Lord Andarack's ward, the Eighth. Garet pulled at the collar of his new purple vest, and then adjusted the new, and very troubling, red sash that hung across it. Salick had been delighted, of course, and the other banes seemed happy enough. There had been so many promotions in the hall that his own change in sash brought few comments except "well done" and demands for all the news of their trip north. The only one of his friends who didn't know about this change was Marick, and Garet could only suppose the boy's – no, young man's – reaction would be the most dramatic.

"What are you smiling about?" Dorict demanded. "And you still haven't answered my question about *how* they do it."

"I was thinking about Marick, and I don't really understand how dragons can join together and split apart! I do know each one starts out as hundreds of eggs, all the same except one, the heartstone, Salick calls it, though it might be more of a thoughtstone, since it seems to control the others. It's red where the others are black. They form around it, and it sits in the head of the final dragon shape."

"Like a demon's jewel," Dorict said. He flicked away an early biting fly. "And you say they speak in feelings? Well, so do demon jewels, don't they? Andarack proved they're capable of more than fear, and we know the Caller demon could cast different emotions. I wonder why regular demons, if anything so foul can be called 'regular,' only spit out fear?"

Garet had thought about this, among other mysteries, all the way from the Itaalk valley to the high white walls of Shirath. "Because they're alone," he said. "And they were never meant to be separated, not for long. It must be terrifying for them."

"Well, we know fear can twist a person," Dorict said. "So why not a dragon egg?" He pointed into the ward where the group they were expecting were coming past the livestock paddocks. An old woman led them, followed by two younger ones, one Garet's height and the other considerably taller. They passed through the outer gate and greeted the waiting banes.

"Hah! The smart one," the old woman said, pointing at Dorict. She wore a green hooded cloak with a thick red scarf wrapped around her neck. "Demon killer, I greet you. May the winds favour you. But you, with skin like mine, who are you?"

This last comment was directed at Garet. Dorict stepped in to make the introductions.

"Ke, this is Garet, who just came back from the North. Garet, this is Ke, a sandwalker and leader of Old Carving Well as well as grandmother to Yala and Brada," he said pointing first at the young woman in blue and the larger one in yellow.

"Yes!" Ke said. "Dasa told me. The one who came to the city from the east. She has good thoughts about you. That cloth you wear. Are you a bane? Dasa said you were a king's man."

"I just came back to the hall," Garet said. He clapped a hand on Dorict's shoulder. "I'm not sure who Dasa is but thank you for looking after my friend."

Ke pulled Yala forward. "He was this one's trouble, not mine. Dasa is Andarack's woman. He is her man? I do not know how to say it here."

"It is *wife* and *husband*, Ke," the young woman said, and took Garet's hand in a strong grip. "I'm Yala. Vinir and Marick have good thoughts about you too. Did the other return with you?"

"Salick? Yes, she did, but she's with the hallmaster, writing a full report of our journey."

Yala nodded. "That is good. I would read it when she is done."

The tall woman, Brada, pushed her sister and laughed. "Do not boast about knowing their wriggling lines, sister. Trade symbols should be good enough for a sandwalker."

Yala did not reply, but Ke frowned at the big woman, silencing her.

"My other granddaughter is not as clever as Yala but not as troublesome either. Sometimes. She came with the other sandwalkers and stays with me in Andarack's house."

Yala smiled behind her hand, and Brada elbowed her hard enough to make the younger woman stumble.

Ke looked up at Garet and sighed. "There is a trouble forever with grandchildren, bane. Come, Dorict said he would show us the way you make food."

They left the ward and walked out into the fields. Teams of horses pulled a hundred plows, and so many people followed with baskets of seeds that Garet now knew why the streets had seemed so empty. This sowing was the first large fieldwork of the year, a time when the greater part of each ward worked outside the city walls, making sure Shirath would have enough food for its many mouths.

They crossed a wooden bridge over a ditch and Dorict led them west on a footpath between two fields.

"The men of our well would dance and sing to have lands as broad as this," Brada said. She made to pull off her cloak, for the morning was finally warming, but Yala grabbed her hand.

"We wear these to fool any spies who may be watching," she said. "Keep that hood up to hide how dark we are next to these Northerners." Garet was confused for a moment before he realized what he knew as the South must be the North to those of the Far South. Yala turned to Garet. "You should do the same."

Garet smiled and shook his head. He had no hood to pull over his black hair, and besides, he was well-known in the city and his return was a fact that wouldn't have escaped Tiralsh's spies.

"Garet!" someone yelled, and two banes on horseback trotted up before one, a tall young woman, jumped down from her mount and enveloped him in a hug worthy of a Crusher demon.

"Kesla!" he wheezed, and had to wait until she released him to manage other words. "Good to see you again," he coughed. "You too, Ratal."

A man even taller and broader than his companion clapped him on the shoulder, indenting the ground beneath Garet's feet. He had forgotten how strong these two were, though he had seen much of their strength and demon-killing skill when they served together under Master Tarix. Kesla wore red now, but Ratal still bore a gold sash.

Kesla smiled broadly. "We heard you were back, but the hallmaster had us out on field patrol and far-scouting for days. Congratulations on getting the Red. Tarix will be pleased to see you, unless you've already talked?"

"Only a little, when we returned two nights ago, and it's been reports and not much sleep since then. Well done to you too, Master. I hope that hasn't put Ratal's nose out of joint?"

Kesla looked to where the big bane stood, eyes lowered and hands fiddling with his horse's reins.

"Oh, he's moping, but not about that. So, what dragged you away from all those reports this fine day?"

"I came out with Dorict and our friends this morning to

show them the fields and orchards, and to see for myself what's changed here."

Kesla nodded, then smiled at Yala and Ke, whom she seemed to already know. Her smile vanished, and she backed up a step when Brada pushed forward to examine her very closely.

"You are big," the sandwalker said approvingly.

Kesla looked back into a woman's eyes on her own level, a strange experience for her, and nodded. "I am, but so are you. You're the tallest woman I've ever seen outside a mirror!"

Brada nodded, her expression fierce. "Let us wrestle then," she said, and spread out her arms.

Kesla swore and jumped back, but Ke stepped between them.

"Brada! Would you tear up these fields with your playing? Act as if you were indeed Brada, and not Bradasana."

Brada hung her head, but Kesla grabbed the young woman's shoulder.

"Wait a minute. She's right. This is the wrong place, and we're just off night patrol so I'm too tired to fight, but come to the hall before the evening meal and we'll use one of the training rooms."

"You will wrestle with me?" Brada said, hope lighting her eyes again. "Friend?"

"It would be my honour to practise with one of our allies," Kesla said, sketching a little bow. "Friend."

Ke shook her head. "I hope you are not so polite when you fight, or you won't last long."

The two banes waved goodbye and walked their mounts towards the walls. The others watched them go.

"Ratal is quiet today," Garet said. The big Gold had never been shy about giving his opinions.

Dorict shook his head. "Remember how ready he is to fight? I'm not sure, but I think he misses the days when there were demons coming over the walls like water over a fountain curb. You saw that odd axe he carried?"

Garet nodded. "It had a back spike like my hammer and trident points on top! Where did he get it?"

Dorict motioned for the party to start walking again. "We'll go as far as the orchards. We could travel even farther, into the tree fields where wood is cut for fires and building – my family works there – but Trax has ordered them abandoned save for the guard patrols. As for Ratal's axe, it's new, but he had a similar one made before he went into the forest, where they found that hidden road. He left that in the two-headed demon you've probably heard about."

"Marick told me," Garet said. "Though I don't know if I should believe him."

"Then believe Master Tarix, Kesla, and Dasanat," Dorict said, holding up three fingers. "They saw it too. I think now that poor Ratal has a new axe, he's pining for another big monster to kill. Sadly, the Itaalk haven't sent him one, not yet."

"Ah," Ke said. "These trees are small like the ones the men tend in their fields. But I do not know this one."

"Apple," Dorict said. "I'm sorry that we don't have any for you to taste. The fruit from its flowers won't be ready until the fall. Picked apples don't last till spring, except as cider."

"Cider is good," Brada said. "It is better than the wine Andarack serves, but . . ."

She stopped and reached into her robe, bringing out a small bone tube. She pulled the stopper from the end and peered inside.

"She is afraid," the sandwalker said, and looked at her grandmother and sister.

They were also checking the little fear lizards all women of the wells carried to warn them of the desert's greatest danger.

Garet looked at Dorict.

The younger bane's brows were drawn together. "Those lizards sense demons, what sandwalkers call 'poison winds,' from far away and much sooner than we can, but I thought the demons coming now were fear-blocked by silkstone plates."

"Chit-chit is very good," Yala said. "She might know even if one such was coming, if it was close."

She turned the tube in a slow circle, one finger inside to feel the lizard's movements.

"North-west," she said, and replaced the stopper, then put the tube beneath her robe. She took the long, heavy scarf from her neck and wound it around her head, leaving a slit for sight. The other two sandwalkers did the same.

"Silkstone inside?" Garet asked. He loosened the coils of his rope-hammer.

Dorict nodded. The younger bane hefted his staff, a six-foot length of oak bound at the top in ridged iron. The sandwalkers, their faces covered now, strung their bows.

"These arrows are not poisoned," Yala said, pulling down a loop of cloth to speak. "But we will aim for the eyes."

Dorict smiled at Garet's disbelief. "They can hit something that small, I've seen it done! Let's move in that direction, slowly so as not to cause a panic if we're wrong."

Brada shook her head. "Not wrong. All lizards say the same. That way."

They zig-zagged across the fields, avoiding the sowers

and teams of plow horses. Garet could still feel no trace of demon fear and began to wonder if the lizards were just reacting to some other frightening creature, like Ratal and his axe. They approached a grove of early blooming cherry trees, brilliant in pink and white flowers, and stopped when Ke raised her hand.

"Even I can sense it now," she said.

"You feel fear?" Yala asked. She looked around, one hand raised to touch her quiver.

"No," her grandmother replied. "I smell it. Coming from these trees."

Garet sniffed. The aroma of the blossoms could not mask another odour, a faint reek of old blood and corruption. There was a cracking sound, the flowers trembled, fell like snow, and a demon broke through the grove and came into the fields of Shirath.

It knocked down an old man who barely had time to turn away before he was ground into the dirt. Others ran, stumbling over the furrows and dodging the rearing, screaming plow horses that thrashed in their traces.

At first, Garet saw none of the deformities Dorict and the others had spoken of. He recognized the beast at once from *The Demonary of Moret*; it was a Bull demon, heavily muscled in front, with forward-sweeping crests that ended in wicked points. Moret said it trampled its victims before devouring them, and the demon seemed willing to prove him right.

Dorict pointed, and Garet saw the silkstone plates fixed between the crests.

Fear-blocked! And yet those little animals sensed it.

The demon jerked a leg free from the split trunk of a tree and clawed at the bloody ground. Garet pulled his rope-hammer from its belt hook and ran to one side, looking for an angle from which he could cast his line and tangle the beast. The thing paused to howl and shake itself all over, like a wet dog. Terror exploded from it, though the plate was still fixed to its skull. The bane fought against the terror, ground his teeth, and began to swing the spiked weight around and above his head. Something was different about the demon's shape now, but fogged by fear, he could only concentrate on his own attack.

An arrow bounced off one of the monster's crests, just above the eye. Another followed, its needle tip piercing deep into the thick neck. The beast's cry was echoed, no, joined by many smaller, higher shrieks. The rope slipped through Garet's fingers and he stood, frozen by a stomach-churning sight. Things were erupting from the monster's back, not the usual tumour-like lumps that added armour to the skin, but creatures, Rat demons, by their look and sound, that pulled themselves from ruptures in the Bull demon's body and dropped like lice from its hide.

That's where the fear's coming from. It's giving birth to them, like a litter of piglets from a sow.

The fieldworkers running from the beast collapsed on the ground, paralyzed by the Rat demons running towards them while the Bull, its birthing done for now, charged the small party of banes and sandwalkers.

Garet was still reeling in his line when Dorict, with an agility Garet did not remember, dived between the demon's front legs and turned his staff crosswise. The beast's smaller back legs collided with the shaft and the demon fell into a slide, tearing at the ground but unable to stop its tumble.

Yala and Brada ran past the banes, chasing the Rat demons and firing arrows as they sped. Angry shrieks reported their accuracy. Ke remained, shooting shaft after shaft at the Bull demon's face. The great beast hooted in pain when Dorict crippled a back leg with repeated strikes. Garet used that distraction to throw a loop around the horns and try to hold it down, sending a fervent request to Heaven that Ke would find a weak spot before she ran out of arrows and they all ran out of luck.

The massive head jerked, almost pulling him off his feet, and he saw feathers sticking out of a bleeding eye socket. The wound inflicted by the sandwalker's last shaft had not been fatal. Using all his strength, Garet held the beast while Dorict worked on its ribs and Ke scoured the ground for useful arrows.

The beast's shoulder twitched, and the skin parted to reveal another Rat demon. It squealed at Garet and tried to claw its way out of the larger monster. Burdened as he was, the bane knew he couldn't reach the hammer end of his weapon. The best he might do was to try and kick the little demon when it freed itself and came for his throat.

There was a roar, and Garet feared another beast had come to kill them. He was partly right, for it was Ratal that leaped over him, axe in hand, and he was beast enough. The heavy blade fell, cutting into the big demon's neck. Blood spurted, mostly from the Bull demon but also some from the Rat, cleaved as neatly as a cook's knife might split a beef sausage.

The axe fell again and again, until the Bull's head dropped away and the beast stopped twitching.

Dorict, who had retreated to a safe distance, ran around the corpse to give help to the others, but they were already walking towards him, accompanied by Kesla, who carried a seed basket piled high with little leathery corpses. Beyond them, he saw a horse down and clawed, but no other bodies save that of the old man killed in the demon's first charge.

Brada had an arm around Kesla's shoulders. "I've seen men use such a flail to beat seeds," she said. "But it's good for beating demons too! Hah, and you said you were too tired to fight."

The bane shook her head. "I said I was too tired to fight you. No bane's ever too tired to fight a demon. Garet, Brada says these Rats came out of that Bull demon. Is it true?"

Garet nodded. He reeled in his line again, but only half came back. The wire-reinforced rope had not survived Ratal's enthusiasm. He gathered the remnants and tied them in an angry knot before smiling to himself. *I suppose since I'm a bane again, I can ask for another.*

Kesla dumped the dead Rat demons on the ground and took out her belt knife. One by one, she used the point to pry out the small demon jewels and put them in a silkstone box, but when she closed it, the fear remained.

"Put this in too," Ratal said, a bloody hand holding out the Bull demon's jewel. That didn't work either, and the banes and sandwalkers looked at each other.

"You don't think," Garet said, and Dorict turned slightly green.

"We'll have to cut this thing apart," Kesla said. "And I was hoping to get to my bed before noon."

It took much of the morning to find all the Rat demons, and their jewels, still inside the larger beast. They twitched in rows along either side of the spine, tucked into little sacs under the skin. They were all moving, trying to attack the fingers that pried them out of the larger demon.

"Storms and sand!" Brada said, rubbing her hands on her blood-flecked yellow cloak. "I touched one of those little beasts and the fear hit me like a spirit wind."

"Why did you touch it?" Ke demanded. She was using

her sand shovel, a sharp square of metal on a short handle, to cut out the struggling demons and split their skulls.

Yala smiled, or might have, for her face was still wrapped in silkstone plates sewn into a scarf. "Because she can't tear something in half with her hands unless she touches it. Use your shovel, sister."

When they were done, and the fear stopped, the sand-walkers took off their scarves and breathed in the cool air from a distance, for the smell of blood was overwhelming near the disassembled beast. News had spread throughout the city, as it always did after a demon attack, and temple priests came out to collect the body of the dead man. The horse was dragged away by knackers from the Sixteenth Ward. While this happened, Dorict was busy explaining to Lord Andarack, who had come out with his ward guards, how the smaller demons had emerged.

"And yet you felt no fear until they did," Andarack said. "Or until the larger one died. Something kept them – and their jewels – quiet." He stared at the hulking corpse. "Maybe the Bull demon did this. Was it because of those inner sacs? Or perhaps there was an Itaalk heartstone staff nearby? Heaven shield us, Dorict, from yet another mystery of these new demons! Get me one of those sacs, please. No, two or three. I'll take them back and examine them." He turned to his guards to arrange for the remains of the beast to be taken to the shambles beyond the orchards where de-jewelled demons were allowed to rot – unless Lord Andarack or his wife, Lady Dasanat, wanted them dragged to the mechanicals' hall.

Ke tugged on Garet's sleeve. "I think we have seen enough of your fields, bane," she said. "Now we will go back with Andarack to his house. I must also help your physicians with the poison, for I think sandwalkers must cover their arrows now when they walk in your city."

Garet nodded. "I think you're right. Dorict tells me that poison is very strong."

Ke laughed as Dorict came up to join their conversation.

"We make it stronger now, since it is only put on our arrows, not poured on strangers like little Marick."

"Lord Andarack will escort you back," Dorict said, frowning at the sandwalker's words. His expression softened when Yala came up to hand back some of Ke's arrows.

"Using strangers to poison demons was always bad," the young woman said, and Ke nodded.

"Yes," she said. "It was, but remember sometimes sandwalkers offered themselves to kill demons and save our wells. I am sorry for Marick, but he lived and brought us here to kill the poison winds at their birth. So, some good came from it."

She nodded a goodbye to the banes and left with her two granddaughters. Yala paused a moment to lay a hand on Dorict's shoulder. They shared a look that wasn't romantic, Garet thought, but spoke of a shared memory, something important to both of them.

"What did she mean about feeding strangers to demons?" Garet asked his friend when they were alone again.

"Like Ke said, they poured that poison over Marick, after he lost his leg," Dorict said in a flat voice. "Then they tied him up and left him to be eaten by the Horned demon their little lizards sensed. Yala and I rescued him, and then the sandwalkers changed their minds about that . . . practice."

"How can you still be friends with them?" Garet said, the words pouring out before he could stop them.

Dorict glared at him, a strange reaction for the normally placid young man.

"You don't know everything that went on in the Far South!" he said, shouting out the words. "I do, Yala does. Marick, Vinir, Son-neen, and Chal-lat do. You don't, so don't lecture me . . . Master."

Garet stepped back, mouth open. "I'm sorry, Dorict. You're right. I don't know. I'll take your word that the sand-walkers are worthy of your friendship, and mine."

They were halfway back to the walls before Dorict spoke again.

"Sorry. I suppose I shouldn't yell at a Red, but it was a hard journey for me, in many ways. Marick and I, well, things are good between us again, but it's not the same as before."

Garet nodded. "Nothing is, is it? The North was hard too, not just finding those caves. When I met my father, well, it brought back a lot. He'd changed, but not in my memories."

He stopped short of the gate and looked at the other bane.

"You still wear the same sash. Why aren't you at least a Gold, if it isn't a sore spot? You should have been promoted before a dozen others I saw this morning with new sashes." He grimaced. "Including myself."

The Green Sash blushed a bit and shrugged.

"I refused. It doesn't matter to me anymore, I guess," he said. "In the Far South, I saw so much. They really have a good way of living in the City of Fountains, and I thought that if we survived all this, I'd like to go back, not as a bane, just as a regular person."

Garet looked at him. "Did you meet someone there. Is Yala . . ."

Dorict shook his head. "No, we're just friends. Good friends, though. We've fought together, and we learned from each other. In a way, I was like a distance viewer for her, letting her see something far away from her own life. She was the same for me. She made the world so big that the colour of my sash seemed very small." He shrugged. "Besides, the people in the City of Fountains are like me, you know, 'boring,' as Marick would say."

Garet smiled. "I wouldn't say that, and besides, I met Son-neen last night. No one would call her boring."

Dorict chuckled. "No," he said. "No more than you'd say that of Marick, but in most ways, she's like the rest of her people. They value work. They like detail. And they all read! How many people in one of our wards can read? One in fifty? A hundred? The City of Fountains is an educated place, Garet, and I think I could be at home there."

He paused to look up to the top of the walls. A figure beside one of the arrow-throwers waved. Dorict waved back.

"That's why I refused the Gold," he said. "I don't want to be a bane when this is over."

CHAPTER 5

THE SLEEPLESS KING

Trax looked down at his miniature city and placed a piece from a Surround game outside the gates of Lord Andarack's ward. There were more pieces in and around the model. This was just the most recent to be placed.

Andarack looked at the harrier facing his ward's gate.

"At least it's not to scale," he said. "If it was, that Birthing demon would have been thirty feet tall!"

Trax looked sideways at the man. "You joke," he said. "But think what this means. A demon like this within the city could drop off new demons as it ran through each ward. That would mean more than the one death today, and however many there would be, they would be on our heads, mine in fact, Lord Andarack, so forgive me if I don't laugh."

Andarack looked at him and sighed. "No, Your Majesty, it is I who should beg forgiveness. I shouldn't jest when you are so troubled. Perhaps the royal physician can give you something to help you to a deeper sleep?"

"No," the king said. "I was asleep once when demons invaded the palace. I'll not be caught so easily again."

"You have guards," Andarack said, gently, for the king wavered as he stood at the table, both hands braced against it to keep himself upright.

"They aren't enough," Trax replied. "Do you know who the safest people in the city are? Gost and Tarock, locked below the palace and guarded night and day. When the demons came here to kill me and my queen, they sheltered in their cells, happy as could be. They don't deserve it, Andarack. I'd call for their exile if I wasn't sure that Tiralsh is out there somewhere ready to scoop them up and use them against us."

Andarack sent a glance at a steward who left discreetly. "If we can't exile them, then the cells are the only answer," he said, guiding the king to a chair.

Trax didn't resist, but he did argue.

"I don't have time to sit, Andarack. And as for the cells being the only answer, they aren't. Shirath's kings were not so pleasant in the early days, you know. They had sharper methods for dealing with traitors."

"Necklacing?" Andarack asked, shocked. In the old days, criminals would be thrown out of the gates with a string of demon jewels around their throats, sentenced to madness and death in the wilderness beyond the city.

Trax grinned, a ghastly expression on his exhausted face. "No, though the neck had a part in it." He made a chopping motion with one hand. "A sword can be used on more than demons, when needed."

The door to the Shouting Room opened and Lysere came in, followed by the royal physician.

"My husband," the queen said, and held a hand against Trax's forehead. "You are exhausted. Come to bed, please."

The physician opened his mouth, but Trax glared him into silence.

"I will," he said. "For love's sake, but send that man away! I'll not have him dosing me with his potions."

"Nor will he," Lysere said, somewhat sternly. "As long as you get some sleep. If not, I will ask Lord Andarack to hold you down while our good physician pours every medicine in his stock down your royal throat. Come, my love, please."

The physician helped the king rise, but Trax stopped before leaving the table.

"Andarack, there are reports in the northern wards of a shaking in the ground. Not strong, but like a great beast walking though none is seen. Look into it."

Andarack nodded and bowed as the royal couple left. He looked down at the model of the city and ran a fingertip along the northern wall.

"Hmmm. Nothing felt in my ward," he said to the empty room and smiled. "So, for once, my lady wife and her machines are not responsible."

CHAPTER 6

THE MASTER MECHANICALS' HOUSE

Dasanat, the lady wife in question, wiped grease from her hands. She tossed the rag back to another mechanical and shouted, "Connect the jars."

A thin man in the mechanical's grey tunic and pants ran across the yard and pulled down a switch. The copper-plated section touched a receiving plate and there was a loud snap. The wheel beside Dasanat began to move, turning slowly at first but gaining speed until the spokes were a blur.

"Pull the release," she shouted, and the man worked a chain that slowed the wheel, and when Dasanat judged it ready, she pulled a lever that moved over a set of toothed gears. The wheel meshed with a jolt, and the spark motor transferred its energy to the gears, sending it to a shaft, which set flying a wide leather belt, which turned a lathe. The thin man ran back and forth, checking all the moving parts, then looked at Dasanat, who nodded. He waved at others to come forward and bring tools to bear on the piece of metal that now spun like a whirlwind in the lathe's jaws.

The master mechanical turned to Ke, who was fairly hopping up and down in joy at such purposeful chaos.

"The spark jars won't last very long," Dasanat told her, "unless we connect many at a time, but they'll last long enough to do some good work on that piece."

"It is very good, Dasa! Very good! What will you make of it?" Ke asked. "A weapon?"

Dasanat nodded. "Yes, part of one, though the lathe can do more than that. This cranking shaft is for a dart-thrower of my own design. If it works, which it should, it will launch a hundred darts at a time, each covered with the poison you brought from the desert."

Ke paused, her eyes on the gears still turning. "A hundred dead poison winds – demons – at once?" she asked, and shook her head. "This is beyond good – like a sandstorm is beyond a breeze."

"Maybe not a hundred," the master mechanical replied, "but it will kill many, depending on how the darts fall."

The sandwalker followed the master of the mechanicals into the main hall of her husband's house. While other lords might use such a space to keep banquet tables and room for dancing, Lord Andarack's hall was full of mechanicals, stewards, and skilled workers brought from every ward. King Trax had decreed that Dasanat's needs came before all else, and the woman, single-minded as always, had taken full advantage of that command. Glassblowers worked in teams to make larger jars that could contain enough spark energy to move machines such as the one in the yard – or the arrow-throwers on the walls. Metal screeched as wire pullers swung back and forth on swings, using their own weight to coax thin copper wire through holes in an iron plate. On the dais, where the lord and their spouse should sit and give instructions to their ward's citizens, a group of physicians muttered over retorts and small furnaces, brewing the poison Dasanat had mentioned.

A dozen other wonders were happening around them, but Dasanat went straight to the wire pullers. They proudly presented spools of copper wire, more than the city usually produced in ten years, but their master was not impressed.

"We need more. Set up three, no, four more stations. Use the stables if you need to and bring in every smith who has ever drawn out wire from any metal."

She left them crestfallen but resolved to do better. Dasanat was not one to lavish praise but neither was she unduly critical, preferring to fix problems rather than lay blame. They also knew her words were born of necessity, for the whole city was holding its breath, waiting for the next move of the demons and their masters.

"Why do you need so much wire?" Ke asked. "Will you use it to tie the beasts?"

Dasanat shook her head, then ran a hand through her hair. She paused in her quick strides, leaning against a wall. One of her mechanicals ran up with a ladle of water, which she accepted without comment, though she put a brief hand on the man's shoulder when she handed the ladle back and said to Ke, "The king demands more arrow-throwers, and they need spark gears and turners, which need a lot of wire."

Ke looked at the woman, peering up into her drawn face.

"Ah, you are too tired to think, Dasa, and I am too . . . wondering to think! This all seems like magic to me. I don't know how such things can be."

Dasanat straightened up and nodded. "That much I can show you," she said, and led the sandwalker to a small side-chamber. A steward followed them in with a plate of food, which he put down on a table before he left.

This was the bed chamber of Lord Andarack and Lady Master Mechanical Dasanat, but aside from the bed and a baby's wicker cot, the room was much like the great hall, cluttered with things half built or half taken apart. One such device was a bronze hawk, each feather a separate work of art, its sharp beak open, and its jewel eyes red as fire.

Dasanat waved the older woman to a nearby chair and leaned over the bird to attach the wires to knobs on the statue's base. When she was done, the wings of the hawk began to move like the big wheel in the yard, slowly at first, then faster until the clashing, ringing feathers looked like they might lift the metal bird from its place on the workbench. At the same time, the beak opened and closed, and a creaky, wheezing cry came from inside the automaton's body.

Ke jumped out of her chair and laid one hand on her sharp sandwalker's shovel. "By twelve winds and every storm, is this town-magic then?"

Dasanat looked up from the clashing, clanking bird and shook her head. "No. There is no magic. Not in this."

She released the wires and the bird froze, wings lifted, feathers spread like fingers.

Ke looked at the mechanical, her head tilted to one side. "Town people always say they have no magic, even in my lands, but everyone knows they cast spells that build their towers and send sleds over the deep water."

"Ships," Dasanat said. "Ships, not sleds."

Ke shivered and turned away. "Whatever you call it, travelling over such deep water is death. Here is better. Your water is held tight in the river that cuts your well, I mean your town, in two. We do not like walking over it on those bridges so much, but it is easier than travelling the Dying River between our wells, and even Yala can do that. This much water is enough, Dasa. You are lucky this town is so far from the sea."

Dasanat frowned and said, "I don't think much about luck. If I lived near the sea, I would make better ships. If I lived in your desert, I would make better sleds." She paused for a moment and then added, "At least, that is what my husband tells me, and he is usually very logical."

A steward entered with cups and a pot of tea. The two women took them and the plate of food to a bench by the windows, far from the mechanical bird for Ke's sake. From this vantage point, they could see the forges in the yard glowing red against the last of the day's light. The grey-clothed mechanicals worked sheets of iron with the great hammers that moved up and down using "motors" such as the one Dasanat had demonstrated.

"Do you truly have no magic?" Ke asked, and wrapped her thin hands around her tea, for this was a cold country for a woman of the desert.

"When I was a child," the mechanical said, between sips, "I went with my mother and brothers to the market every five-day. We sold what we made, spindles and loom parts mainly, but I would always look for the entertainers, especially the magicians."

Ke leaned forward. "See! I told you, Dasa, town people always have such things. Did they cast spells?"

Dasanat shook her head. She watched through the window as several men and women strained to carry an iron support to the riveting station. "No, it wasn't real magic, just tricks. They would make a scarf disappear from before your eyes and then take it from out of your own pocket. Some could make a ball float in the air or join metal rings together in a chain."

Ke leaned back and frowned at her host. "Is this not magic then, to make things go away and join two things into one?"

Dasanat smiled, a rare occurrence, but one more common since the birth of her son.

"No, it was a trick," she said, "but I always wanted to know how the trick worked. So, I looked and looked until I found out. Those rings had a break you could not see from far away. The ball had a slim thread to hold it up, and the scarf was hidden in the performer's sleeve. They weren't real magicians; they were usually just actors who made money between plays by putting on market shows. They were competent, skilled even, but it wasn't magic."

Ke thought about this. "Were you sad when you saw it was not magic?"

Dasanat took up the pot and refilled the older woman's cup. "No, because I was truly fascinated by the method of it. How the trick was done was more interesting than some magic I'd never understand."

Ke laughed. "Dasa, I think you are another trick, and I am trying to see how you are done! You are like a wind blowing away the sand to show what was hidden. Hah! I think you will keep going until all secrets are plain and fair under the sun. But, tell me no-magic woman, will your tricks kill the poison winds coming to this city?"

Dasanat let out a long breath. The door to the hall opened and she looked over to see her husband, Lord Andarack, entering with their son balanced in one arm while the other held a device for measuring vibrations in spinning shafts. He was making nonsense sounds and Mandoran was replying in sleepy gurgles.

She turned back to Ke. "No, it will kill many, since your poison is so effective, but it won't kill such numbers as Salick and Garet reported. There's also the staff Tarix recovered. It might be very useful, if we can figure out its trick, but no, we cannot win, not without something else. Something more than what we already have. A strategy rather than a machine. Something . . ."

Andarack dropped the device on the bed and stood there, rocking the child in his arms.

"Magic?" Ke asked, her face wrinkling up into a smile. "I thought you do not believe in such things. Is it not all tricks?"

Dasanat went to her husband and took the baby from his arms. She looked down into his little face, half asleep, half awake, studying it.

"Maybe there's some magic that isn't a trick," she said.

At that, Ke laughed aloud and the baby opened his eyes to find his mother smiling down at him.

CHAPTER 7

BLOOD ON THE STAGE

The day had been wonderfully warm, a sure sign that spring had truly replaced winter. The warmth had lingered after the sun eased from the sky. The birds, more of them every day, it seemed, called sleepily from the rooftops. It had rained briefly in the afternoon, and the fresh smell of it remained after dark.

Marick could not imagine a more perfect evening on which to stage a play.

"This is a disaster," Son-neen said. "Why can't we collect coin like we always do? 'Royal Performance.' More like royal thievery!"

Marick raised an eyebrow. "I'll let *you* tell Trax that. I'm surprised he didn't demand we show the new play, even though it's only half written."

"But this one's not even half paid!" Son-neen said.

Marick put an arm around her shoulders. "Think of tonight as promoting the success – and profit – of every other night to come. Those seats can't hold even a ward's worth of people, let alone a city, but if the king watches it tonight, everyone will want to watch, and pay, tomorrow."

The girl grumbled but didn't reply. She pulled away and went back to checking the newest paper demon. This one was much more complex than the simple models of other plays. It stood higher than the girl herself and could be raised in sections, each one hidden within the last, until it topped the back curtain on the stage. Instead of holding it up from behind a piece of scenery and waving it about, Son-neen would have to wear this false beast like a suit of paper armour and manipulate the parts from within.

"Nobody will pay if the earth shakes again," she said, "and if it does, I could fall over in this thing and kill Toonan instead of the other way around. Maybe someone else should do it."

Marick frowned at this rare display of doubt. An uncertain Son-neen was as unlikely as a humble Trax. "What do you mean? No one plays a demon better than you, well, maybe Allifur and I did, but neither of us want to try that again! I'm serious though, you really are better than anyone else here. What's wrong?"

"Nothing," she said, turning to hide her face.

Marick swung her back around on her stool and took out a handkerchief from his pocket. He put it in her hand. "There, that's a very famous piece of silk. I want you to have it."

"Why?" Son-neen said.

"Well, I still owe you for all the trouble I got you into, don't I?"

"No," she sniffed. "You're all paid up. I can show you the accounts, claw it all!"

Marick looked at her. "Your cursing like a citizen now, but why does that make you sad? I thought you'd be happy when I finally paid off my debt."

The tears started again, and he pulled his own seat

closer until he was facing her. Son-neen looked very small sitting there, long arms wrapped around her body, long legs twisted around the stool's supports.

"Because you don't have to be my partner anymore! And you'll all send me back to the City of Fountains because I'm too loud and too impolite, and too . . ."

"Too much like yourself?" Marick asked. He leaned forward and lifted her chin. "Who says we're not partners? Listen, I couldn't do this without you anymore than you could do it without me, yes? And besides, I still owe you, and probably will for the rest of my life, claw it!"

"Are you saying my accounts are wrong?" she demanded and used the handkerchief to blow her nose.

Marick smiled and shook his head. "I'd never dare! But listen, when I was in your city, and after that disaster at the Mother of Waters, I felt, well, helpless. Believe me, that was a new experience! But it's true. I thought my place in the world was gone and I was . . . left behind again, like I was in Old Torrick when my mother . . . Claws and teeth, it's hard to talk about that, even now. That's why I stole those things from you and Vinir. I wasn't anything anymore, and I wanted to be *something*, even a thief."

"You're a terrible thief," Son-neen said, smiling a bit. "You always get caught."

"And punished!" Marick said, tapping his wooden leg. "The fact is, I couldn't find my way back from that deep pit on my own. It was like an open wound that wouldn't heal. Dying under that Horned demon's claws would have been a relief."

"Not to me!" she said, then quickly added, "Not to any of your friends."

Marick smiled. He saw the mechanical who set the

scenery give him a wave. He waved back but did not move from his stool.

"Thank you for saying that. The point is, you brought me back. Every time you told me I owed you, and you were going to get it out of my hide one way or the other, you were really telling me I had some worth left, if only a little and only to you. You know, I think I would have died in body as well as spirit if you hadn't been such a terrible pest."

The mechanical waved again, frantically, and Marick stood up. "I have to go see what his problem is," he said.

Son-neen unwrapped herself from her own stool and faced him. "Are you saying I saved your life?" she asked, in a very small voice for the girl. She shifted a step closer.

"Yes, and I want to stay partners, and no more talk of who owes what," he answered, moving a bit closer himself.

"Are we going to kiss?" she asked.

"Maybe," Marick said. "I think I've written enough kissing scenes now to give it a try myself. Is that all right?"

"Maybe," she said, then stepped back. "But I want to think about how to do it first."

The mechanical was fairly jumping up and down in the corner of Marick's vision.

"Think during the performance then," he said, and picked up his cane. "But not while you're playing the Stalker demon. I don't want it blowing kisses at the audience."

"It won't," Son-neen said, flashing a smile that was at odds with her tear-streaked face.

"Coming Canarr," Marick called out, and went over to see what new disaster had befallen the movable, and often breakable, scenery.

Son-neen watched him go then looked to where Meesa

stood, dressed as a fine lady, practising graceful turns, and looking nervous. Those nerves were not improved when Son-neen grabbed her arm and dragged her behind the curtain.

"I'm busy!" the actor protested, but to little use.

"Forget about that," Son-neen said, staring intently at the pretty young woman. "There's something I have to ask you about."

THE KING and queen arrived just before the curtains drew back to reveal an image of the palace, painted on cloth and wood, covering the back of the stage. The royal couple sat in a middle of a row of comfortable chairs placed among the benches used by less notable folk. Branet and some of the other masters were there, Garet, Salick, and Tarix included. Several lords flanked the royal couple, and beyond them, a line of masked guards led by Bixa stood near.

Lord Kirel stood and bowed to the king and queen. When he was seated again, his wife, Lady Kaela, snapped her fan against his thigh.

"Don't fawn over them, my husband," she said, keeping her voice below the chatter of the crowd. "Trax may pretend he likes flattery, but he knows the weakness of those who use it too much." She nodded pleasantly to Lysere. "And the queen is too shrewd to let any compliments go to her head."

"And what about you, my beautiful, clever wife?" Kirel said, leaning in close to whisper in her ear.

Kaela smiled. "Flatter away, my love. Fortunately for you, I believe you mean it."

The audience in front of them was doing a peculiar dance. They sat, then stood, sat again, then turned on their benches to get a glimpse of the king and the sparkling luminaries around him. Eventually, at Lysere's urging, Trax stood and waved to the crowd, motioning them to sit.

"My friends," he shouted out over the applause. "We are here to watch a play and honour those who fought against the demons on the bridge and between the Clawed Walls. Of all of them, I was the least, but I am the first to thank young Marick for his efforts to preserve the memory of the fallen."

"He looks tired," Lord Kirel said. "With a new child in the palace, he'll get little sleep. I do sympathize with the man."

Kaela studied the king while he spoke. She shook her head. "His restless nights come from another source, I fear. Heaven shield him and us all. You fretted at my hunting down Tiralsh's spies, but I think I had an easier job than poor Trax."

The applause went on for some time, even after the king sat down again and received the congratulations of his nobles. All such noise and trouble vanished when the tall curtains opened and Marick limped out upon the stage. His silver cloak gleamed in the glare of the stage lamps. The demon-headed cane, raised for silence, shone like a baleful star. He paused, dramatically of course, and then spoke to the assembled citizens and lords of Shirath.

"Your Majesties, noble lords, banes, protectors, and citizens of Shirath, welcome! Tonight, we present *The Battle of the Bridge*, a new version with added dialogue, improved scenery, and the always excellent performances of our players. We chose this play to remind us all that though we may fear what is to come, it was not long ago when our city also faced certain destruction. An army of demons descended upon us, and all that stood between Shirath and its end was the bravery of its defenders."

He paused and dropped his hand to thump the tip of the cane on the stage.

"But perhaps it is too terrifying to start our evening with such a bloody battle. Let us raise our spirits before we harrow them! I present to you, the clowns!"

As he moved aside, Garet leaned over to Salick and said, "He plays the crowd like it was a child's toy drum! It's a good thing his voice has deepened, but how did he learn to talk like that?"

Tarix, sitting behind them, leaned forward and answered his question. "By pestering every playwriter in the city for a whole season," she said. "And reading every play he could beg from them or from Barick, our good historian. I'll give credit where it's due; his reading has much improved under Son-neen's gentle teaching."

Salick smiled. "That girl is as gentle as a Northern winter! Look, it's that Meesa woman. Well, at least she's not playing me tonight."

The actor was not in a bane's uniform. Except for a ridiculous amount of makeup, she was dressed as elegantly as any lord and waved a fan about as if shooing away bothersome flies.

"Unless I miss my guess," Tarix said, leaning in again, "Meesa is supposed to be Lady Kaela, a tribute of Marick's, perhaps, from one schemer to another. It also shows the city has forgiven her for any association with Kirel's uncle, Gost."

"There was never any real proof she joined his conspiracy," Garet said. "And she did hand Gost over to the king."

He turned to watch the stage. The Kaela character was

hopping and dancing around the stage until she froze, fan held up to an ear, listening. With a smile and a twist, she hid behind a false pillar. Three men came out from the other side of the stage. They wore red paper masks bearing twisted noses and open grimacing mouths. One unfolded a large piece of paper, a map from what Garet could see, and began to skulk around the stage. Another pulled out a child-sized creature made of cloth and stuffing and began petting it.

"I think that's supposed to be a demon," Salick said. The boos and hisses from the audience showed they thought so as well.

The Kaela character slipped out of hiding, the fan held open before her face, and began to follow the three. At every few steps, they turned to look, at which point she would freeze in mid-step, often comically, while appearing to remain hidden from the rogues, if not from the audience. This chase became more and more absurd, until the actress was walking step-for-step behind the leader, almost touching him. The other two spies broke away and crept to the back of the stage. Meesa pointed her fan at the two while their leader looked the other way, and actors dressed as guards leaped out from behind the back curtains to clap hands on the spies and drag them off.

This led to much frantic searching and even more frantic following. The audience roared with laughter, and even Salick chuckled.

"She's better at comedy than drama," she said, then pointed to where the villain was circling Meesa, looking around suspiciously.

The woman skipped across the stage and snapped open her fan. The man turned, his grotesque mask facing her, straight on. He pantomimed discovery, and drew out a curved, painted knife as exaggerated as his features. He began to creep towards his prey, raising each foot waist-high before setting it daintily down. When he reached a spot in the centre of the stage, the Kaela character held out a warning finger. The spy paused, one leg still lifted. Meesa snapped her fan shut, and a trapdoor opened beneath the man's foot. With a shriek, the only sound made by any of the clowns so far, he fell out of sight, and Meesa twirled around the stage to thunderous applause, stopping just before the lamps and bowing, first to the king and then to where Lady Kaela sat blushing nearby.

The approval went on for some time, and Kaela and Kirel were forced to stand and bow to the actor before people returned to their seats. Kaela found Trax's spymaster, Shula, standing with the rest and saluted with her own fan. Shula winked in return.

The curtains closed and remained that way while the scenery was switched and the actors changed clothes. When it opened again, Marick stood before them, not in silver but in red.

"Now from laughter to tears, from comedy to the clash of spears. I give you, *The Battle of the Bridge!*"

He left the stage and Toonan arrived, dressed as the king, crowned and with a mask covering the top half of his face. Ten or so others followed, bearing spears and wearing similar masks.

"Upon this bridge we make our stand, to clear the beasts from Shirath's land. With guards and Masks and banes as one, let no one rest till the day is won."

Several other actors then made brave statements. Garet and Salick tried to ignore them, since they were sure two of the players were supposed to be them. When the speeches were done, the group stood ready and a hooting roar was echoed over the plaza.

"Son-neen's gotten good at that," Tarix said, shuddering. "It sounds very like a demon."

The trapdoor exploded upwards, leaving its hinges and smashing scenery at the back of the stage. Black claws, bigger than any the banes had ever seen, emerged and scissored together. A beast followed, coming up in sections, each propelled by a pair of stick-like arms. Where the head should have been was a row of black eyes and those sideways claws, or perhaps jaws, clicking together like an iron-smith's tongs. The creature pulled itself forward, until it was all on the stage, facing the stunned actors.

"That can't be one of Marick's tricks," Salick said. "But what is it?" She fumbled for the trident at her feet but found others stepping on it as the audience realized that the attacking beast was indeed too like a real demon, despite the lack of freezing fear. People began to run, turning over benches in their haste to escape. Bixa tried to bring her guards closer to protect the king but could not move against the press of fleeing humanity.

Toonan stood on the stage, wooden sword raised and gaping at the creature approaching him – a poor strategy, but the beast was worthy of close examination.

Like the other demons who now plagued the city, this one bore silkstone plates fixed just behind its odd crossways jaws. As it advanced on the actors, it snapped the tips of those black blades together, making a sharp clicking sound. To Garet's eyes they looked big enough to cut a man in half.

Even without a paralyzing wave of demon terror, the men and women on the stage stood there, frozen by the hypnotic dance of the demon's many legs. Thankfully, that paralysis broke when another hooting call came rolling over the stage, this one higher and undulating like a lunatic flute. The demon whipped around and found itself facing another of its kind, more or less. This one stood swaying, its arms flailing back and forth in a menacing manner, while its body grew by degrees until it was twice as tall as before.

"WhoooOOOoooooOOO," cried the wood and paper demon, and the real one retreated in some confusion, giving Toonan and the others time to shake off their daze and dive from the stage into the benches below.

Salick, Garet, and the other banes tried to reach them but like Bixa and her guards were held in place by a mass of screaming, struggling crowd. So held, they could only watch when the beast swung its fearsome jaws at its challenger, tearing off its top half and revealing the chalk-white face of Son-neen sticking up from the remains. Toonan, Meesa, and the other actors began throwing benches at the beast, but the thing's skin was armoured in broad plates and it didn't seem to notice.

As Son-neen stumbled back, something flew across the stage and hit the demon where its face should have been, and now the demon did pay notice. It picked up the object, a shaft of wood tipped in silver, in its jaws and snapped the thing in two. The creature then turned and turned again, seeking its new rival. When it focused on the tumult in the plaza, Marick slipped out from behind a painted tree, leaped off his good leg and landed on the demon's back, his red cloak flapping behind him like a set of wings. One hand gripped the nearest jointed leg to hold him in place, and the other came down again and again around the edges of the silkstone plate. Blood spurted across the stage, and the beast finally threw him off, its small legs picking at, but not dislodging, the demon-headed dagger sticking out from between its crosswise jaws.

Son-neen tore herself free of the demon costume to pull Marick away from the thrashing beast. Branet, the bane best able to ford through a sea of bodies, reached the stage and brought his axe down on the creature's back, once, twice, and a third time, nearly cutting it in half. The writhing stopped then, but new cries came from behind them.

Garet and Salick turned, ready to fight another monster, but it was no demon that caused this uproar. A man dressed as a mechanical and bearing a knife was charging towards the king and queen. They were still in their seats, and still without the protection of their harried guards. Lord Kirel grabbed at the man but fell back with an elbow to his face, smashing a bench in his tumbling. The attacker raised the blade and started forward again, but a small figure, elegant in silk and lace, grabbed that arm with both hands and a strong set of teeth.

"Claw you!" the man said. He looked wildly around. The guards were getting nearer, and the banes had reversed direction and were closing from behind. He shook off Kaela, losing some skin in the process, and made to kick her away. At that moment, a squat and muscular woman jumped between them. She wore a silkstone mask and the crest of Lord Kirel's guards. With a truncheon in one hand, she blocked the knife. With the other, she grabbed the would-be assassin by the front of his grey tunic and drove her stone-covered head into his face.

The mask shattered and the man was driven back, nose gushing blood. He kept hold of his knife, screamed in frustration, and raised his arm to fling it at where the king stood shielding Lysere with his body.

That arm never fell, but the dagger did, dropping to his feet as his head was driven forward by the impact of a spiked iron ball against the back of his skull. He was very likely dead before he fell face-first onto the stone paving.

The guard who had protected Kaela pulled the shattered remains of the mask off her face. She was in no way lovely, but the smile she bestowed on the body was almost beautiful.

"Serves you right," Cruster said, swaying on her short bowed legs. Blood trickled down her forehead.

Kaela scrambled up and took her arm. She guided her bodyguard to an empty chair. "Cruster, you're bleeding! Sit here while I tend you." She tore a sleeve from her dress and dabbed at the wound, carefully picking out slivers of stone before she wrapped the cloth around the woman's head.

The injured guard tried to focus on her surroundings and seemed to notice the woman hovering over her for the first time. "Sorry, Lady Kaela. I should have grabbed him so he could be questioned. Think I hit him too hard."

Kaela clucked her tongue and said, "Not at all. It was the bane's hammer that finished him. You did nothing wrong. Indeed, you saved both me and the king. Why, if it wasn't for you, I wouldn't be seeing my baby tonight, nor ever again! Don't think that I will forget this, Cruster. Captain Cruster, I should say, for so you are now. My lord husband, help me get this brave woman to a carriage."

Lord Kirel did as he was told, and smartly too, perhaps remembering how he had failed to stop the traitor's knife where Cruster had briefly succeeded. The two led the guard away and Garet watched them go, shaking a bit while he drew back the rope and the bloody weight attached to it.

"Kaela's quite the woman," a voice said, and he turned to see Shula standing behind him. The woman, motherly looking despite her role as the king's chief spy, held the assassin's dagger, the handle wrapped in a cloth.

"Look, but don't touch," she said, and held the blade out for their inspection. An oily sheen showed on the blade, and a viscous liquid dripped from the tip to stain the ground.

"Poison!" Garet said. "He really meant to kill the king, didn't he?"

Shula wrapped the cloth around and around the weapon before handing it off to a man who disappeared into the crowd. "Lord Andarack will want to see what's on that blade. Yes, ex-agent, ex-and-yet-once-again bane, they do want the king dead. Enough to bring a fear-blocked demon into the city – though how they got past all the patrols, I don't know – and loose it upon Marick's play as a diversion. The lad was quick with his dagger, wasn't he?"

Her voice held admiration, and Garet remembered that the two had once been allies in the fight against traitors within the city's walls.

"So, was he Tiralsh's man?" he asked, deliberately looking away as Bixa's guards rolled the body in a cloak and carried it off. He looked down and wished he hadn't, for some of it had been left behind.

"Makes a mess, doesn't it?" Shula said. "That weapon of yours. But think on this, bane, how much of a mess would Trest there have made if he had managed to kill the king? The city's hope depends on his leadership, not mine, not yours, not even the hallmaster's. With the king dead, the panic alone would have killed thousands."

"Trest," Garet said, not really wanting to put a name to the man he killed.

All those words I poured onto Salick's guilt about killing that brigade thug in the North. I can't say they mean much now, not when measured against a pool of blood and brains on the ground at my feet.

Shula nodded. "He's the Trader who fled with Tiralsh in the winter. Kaela, tricky little plotter that she is, found some of Tiralsh's hidden caches and left them untouched to see if anyone came back to use them. We found one emptied two days ago, and we've been searching ever since. We've also tripled the patrols outside the city."

Salick came up and laid a hand on Garet. She looked him in the eyes and understanding passed between them. Half smiling, she gave him a shake, then turned her attention to Shula.

"Bixa is taking Trax and Lysere back to the palace. Shula, if the patrols outside the walls were increased, how did this demon get past both the banes and your guards, then through the walls and into the Palace Plaza without alarm?"

While Shula frowned, Garet thought back over the events of the last few days.

"That shaking," he said. "Maybe it wasn't some Heaven-sent warning but something digging below the city. Come on."

He led the others back to the stage, where the actors were examining the twisted body of the demon from a distance. The impossible creature still lay draped over the edge of the pretend bridge. "Marick!" he called out, and the young man, sitting beside Son-neen with his arm around her shoulders, looked up.

"The king?" he asked.

"Safe, and the queen as well. They've returned to the palace. The only one . . . injured was the assassin."

"It was Trest," Shula said, and Marick growled.

"Claw that traitor! He's the one who beat me in

Tiralsh's house and dumped Allifur and me in that demon cell. So, he dared to sneak back into Shirath to kill Trax? I'd write a play to show his evil heart, but I'd never find an actor base enough to play him!"

"I'll try," one of the actors said, and Garet recognized him as the man who had portrayed Draneck in the other play.

Marick ignored him. After a measuring look at the still-shaking Son-neen, he stood and came forward to the edge of the stage. Without his walking stick, his limp was more notice-able. Toonan skirted the beast's corpse – giving it no wider a berth than a hero should – and handed him back the dagger.

"I took it out and cleaned it, Marick. Maybe you should play the hero next time," he said, smiling, and the actors all applauded, one hand slapping the back of the other until Marick waved them to silence.

"No, thank you! Though I hate to say it, you look better in the role than I do! Let's just say that tonight we had to deal with an unruly critic."

There was laughter at that, and Son-neen came over to climb off the platform and stand beside Salick. The bane hugged her, pressing the girl's tear-stained face against her shoulder.

"Easy there," she said. "You did well against such a beast. It was terrified of that paper demon you waved about."

"No more than I was of it," Son-neen said, and turned away to wipe her eyes on a silk handkerchief. "But Marick wasn't afraid."

"He wasn't?" the subject of their conversation asked. "I'm sure he was terrified!"

Son-neen reached up to offer him a hand, and he took it

to ease himself over the edge and stand beside her. Salick looked at Garet and smiled.

"I really was though," the young man said. "Afraid, I mean. Enough to make my toes curl, even the wooden ones."

"Fool," Son-neen said, but there was more affection than heat in the words.

Marick turned to stare at the dead demon. "I've seen something like that before, but not a demon. The sand-walkers call them pit-killers. We should have Yala or Ke take a look, but I'd guess the slavers brought it north for the Itaalk to make into a demon. Funnily enough, that first one was trying to kill me too."

"The things you people think are funny," Son-neen said, and leaned against him.

Salick coughed, capturing the couple's attention.

"That beast got here very quietly, Marick. Is there a drain nearby, one that leads into a main sewer tunnel?"

Son-neen nodded. "Yes, behind us by a dozen of your yards. We had to move the platform forward to avoid it when we first set up. It was only a minor problem, and not costly to fix."

She led them around the stage supports and back to the drain, only to find it open. It was more than open, for the iron grate was lifted off, the pins ripped from the surrounding stone, and a black hole gaped beneath.

Salick sighed. "Well, it wouldn't be the first time." She handed her sash and vest to Shula. Garet did the same.

The bane dropped her trident into the hole, judging the distance when it rang against the bottom.

"Like before?" she asked, and Garet nodded.

"What's going on?" Son-neen demanded, then at

Marick's whispered explanation, she ran off and returned with two surviving lanterns from the foot of the stage.

Marick held up the demon-headed dagger and offered it to Garet. "This will work better in a tunnel than that skull-splitter on your belt," he said, and took the rope-hammer from the frowning bane. Marick tied the pick end around his waist. Son-neen anchored him with her arms around his waist and shoulders.

Shula, looking rather odd with two red sashes hanging around her shoulders, smiled encouragement. "We'll tell Branet – he's still around here somewhere – and make sure others follow. Oh, and I'll ask him to have towels, hot water, and, hmm, clean uniforms ready for you at the hall."

"Remember to make notes so I can use them in—" Marick began, but Son-neen interrupted him.

"Your next play. There's always a next play, so don't worry about that. Just don't die."

Salick laughed. "We won't, I hope! Are you sure you don't want to join us, Marick, for old time's sake?"

The ex-bane shook his head. "Hah! Everyone wants me to play the hero again when it took me so long to learn some sense. No, thank you. I have some important business to take care of here."

Salick smiled and was lowered down first, followed by Garet. The rope-hammer drew back and the three faces, dim against the stars, disappeared.

The banes held out the lamps and saw the marks of claws and patches scraped clear of slime leading off in one direction and nothing disturbed in the other.

"Well," Salick said, holding the lamp in one hand and her trident in the other. "The smell is much as I remember. North?"

"North again," Garet said, and followed her lead.

THE HALLMASTER CAUGHT up with the king and his guards just before they reached the palace. Lysere was already inside and Bixa was trying to convince the king to follow.

"Please, Your Majesty. I'll send for the hallmaster and Marick as soon as you are safe inside."

"No need," Trax said. "Branet is here."

The king's sword was in his hand, the shining length of it resting lightly against one shoulder. Trax eyed Branet and slowly dropped the point of the blade until it rested on the stone between his boots. "What happened?" he demanded.

Branet wiped sweat from his forehead. Running across the whole of the plaza was more work than killing a demon. He took a deep breath and said, "The assassin – Trest, it was – died by Garet's hand and the demon by my own, though Marick of all people had a hand in that. The audience fled, perhaps taking any of Trest's accomplices with them. Shula sent word there's a sewer tunnel behind the stage that Salick and Garet are now searching. I've sent word for as many Golds as possible to travel above ground in the direction it seems to lead. With Heaven's luck, they'll meet at the tunnel's entrance and find whoever sent that man to kill you."

Trax's expression was guarded. "And if they find these killers?"

Bixa answered. "They'll bring them back to be questioned. We need more information."

Branet nodded, but Trax shook his head. He sheathed his sword and looked down at the captain of his guards. "We need only know how to kill them better, Bixa. Killing them on sight will tell our enemies more than any of their lies would tell us."

The king went inside the palace, both preceded and followed by many guards. Bixa and Branet looked at each other.

"Claws," the captain said. She pushed back her sling to scratch the skin above her wrist. "He's wrong about that! If Master Tarix had killed Tarock in the forest, we'd know nothing of what's to come. And as much as I hate these traitors, you can't treat people like demons . . . can you?"

The hallmaster shook his head. "We don't kill in Shirath, do we, Bixa? Not unless we're attacked and have no choice. Think of it, how many murders have we had in the wards, by people, I mean, not demons? A handful in drunken brawls? And that's in my entire life! We work too hard to stay alive for us to easily end a life, even a life we hate. And there was Shirin . . ."

Bixa nodded. Exiling the Mask had led to her death, and Branet would never forgive himself for demanding it. The hallmaster said nothing more, and the captain, after one more searching look into the man's face, turned and followed the king.

The hallmaster looked up to Heaven's dome and found the Plowman, the constellation he had been born under. Perhaps he should consult an astrologer like Mistress Alanick and learn what his future held. At the very least, she might give him advice on how to deal with a difficult king.

He decided against it and began the long walk back to the banehall. He had never been a man to seek his future in the stars, and given the desperate times, it was doubtful whether or not those tiny trembling lights would have any clue about what would happen next.

∾

THE SEWER TUNNEL ended in a maze of smaller outlets save one, a demon-sized hole torn through the stonework and leading – as best as the two banes could guess – under the walls and into the northern fields. Garet touched the roof and jumped back when a head-sized clod of dirt fell at his feet.

"It's not safe," he said.

Salick held her lamp forward and sniffed. "It wasn't safe when we started, was it? Shall I go first?"

Garet frowned. He hated to think that what he considered caution would be seen by Salick as cowardice. "No," he said. "I'll go. I'm not afraid, just . . ."

Salick looked at him, eyes wide. "I didn't mean . . . Claws, you know I speak without thinking. I just meant I don't mind going first. If you don't want to?"

"Go ahead," Garet answered stiffly. "I'll follow."

Salick looked at him for a moment then hung the lantern hook on the central prong of her trident. She held the light up and moved forward, stumbling a bit over the loose dirt of the new tunnel's floor. Mud and dirt kept dropping from above, but she kept walking and Garet followed close behind. The floor slumped down for some yards, then rose sharply, and a raised lantern showed the foundation of the wall overhead, the stone scraped by the demon's frantic passage. The climb back up on the outside of the wall was difficult. The floor shifted several times, making little landslides and forcing the two banes to crawl upwards against the flow of dirt.

"Here," Salick said. "It's better now that we're past the wall."

She reached back but no hand took her own. She looked over her shoulder and saw Garet's lantern guttering on the slope. The young man huddled beside it, face buried in his muddy hands. She carefully slipped back down until she could lay a hand on his shoulder.

"What's wrong?" she asked, and when she got no answer, shook him. That made the lamp slide all the way back down to the lowest point of the tunnel, and she had to grab Garet's collar to keep him from following.

The only light was above them, left with Salick's trident in the part of the passage outside the wall.

"Garet, come up, please," Salick said, and pulled him up by the strength of her arms and legs, creeping up the incline until they rested on a level floor.

Garet stayed curled up, and Salick could hear his harsh breathing through the mud and felt his chest rise and fall beneath her arms. She gently but firmly pulled him up to face her. With one hand, she wiped the grime from his face and stroked his forehead.

"What is it? Tell me, please, my love."

Garet stopped gasping long enough to look at her and say, "It's too close in here. I can't breathe!"

She looked around them and nodded. The sharp circle of light showed mud walls barely four feet apart and not much higher. Even the sewers were bigger than this, and less likely to collapse and bury them alive.

"I know, I know," she said, holding him tightly. "I feel it too, but we have to keep going. We must find the exit and see if any more of Tiralsh's traitors are there with more demons. Listen, if it gets too much, we'll just dig ourselves out! Between my trident and Marick's fancy dagger, I'm sure we can climb up to the fields and free ourselves."

Garet nodded, his mud-streaked head dropping against her shoulder. His jerking breaths paused, slowed, and he pushed himself upright, bracing his back against the tunnel wall. "All right. Sorry, Salick. It's just . . . what happened back in the plaza. It seemed to follow me here like a ghost out of an old tale. This tunnel is so tight, I couldn't get away from . . . thinking about what I did."

Salick held his face in her hands and looked into his eyes. Her own shone in the lamplight.

"Do you remember what you said to me about that spearman I killed in the North, the one taking those children?"

Garet nodded. "I said you didn't do it on purpose, and you acted to save those children." He sniffed and smiled. "Branet and Tarix said the same thing when they read your report."

She nodded. "I remember! But listen, they will say the same thing to you. You acted to save the king."

"But I did it on purpose," Garet said, tears starting again. "You didn't. You just meant to knock that brigade man off his horse, but Salick, I knew the blow would kill Trest when I sent the weight flying! It was my choice." He looked around him and shuddered.

Salick didn't let go of him but forced the bane to look into her eyes. "Yes, your choice, like when you chose to protect Master Mandarack two years ago by throwing a stone at that clawed fool Adrix."

She was referring to a time when the banehall was in the middle of a civil war, when the old hallmaster, Adrix, had sought the death of Mandarack and the capture of any who followed him. Adrix had attacked Mandarack with a spear at the most desperate point in that struggle, and Garet had used his skill with a thrown stone to cripple the man, shattering his knee and ending the struggle.

"I didn't kill Adrix," Garet said, but he stood up as much as possible in that cramped space and tried to brush the sludge off his pants and boots.

Salick stooped beside him and picked up her trident, lifting the lamp with it. "No, you didn't. But if that had been your only choice back then, you would have made it, like tonight. I would have made the same choice, you know that, don't you?"

Garet nodded. "I suppose so. Let's get on with this, before I break into pieces. I wonder what happened to him?"

"Who?" Salick asked. She began moving forward, trying not to brush the walls or ceiling and dislodge more dirt.

"Adrix," Garet said. Despite his light tone, he crowded Salick's back, still shaking under the weight of the night's events.

"No one cares," Salick said. "There, smell that. Fresh air, fresher than the smell coming off these clothes, anyway."

"Hurry up," Garet said, and pulled Marick's demon-headed dagger from his belt.

The moon was long down when Branet leaned over the counter in the records room and examined the two towel-wrapped banes. He sniffed suspiciously. Vinir and Lord Andarack, also watching, smiled.

"And it went under the walls?" the hallmaster asked.

Salick nodded, brushing back a strand of damp hair behind her ear. "Yes, deep below the foundations," she said. "Marick thinks this demon was made from a pit-killer from the Far South, a very large insect that digs with those big sideways jaws, so we guess it made the tunnel. Trest could have controlled it with one of those staffs Tarix took, but we haven't found one yet. It could be buried in the tunnel, or he might have had an Itaalk helping him, one who got away and took the staff with him. We'll probably never know. What we do know is the digging goes for well over a league past the walls, under the fields and nearly to the edge of the hills and forest proper. It was made quickly, maybe only for this attack, since parts of it are already falling in. The people in the Sixth Ward will have to do a lot of filling in or some streets might collapse."

Garet looked up and nodded. "It was too dangerous to come back the same way, so we returned above ground with the Golds you sent to help us. Thank you for that, Hallmaster."

The man waved it away and looked at the line Garet was drawing across a map of the city and its surroundings. He held the brush gently in one hand and the towels that protected his dignity tightly in the other.

"It came out here. We filled the entrance with rocks, though I suppose a big enough demon could just dig it out again. We'll need to pay attention to reports of any more tremors."

Lord Andarack nodded and looked down upon the map. He took the pen from Garet's hand and began making lines and notes along the border between Shirath's last stands of planted timber and the Itaalk's forest.

"We could set up patrols farther out, but that requires even more trained guards, and we don't have them," the ward lord said. "Yala's people might help, but the king doesn't want to give away their presence. Though, perhaps our enemies know of them already, if they're coming in and out of the city so easily! In the meantime, I think the devices we use to check for shaking in the big spark-gear motors could detect another tunnel being dug. We can set them above each ward on the north side, and the banes looking after the arrow-throwers could watch them."

He blew the ink dry, rolled up the map and tucked it into one of the many pockets in his coat. "That is one problem dealt with," he said. "But we are faced with another. With a tunnel so long that it avoided all patrols, perhaps a spy did make their way back to the forest. Tiralsh and the Itaalk might already know of the sandwalkers and their poison."

Branet shook his head. "I don't think so. Shula and Kaela are two spiders that let nothing out of their webs, no matter what finds its way in, and the outside patrols are looking for anyone trying to leave the city. No, this attack speaks of desperation. I'm sure Tiralsh's previous failures have made her anxious to prove her worth to the Itaalk. I think she sent her lieutenant, Trest, to make whatever mischief he could manage, which makes me think this was a plot birthed by opportunity, not planning."

Salick ignored a proffered cup of tea from Vinir, preferring to hold on to her dignity with both hands. "I don't think I understand you, Hallmaster," she said.

Branet sat across from the young women. "I'll explain this much, then to bed for both of you. Travelling through the sewers, for a second time now, if I recall correctly, is much to ask of anyone, even such diligent Reds."

He leaned back and tapped the arms of his chair twice before continuing. "My belief is that, yes, Trest wanted to kill Trax if he could, but he had no set plan of how to do it. After the last attempt on his life, the king goes nowhere without a squad of masked guards. Neither does Lysere, and the palace is now better protected than the hall. Any demon digging there would find a dozen spears in its back before it could clear the hole."

He rubbed his chin and grimaced.

"No, I think Trest had some of the luck Heaven gives the

bad as well as the good. No doubt he saw one of Marick's clawed posters about the 'Royal Performance' and realized that – with a demon as a diversion – he might kill the king and escape in the confusion."

Vinir put the cup on the small table beside her friend and asked, "After he saw this gift of a royal performance, did he go back to the Itaalk's valley for the demon? Or did he have it nearby, in case of need?"

The hallmaster shrugged, but Andarack spoke up from his seat by the door. "The latter, I think. And it's no surprise, since they seem to have so many at hand. Branet, I can't fault your logic. You really should have been a mechanical!"

He smiled at the hallmaster, but Salick noted how thin Andarack had become since they had left for the North. His cheeks were gaunt, his eyes shadowed, and she wondered if he slept at all these days.

"I fear this attack of fear-blocked creatures is having an effect," the ward lord continued. "Before, when the terror came, you knew that banes would be alerted and could hope they would arrive before the beast found you. Now, the demons appear without warning, and in even more grotesque forms than before. The banes and guards are forced to chase every shadow and noise. Some say it's an omen of the city's downfall, though they said that about the shaking too."

He yawned and Salick forgot her dignity enough to reach out one hand to grasp his thin fingers. "Lord Andarack, you are so weary! Stay here in the hall tonight. I'll take a message to Dasanat and let her know. I'd feel I was betraying your brother's memory if we didn't host you tonight."

Andarack started to protest, but Branet cut him off.

"She's right, you know. Between babies and demons, you've had no sleep at all. We will send word. Not you, Master Salick, but another, for you are off to bed as well."

He yawned prodigiously and shook himself all over. "And it seems I could also use some rest. Enough! To sleep, all. Master Vinir, would you see a message sent to Lady Dasanat and one to Trax with news of what these two found?"

Vinir nodded. "Gladly, Hallmaster, for I'm fresh from night patrols and I'll not sleep till dawn! Go. I'll deal with the messages."

She helped Salick up and pulled the towels tighter around her friend. Sniffing, she said, "No more bathing tonight. I judge, my fellow master, that you're finally scrubbed clean of sewer smell."

"Find me a uniform, will you?" Salick whispered. "The one they left in our room is too big."

"That's because it's one of mine," Vinir said. "But I'll see what I can do."

When the room was cleared, she sat down at the nearest table and began to write messages to the king and the mechanicals' hall. Garet had left the demon-headed dagger there, and after a moment's thought, she added one more note for Marick.

"I told that brave little imp my gift would come in handy someday," she said to the empty room, and picking up both the pages and the dagger, went out to find the duty messengers, a group of sleepy Black and Blue Sashes, to send them running through the night.

CHAPTER 8
A LACK OF VISION

The sun was low, red, and shining directly into the king's eyes. He blinked and turned away, slipping between the curtains to step back into the darkened room. The royal bedchamber boasted much overstuffed furniture: chairs big enough to curl into, couches as wide as a weaver's cot, and a bed of kingly proportions, but Trax stood there, swaying a bit and resisting the call of comfort.

Fifteen days until the equinox when Tarock claims the demons fall on us in force, and I have no hint of a plan to stop them.

Lysere moaned in her sleep and turned beneath the quilts. The lines of worry deepened briefly, then disappeared as her breathing slowed. Part of Trax wanted to go to her, hold her in his arms, and protect her from the bad dreams that plagued her, but he didn't.

He couldn't.

No one could take away dreams. He had his own, in which waves of demons came over the walls of Shirath. The city buckled and burned and the screams of its citizens were drowned in blood. In the worst of these nightmares, the horde came into the palace, up the broad, curving stairs to the door of this room. They tore Lysere apart while he watched, frozen, then went to the crib. He often woke screaming his daughter's name.

"Noella," Lysere said, turning again. Relenting, Trax went to her and laid a hand against her cheek. She opened her eyes and the green irises, like spring leaves, looked up at him.

"My husband," she said, her voice soft. "Did you sleep any better?"

"Yes," he lied. "You rest now. I'll have the nurse tend to Noella and bring her to you later."

Not awake enough to protest, Lysere nodded and closed her eyes. She did not know Trax stood over her for a long time, gazing at her, and sometimes past her, until he left their rooms and went down the stairs. On the way, he instructed a steward to take the child and let the queen rest for now and to summon Bixa and Barick.

The man left as quickly as one could with the dignity of a palace steward, and Trax stood there, neither upstairs nor down, thinking.

What good will it do to argue with Bixa again? Or Branet? Or even Garet? They put their hopes in arrow-throwers and maps, while I just see the folly of it all. We would need five hundred machines and a lake of poison to guard every foot of the city walls. And guards? With barely one hundred and twenty banes in fighting condition, we'd need to double – no, triple – the number of trained guards, and yet half the ones we have now know a shovel better than a pike!

He continued his descent, turning at the bottom of the stairs and moving more by memory than sight until he came to the open door of the Shouting Room. It was empty, save for a pair of stewards. Trax stalked over to the map-table and stared into the model of Shirath. From this vantage point, it looked so . . . open.

Like that cursed box. I tried for two seasons to close it on that jewel. I suffered the tortures they say Heaven saves for the likes of Tiralsh, but to no use. I couldn't close it. My city is just as open, and I fear the demons will have no trouble shutting the lid on it forever.

He shook himself at that and signalled the stewards for wine. They brought both that and a platter of toast and tea. Trax ignored the food and began drinking. While he drank, he stared at the miniature city and waited for his advisors.

"MORE MASKS," Bixa said. "We can use all our silkstone and hand them out wherever the demons attack, along with weapons. Then we can blunt the attack until—"

"They attack somewhere else?" Trax said. "The walls have never kept demons out. Branet claims they're meant to keep them in, along with every other wall in between the wards, on the roofs, and so on."

He leaned forward and put a finger on top of the model of the wall. "How many arrow-throwers now, one per ward? And Dasanat will only double that in the time we have."

"If we put every archer—" Bixa began, but Trax cut her off.

"Then the demons will take slightly longer to enter the city than if the archers were not there at all. They'll pick a spot and a thousand of them will claw their way to the top and butcher all the defenders while the rest of us are running across the city to help them."

While Bixa ground her teeth, Trax stared into the model.

"No," the king said, leaning forward in his gilt chair. "Don't you see? It's the city itself that's against us. We fight two enemies. One inside and the other outside."

The guard captain shook her head. "Then strike against them before they can bring their army! Let me take a hundred guards and Masks up that forest road . . ."

Trax didn't even bother to turn towards the woman when he answered. "Don't be a fool."

Barick looked at the stunned captain, coughed behind a hand, and said, "Perhaps, Your Majesty, Hallmaster Branet or Master Garet could—"

"What," Trax demanded. "Change the shape of the city? Make the walls fall upon our enemies? I'm sorry, Barick, but this is outside your area of expertise. Leave us."

Bixa waited until the man had left before speaking again. "That was unfair. Barick did well in the Far South, arranging for the sandwalkers to come to our aid and even opening trade routes to the City of Fountains."

Trax shook his head. "The sandwalkers are welcome, but they won't be enough, even if more arrive in time. As for trade, we'll have nothing to trade but our bones in fifteen days. Leave me, Captain, for it seems I'm the only one in this city who sees things as they are."

The woman set her jaw and protested, "No one can do this alone! Branet and Lord Andarack might give some counsel—"

"No!" Trax shouted and slapped the top of the model wall, cracking it from top to bottom. "They can do nothing! Nothing! Remember, Captain, who the demon masters wanted dead tonight. Me, not Branet, nor Andarack, and certainly not you. If there is an answer here, they know I will be the one to find it and no one else. Go!"

Bixa left, and the king was alone, except for two stewards who, when the king turned away, exchanged worried glances. Trax looked down into the broken city and drummed his fingertips on the tabletop.

"What am I missing?" he said and began chanting those words over and over again while the stewards stared.

CHAPTER 9
A BROKEN WAY

Called after little sleep and sent running through the Banehall Plaza, Garet followed a panicked guard over the Centre Bridge and then to the East Bridge gate on the palace side. Coming past the waiting palace guards and onto the span, he found the king standing near the break between the south and north ends. Lights were showing on the other two bridges, but this one, still not repaired from bank to bank, was empty save for the king and the bane. The king's personal guard had allowed Garet through the gate but did not follow.

"Your Majesty?" Garet said. The king stood dangerously close to the edge of the new construction, only a few feet from the dark gap and the water below. He did not turn at Garet's words, so the bane came carefully up beside him.

"I suppose you haven't come to beg for your job back," Trax said. He kept his eyes on the emptiness in front of him. His voice was as flat as a sword blade, and Garet began to fear for the man's sanity.

"Come back to the palace, Trax," he said. "The attempt

on your life must have been upsetting, but your city needs you."

He lay a careful hand on the king's arm, but Trax shook it off. Garet glanced back at the guards. They were whispering to each other and one went running off, probably to the palace.

"Upsetting?" the king said. "We both know there are things more *upsetting* than a single man with a poisoned blade! And what of you? Aren't you upset? After all, it was your weapon that scattered the man's brains."

Garet swallowed. "To protect you," he said. "I did it to save your life."

Trax rounded on him. "As if I couldn't protect myself – and my queen?" He slapped a hand on the temporary railing. The poles vibrated for a moment then stilled. At the same time, the king's anger seemed to lessen. "You never saw the demon that broke this bridge, did you?" Trax asked, turning away to look down into the darkness.

The bane shook his head. "I saw Vinir's drawing. The thing was a brute! I'm surprised the guards and Masks fought it off."

"They did, and they didn't," Trax said. "The ones on this bridge and the centre span did push it off, though not without damage, as you see. And deaths, yes, there were many deaths. But it was one of Dasanat's big bows that killed it. I don't know the bane's name, but he had the brilliant idea of picking the whole thing up and moving it along the wall until he had a clear shot. Tell me, Garet, why weren't we that smart? Why didn't we put arrow-throwers on the bridges, or at least on the walls facing them?"

Garet shook his head. "It probably never occurred to Bixa, or Branet, or anyone, Your Majesty. Swimming demons are rare, and we forgot about this weakness in the middle."

Trax smiled, almost a grimace. "You mean I forgot. You can claim innocence in this debacle, for you and Salick were off in the North chasing dragons. I did this."

He struck the scaffolding again, harder.

"This isn't your fault. You are not the demon!" Garet said, with some force. He pulled Trax around – and back from the edge.

"You, Andarack, Branet, Dasanat, Bixa, and everyone else, me included, can only do what we can see to do, and what we have the strength for! This isn't our fault. We didn't make that demon, and you didn't kill those guards. I killed, last night, saving your life, whether you think I needed to or not, and I'll take that death to the funeral fire with me. Let Heaven judge me as it will, but it won't blame you for the deaths on these bridges."

Trax's face was impassive, and Garet took a deep breath before he continued.

"Listen, we need you, Trax. We need your brains and courage to help us make some plan to save the city." He released the king and was shocked to see tears on the man's mask-like face.

"I can't. Don't you see? No one can. There are too many of them this time. The city can't be saved. Shirath's walls are too long and our trained people too few."

"Even with Yala's people?" Garet asked.

Trax shook his head. "They help, of course, but fifty-odd archers, no matter how skilled, cannot defend all our walls."

Garet thought of all the half-formed ideas running through his head these past days. "What about that staff?" he demanded.

Trax leaned back against the railings. The poles groaned but held. He continued in that flat tone. "Dasanat says she might be able to . . . amplify its effects, but not enough to cover all of Shirath, and it can't be everywhere at once. Neither can we, and our enemies know this. They won't let us choose the battlefield, like we did at the Battle of the Bridge. They'll come at us from all sides, testing our defences until they break them. My guess is they'll take the northern half of the city first then pour across the remaining bridges and wipe us out. If we burn the bridges, they'll just find another way across and repeat the process on what's left of us."

The king turned and looked down into the flowing water, half lit by the lamps of the Centre Bridge. He gripped the railings so hard the wood creaked. "The clawed fact I stumble over, Garet, again and again, is that no amount of wit, bravery, or luck can save this city."

There was a commotion at the gate, but Garet ignored it. He put his hands on Trax's shoulders and shook him gently.

"Even so, you can't be thinking of . . ." He didn't finish, but the involuntary glance he sent to the water's surface brought a flash of anger to Trax's face.

"Fool!" he said, shaking off the bane. "I don't have the luxury of a cowardly escape. I came here to think, to get away from those prattling lords, from Bixa, from Branet, and from banes like you! I needed air, and to think alone, and this was the best place to do it."

"Trax!" a woman's voice called, and Lysere was there, accompanied by a single guard. "What are you doing out here, my love?" she asked. "The guards were fearful."

Trax looked at them both, a cold distance in his manner. He took Lysere's outstretched hands. "Everyone thinks I want to do myself harm. How amusing! Why should I bother when the demons will do it for me without any great effort on my part? No, I didn't come here to drown myself but to make a decision, one that will no doubt sully my name in Barick's histories, if anyone is left to read them."

He walked with the queen back to the gate, pausing only to say over his shoulder, "Bane, tell the hallmaster that I require his attendance tomorrow morning at first light."

The guard trailed after them, confused at such a calm ending to the night's drama. Garet was left alone on the bridge. He breathed out some of the tension in his shoulders and then breathed in cool air. The equinox was fast approaching, and somewhere in the north, the forest Itaalk were preparing their army of Human demons. Tiralsh's son, Tarock, had sworn that they meant to destroy Shirath first before attacking the other cities along the Ar: Old Torrick, Illick, Akalit, even mighty Solantor.

Garet shook his head. This wasn't like the king. Trax acted like he had given up, despite what he said about a decision. There had to be some way to win. What if Bixa was right, and they should gather their forces and take the road Master Tarix found, fight their way along it, and destroy the demons at their source?

After one last look at the black, surging water below, he shivered and walked back to the gate, still held open by a nervous guard. Garet paused inside the gate to try and think it through.

I suppose Trax is right after all. Trying to fight our way through that narrow tunnel of trees Tarix described, facing Basher demons, and maybe worse, sounds more like a desperate last chance than a plan. And what about the Human demons we saw? Those caves were full of them, still sleeping, changing. Are they ready now? If Bixa did lead us all north, would an army of those ruined people be waiting for us, or worse, go around us and attack the city?

He cut west across the plaza to the gates to the Centre Bridge. Branet might still be awake – another man who rarely slept, it seemed – and would want to know of the king's request, and about Trax's strange mood.

The wind blew across the open space, tossing Garet's hair and blowing dust into his eyes. He stood there for a moment, blind and confused, feeling the world spinning around him, out of control.

CHAPTER 10

A DECISION MADE

Trax had slept a bit and seemed more himself in the morning, though Lysere kept a careful eye on him as the hastily arranged council convened. The meeting had moved from the Shouting Room to the grand reception hall on the other side of the main floor. It was rarely used: lords were confirmed here, high justice dispensed, kings crowned, heirs presented, but it stood empty from season to season most years. Now it was almost full. Trax had called together all the notables of the city. Ward lords rubbed elbows with guild officials, as well as the representatives of the mechanicals, the physicians, and the stewards. All the tables from the dining hall and the kitchens had been brought in, and a great square of anxious faces turned to the front of the room, where Trax and Lysere sat on a slightly elevated platform.

The king looked over the hundred or so men and women looking back at him. He glanced at Lysere and smiled to take the worry from her brows.

"Don't fret, my love," he said. "I haven't gone mad, though it may seem so in a moment. Remember, what I say here today is necessary, and not really of my own choosing."

Lysere leaned in and whispered in his ear. "My love, I do not think you mad but perhaps overburdened by events no other king in Shirath has faced, save perhaps the first. I only wish you had told me what you're planning to say today. Don't you want my counsel?"

"Always," Trax replied. "But the reaction I anticipate from everyone, even you, my dear wife, is such that I'd rather take it all at once rather than in many painful doses."

The king stood, and the room fell quiet. He looked around the table, marking those whose reactions would count the most: Branet and several other banes, including Garet and Salick; Lord Andarack and Dasanat, huddled with several other mechanicals and a group of sandwalkers; the new lord of the Trader's ward, Lord Staxan, with his son beside him ready to take notes; and there, glowering in a corner, several Masks gathered around Dirst, their leader.

Trax turned to nod at Bixa before beginning, ignoring her frown. Lysere was not the only one who feared the meaning of this council.

"Lords, masters, banes, and Masks, worthy citizens of Shirath, I welcome you to this meeting, one that will go down in either fame or infamy in Barick's histories, which I see he is writing as I speak!"

He motioned to his butler, and maps were distributed around the room, not enough for everyone to have but enough for everyone to see. The maps showed Shirath and several leagues of its surroundings.

"The question that vexes us all is this: how do we protect our city?" Trax asked. "How do we defend it against thousands, yes, thousands of demons and their masters?"

Some answers rose up from those watching.

"Arrow-throwers," said Lord Bereth of the Second Ward.

"More silkstone," cried Dirst, holding up his own mask.

"That staff Dasanat has," said Cirta, one of Bixa's lieutenants.

The king stepped forward. "Not enough. None of it. If we had a thousand more masks, and men and women trained to use them and fight, perhaps it would do. As for everything else, our arrow-throwers are effective but stationary and may be overrun by a rush of demons, especially big ones. And as for the staff, Dasanat?"

The master mechanical stood. "At best, we can cover a ward, maybe two."

She sat back down, and Ke stood up beside her.

"Town king, you have our poison, do you not? And more of our people will arrive soon to lend our bows to you and your people."

Trax bowed to the sandwalker and said, "I am beyond grateful, Ke, that you bring such help, but unless each of you kills a hundred demons, and does it while running from ward to ward around the city, we will still lose."

Ke sat down, shaking her head.

"The problem is, and always has been, the city itself," Trax said. "It was our home, but now it is a trap. I came to this realization some time ago, and it . . . daunted me. I will not lie to you, of late I have been visited by horrors, both in sleep and in my waking days, horrors that we all have borne, and our parents and their parents back for centuries. I sometimes think we should hear the city walls scream, for all the things they have witnessed."

He paused, but none spoke. The entire room held its breath for his next words.

The king bowed his head for a moment, then raised it again to speak.

"The walls that have helped protect us for six hundred years now aid our enemies. This fact cannot be waved away, no matter how dreadful it is. No bane, Mask, guard, or king can change this."

He held up his hand to stop the distressed murmuring of his listeners. "Once I had accepted this, my course was clear, but it took until this morning to work up the courage to tell you what it will mean for Shirath."

He nodded to the butler, and the man ushered in a group of stewards holding a table high enough so they could edge between the ones at the back of the room. They placed it in the centre of the square and retreated to stand against the walls. The Shouting Room's model of the city stood upon the new table, and Trax descended to enter the space between the increasingly anxious chatter to point at this small Shirath.

"Look here or to your maps. Were we able to send a large army into the field, such as existed before the demons came centuries ago, we might make clever manoeuvres and outflank the Itaalk, lay ambushes and use the land to our advantage. We cannot, for we have only a few hundred ready for that kind of fight. If our limited forces leave Shirath to fight, our enemies have demons enough to confront us in the forest and still send hundreds to spread death and ruin through every ward. If our forces stay behind our walls, we still cannot guard the entire city and all its people. The demon fear will overwhelm anyone who isn't a bane, who isn't masked, or who isn't protected by the staff Master Tarix's team so bravely recovered." He bowed to the group of banes and Tarix returned a wan smile.

"Now," he continued, "if this were a play, I would make some brave speech and we would go forth to destroy our enemy." Some in the room looked hopeful, but Trax shook his head. He took a deep breath and spoke over the model of Shirath in a voice that echoed through the hall.

"This city, our city, is doomed."

It was some time before he could continue, and in the interim, Cirta and some of the other guards had to calm screaming arguments and stop a few fist fights.

When the council was once again seated, some of them shoved back into their chairs, the king came back to the dais and motioned Lysere to stand beside him.

"Listen, all of you! As I have made clear, we cannot save the city because we cannot move it or protect it."

He held up his hand again, and Lysere called out, "Please, listen to him. My husband will not abandon you."

Branet stood. "Yet it seems that is exactly what he is saying. If the city is doomed, what then do you propose, Trax. Surrender?"

The king looked his gratitude at Lysere before answering. "No. That would mean our deaths, for who would expect mercy from a demon? Forget the city and think of your lives, and the lives of those you love."

That brought some silence to the listeners, and Trax spoke into that.

"Not everything is against us. We do, after all, have Dasanat's machines, the silkstone, and the poison and bows of our allies. Also, thanks to Shula and Lady Kaela, our enemies will have no knowledge of our preparations."

Kaela accepted the thanks of several people nearby and smiled knowingly at the king's chief agent.

"As it stands, we have one other advantage. Thanks to banes who risked their lives in distant lands, we know our enemy at least as well as they know us. We will use that to do something the Itaalk will never expect."

"What, Your Majesty?" Branet demanded. The bane was still standing, waiting for Trax's answer.

"We abandon the city," Trax said, and then had to shout over the frantic protests. "Only for a while, I hope. Listen, all of you! We cannot defend the walls, but we can defend our people!"

The last sentence was roared, and that brought some order to the room, if not agreement. One of the lords, Isaken, spoke into it.

"My king," she said, and waved an arm at the gathered citizens. "How can you save us if we're driven out, pursued by demons until we die of starvation? Does Old Torrick have the room or food to take us in? Can we last long enough to reach the other cities with the beasts at our heels? How can we live without Shirath?"

There was much loud agreement to this, and Trax waited for it to subside before answering. "Lord Isaken, let us not doubt each other's intent. We both want the people of Shirath to survive. If we try to save the city, we lose the people, but if we sacrifice Shirath, her people may survive."

Ke stood again. Her high, wavering voice cut across the renewed mutterings. "Town king, you said you would lose it for a while. How will you take it back if you cannot hold it?"

Trax smiled mirthlessly. "At least one person is listening." He came into the centre of the tables again and borrowed Marick's new walking stick to use as a pointer.

The young man looked at him with narrowed, watchful eyes.

Trax used the cane to point to the palace side of the city. "The demons will not use Shirath gently," he said, "but the opposite can also be true. Shirath itself can be a weapon against these beasts. When they attack, we will retreat before them, either from the northern fields or on that demon road Captain Bixa wishes so much to see. Everyone on the palace side must pretend to flee, even those under arms, but in truth most of the ordinary citizens will already be in the southern half of Shirath, or out of the city all together. We will move them, along with supplies to keep them alive, farther south, all the way to the edge of the desert if we must."

Ke nodded. "A few of us can go with them."

Trax bowed. "Many thanks, from all of us, Ke. You are valuable friends indeed! Now, we will retreat over the bridges – Andarack, we must have the eastern one fixed at least enough for some foot traffic – then I intend to lure the creatures into the northern wards and the Palace Plaza both with our retreat and by burning what meat we have to attract the demons. Yala told us that works in the Far South, let us pray to Heaven it does here as well. When the demons crowd in, we fire the northern wards, using oil and burning arrows from the walls."

Dasanat shook her head. "What of the Itaalk who lead them? The staffs they carry could stop the demon's from coming into the flames and send them across the river instead."

Bixa answered for Trax. "If we do this," she said, sounding unsure, but her voice gaining confidence as she spoke, "we could target any Itaalk with the arrow-throwers, even use our own staff and runners to draw the demons in against their will."

Branet looked at the captain and then the king in disbelief. "Are you mad? Any banes using those arrow-throwers would be overrun. And even if they weren't, what do they do when you set half the city on fire?"

"Die, maybe," Tarix said. She stood beside the hallmaster. "Which is what we have been ready to do for this city for six hundred years. Your Majesty, the banes will fight, though we might require some Masks to guard our backs."

Dirst laughed, a rough, braying sound in that polished room.

"Banes and Masks fighting together with the city on fire? How can we resist such a dainty invitation? We'll be there, Trax, but with the wards fired, how will your guards and the rest of the banes hold a thousand demons from escaping? Or do you mean to fight them on the bridges?"

Lysere answered for her husband. "If I read my husband's plans rightly, there will be a fire behind them in the wards and our forces will hold them in the Palace Plaza."

"And we can spray or throw even more oil on the demons when they're crowded together," Lord Andarack said. "I have some ideas for that."

Lord Staxan of the Trader's ward stood up. "Lamp oil is expensive and not transported in great amounts. All the oil we have in the Twelfth Ward wouldn't be enough, and I judge the rest of the wards cannot make up the difference. Of course, all that we do have is available for the defence of the city."

Trax nodded. "Well said, Lord Staxan. You are much more reasonable than your predecessor, may she die under a demon's claws! Luckily, we have other sources to draw on."

A Red Sash unknown to many in the room stood. "Yes, you do. I am Hallmaster Sicarth of Akalit Banehall. Beside me is Hallmaster Chon of Illick. Unlike the banehall in Solantor, we have listened to Master Relict. Between us and Hallmaster Corix of Old Torrick, we can supply much more oil for this, erm, plan of yours."

"And fighters," Hallmaster Chon said. She stood and looked at the others with her one good eye. The other was patched by a strip of red cloth. "We can each send seventy or so banes and still leave enough to protect our cities, especially if the enemy is concentrated here. However, we have no silkstone masks nor any great store of that stone to add to this tally."

"What you bring is enough," Branet said, to the loud approval of the crowd. "And speaks better of your cities than it does of Solantor."

"But what will be left?" a voice said, tremulous but clear.

A middle-aged woman stood up from one of the side tables. She was neither a lord, a bane, nor a Mask, but Trax motioned for her to continue.

"I'm sorry, Your Majesty," she said, ducking her head in a graceless bow. "My name is Harsol. I lead the Weavers Guild in the Fourth Ward. I just want to know, what will be left after the battle? If we win, I mean."

Trax didn't smile. His features were calm but his stance was focused, intense. "I mean to win, Weaver Harsol. As to what will be left, I don't really care. Not anymore."

He walked back over to the model of the city and picked up the wooden building that represented the palace. With no warning, he dropped it to the floor and ground it under his boot.

"Six hundred years of death and deadly fear. Six hundred years of imprisonment within our own walls. Listen, all of you! If the last block of the last wall of Shirath crushes a demon as it tumbles, I will dance on that rubble. As I will dance on the bones of those who want to destroy our people. Do you hear me, all of you?"

He strode around the inside of the tables, fixing each man or woman with a piercing look, his voice rising with each thumping step. "We will use this city as a machine to break them, to grind them to dust. We will end their tyranny forever. We will be free, even if we have only the clothes on our back. Do you hear me?"

The agreement came first as a whisper, then as a roar. The Masks pounded the table and each other's backs. The lords and guild masters screamed agreement, and even the little weaver shook her fist and cried, "Fight!"

Trax signalled the butler before escorting Lysere back to her seat.

"Let them cheer each other for now," he said to the man. "Have food and wine sent in."

Lysere looked at him when he took her elbow. "I see now why you kept this to yourself. You are full of tricks, my husband! Tell me, will Noella and I be sent to the desert while you dance here amid the flames?"

Trax collapsed into the chair beside her. "Yes, you will, and I would be there with you if I could. It may only be for a few days. With luck, half of Shirath will remain to house us, for there is a chance to save the southern wards, but only a chance. After we let them in, I intend to use Ke's archers to keep the demons on the northern bank. Dasanat's new arrow-throwers will help guard the bridges, but I'll burn all three spans if I must."

"Very reasonable," Lysere said, pale despite her light tone. "Since there will be nothing left on the other side to cross over to, why save the bridges? My lord and love, what you have not said is how many of those fighting on the north side will survive to flee across those bridges – before you destroy them."

Trax gave his wife a small, cold smile. "Some things are too grim for even a mad king to say."

Salick grabbed Garet's arm and pulled him into a corner of the reception room. He leaned in to hear her over the noise of conversation.

"Did you know of this?" she demanded. "Did he say anything last night when you spoke to him on the bridge?"

Garet shook his head. "No, not a word, though you could tell he was troubled. I thought for a moment, well, that he meant to jump into the river."

Now it was Salick's turn to shake her head. "No, not Trax. He's too arrogant, claw him. Do you agree with this scheme?"

Garet took a deep breath. "Maybe? No, don't say anything yet. Hear me out. We both saw what's coming out of the forest this spring, if that traitor Tarock is right about the timing."

Salick nodded. "I talked to Bixa. It's true. Tiralsh was ordered to weaken the city until the equinox then stand aside."

"So the final blow could fall while we were still reeling

from her schemes?" he asked, then struck a hand against the wall. "Claw them, they're learning from their mistakes, just like we should. I suppose Trax is right. Last time we won because we lured them into a small space where we could concentrate our forces rather than try to protect the whole city at once. The Itaalk won't be fooled that way again. This time, what's to stop them from attacking a dozen places at once? Or a hundred? They'll have the numbers."

Salick frowned. "And they might have demons that are clever," she said. "Compared to the mindless brutes we've faced before." She shivered. "Do you think the Caller demon was once a human being?"

Garet thought about this. The Caller had arrived in Shirath soon after he did. A different type of demon, one that had been absent for six hundred years, it had the power to control other demons and could evoke a powerful fear, one beyond anything a living bane had faced. He looked at Salick, seeing the worry in her eyes. Knowing how she hated the beast that killed Master Mandarack, he moved closer, comforting her with an arm around her shoulders.

"Not by its shape. Maybe the Caller had a different type of jewel – dragon egg, I mean."

Salick looked at him. "A heartstone? That could explain why there's only been two of them in the city's history. A clutch of dragon eggs has only one heartstone for hundreds of regular ones, and the Itaalk need heartstones for those staffs Tarix discovered."

She relaxed a bit and smiled. "I'm glad we don't have to worry about another Caller, but Garet, these new demons *will* be different. They may be able to think and plan rather than just mindlessly attack."

Garet frowned. "Perhaps. My fear is that they can fight like guards do. Like we do, with weapons."

She shivered and looked up to where Trax spoke with Bixa and Branet. Lysere stood with them, listening and shaking her head. Salick glanced back at the model of the city, the little wooden palace still lying in pieces on the floor beside it. "So, he must destroy his city to save it? I almost pity him. I know he never wanted to be a hero, just a very, very comfortable king."

Garet tightened his one-armed embrace but broke off when Marick came up with Dorict trailing behind.

"Claws, that plan is so mad I thought it must have been one of yours," Marick said, poking Garet with his retrieved walking stick. This cane was a simple one-piece affair, but Garet saw the demon-headed dagger from Marick's old stick hanging in a sheath at the young man's belt.

Salick batted the cane away. "And here I thought it might be you whispering in the king's ear."

Dorict shuddered. "Whoever is doing the whispering, they're madder than all of us put together. The nerve you'd need to even think of it! I don't know whether to praise Trax or demand he be locked in his own cellars."

Marick smiled up at Salick. "I know what fate you would choose for him, but spare some sympathy for the man, a new father and ready to hand his heir a handful of ashes."

He looked at the knots of people eating and talking, waving hands and pouring cups of wine over and over again. "His speech was very stirring," Marick added. "I'll give him that. It has the beginnings of a good scene, and he certainly got the audience applauding. I was jealous, but the thing is, when the demons do approach, how many of these people will still be clapping?"

Garet looked over to where Branet and Dirst were now conferring over one of the maps. Bixa looking over their shoulders.

"Most will be gone, I'd guess," the bane said. "In the southern half or away with the sandwalkers. The rest of us will have to stay and serve our city, enthusiastically or not."

Bixa was called back to the king's side and listened to whispered instructions before turning to the assembly.

"Lords, banes, Masks, and all others," she called out. "The king thanks you for your attendance and wishes to call this council to an end. All of you will be needed in the near future, but for now, go back to your wards and tell people of the king's plan. It's up to you to convince every citizen that this isn't the end of Shirath, but it will be the end of the demons."

The room emptied slowly, Bixa and her lieutenants having to convince many that the king could not immediately listen to their concerns.

Branet signalled the other banes to wait. He gathered them around the model of the city and handed out more copies of the map.

"Study these, all of you," he said. "The king wants us to plan out the position of our forces for his clawed plan."

"Don't you agree with it?" Tarix asked. The hallmasters from Illick and Akalit stood behind her, eyeing the Shirath hallmaster.

He rubbed a hand over his greying hair. "Yes, I do, Heaven shield me! Captain Bixa's idea of charging up the forest road with all our fighters was even more dangerous, I deem. It would have been too easy to see our forces passed and then attacked from both ends of the tunnel, or the Itaalk could just let us go blundering on while they attacked Shirath."

Tarix nodded. "And they might have other roads we haven't found. Ones that lead to other cities. Such a foray might have led to attacks on your homes, Hallmasters," she said to their two guests, who nodded.

"Too true," Hallmaster Chon said. She ran a fingertip along the top of the model's wall. "Though if Shirath falls, my city of Illick will not be far behind."

"Nor will Akalit," Hallmaster Sicarth added. "Or Old Torrick, for that matter. It seems we stand together or fall together, Hallmaster."

"If only Solantor felt the same," Branet said, moving around to the Palace Plaza side.

"They feel very little, at least for other cities," Relict said, bringing a platter of goblets to the group. Vinir followed with food scavenged from the stewards cleaning the room.

"Many thanks!" Tarix said, taking a cup. "I can see why we made you an ambassador, husband. I wonder that you didn't charm the overking."

Master Chon laughed. "The overking and charm have very little to do with each other – speaking as someone who lives much closer to Solantor than yourselves. He sees Illick and Akalit as unsophisticated, Shirath as a rude outpost, and Old Torrick as a barbaric village in the middle of a wilderness."

Tarix laughed. "I'd like to see him say that to Hallmaster Corix."

Sicarth laughed with her. "I have heard tales of that woman and hoped to meet her here. Will she come with the promised oil?"

"I believe so," Tarix said, "for she has been a good friend to this city, and to me. Is there any chance the overking or Solantor's banehall will change their minds?"

Chon shook her head. "No. We all saw the same proofs that Master Relict brought: those terrifyingly detailed drawings of new demons, the power of silkstone to block demon fear, the tale of the Caller beast, and how the demons keep changing tactics. The fact that someone — these Itaalk, it seems – paid for spies in your city was particularly convincing to me. But what was clear to all of us was . . . uninteresting to Solantor. You see, the overking does not care to know about this, and the banehall listens to the overking."

Vinir, who blushed at the praise for her sketches, said, "Their help would have been most welcome."

Sicarth nodded. "Especially for a scheme like this, since Solantor gets lamp oil directly from the City of Fountains by sea. We can only buy what they let us, which is not much, though what we have we will bring to Shirath. It is an odd liquid. They say it comes out of the ground in the Far South, and it burns much more fiercely than what we press out of seeds or make from distilled spirits."

Vinir stood still, mouth open, and spun to race out of the room. Salick followed and caught up with her halfway to the palace's front doors.

"What's wrong?" she demanded, and her friend, instead of stopping to make sense, grabbed her arm and dragged her along.

For a moment, Salick felt as if they were Blue Sashes again, running off to escape some Gold's tyranny or pursuing one of Vinir's mad whims.

"Stop, stop!" she said, but was pulled along until Vinir spotted Yala and Son-neen outside the palace, talking with Ke. She let go of Salick's arm and ran up to them.

"Oil!" she said and stopped to catch her breath.

"Oil?" Yala asked. She looked at Salick and then Son-neen.

"Oil!" Vinir answered most definitely. "Rock oil. Do your wells have any, or do we have to send to the City of Fountains?"

Ke thought about it for a moment before replying. "Each well has some, perhaps a few barrels we trade for at the Mother of Waters. Men use it in furnaces for their makings. Why do you ask?" she said, then her eyes lit up. "Ah! For the demons, yes? Burn them in a hot fire, though this city burns too. You people are very fierce!"

"Can we get them in time? Say, a five-day?" Vinir asked.

Yala shook her head. "No, not even the closest wells can send the oil so quickly."

Vinir's face collapsed.

Salick gave her a light punch on the arm. "It was a good idea," she said. "Don't worry, we'll make do with what we have."

Son-neen looked from one to the other. "Why are you so worried? There're seventy-two big barrels of rock oil in the city right now."

The others stared at her, and she stepped back from the surprised regard.

"You Northerners are mad, all of you," she muttered. "Listen, Chal-lat and I arranged for it a long time ago for Dasanat. She wanted to try it in her forges, and Chal-lat took the order back when he left with Trax's letter to the towers. It came up the Dying River two ten-days ago."

Vinir's look had lost none of its confusion. "But why does nobody know about it, not the king, not Andarack, not even the lord of the Trader's ward!"

Son-neen stuck her chin out and put her hands on her hips. "Don't ask me! Dasanat knew about it, or would have if she wasn't so busy. I knew about it. Even your true love, Chal-lat, knew about it. If the Traders didn't, it was because the king told us not to ship anything through them until he was sure of their loyalty. He hasn't told us anything different, so I guess he's still not sure."

"Hey!" a voice cried from the palace.

They turned to see Marick coming slowly down the steps.

"Don't you dare bully my partner," he called, waving his stick.

"I can take care of myself," Son-neen said, still angry.

Marick used an elbow to nudge her out of an angry stance.

"I was worried about them, not you," he said, which pleased her. He turned to the banes. "Branet asked me to tell you that he and Garet will be much delayed, so you're all to run along and be useful at something. He wasn't too clear about what."

Yala and Ke put their heads together for a moment before the younger sandwalker spoke.

"More of our people will be arriving at Dry Hill soon. Perhaps this day. The Old Torrick people will meet them, but my sister should go and tell them what has happened and that they must hurry here." She turned to Vinir. "Has space been put aside for them?"

The bane nodded. "Yes, though I think we can do better than tents in the Banehall Plaza."

Ke waved that away. "Too much stone. Too many roofs. Go, Yala, and tell Brada to hurry back."

The others left, going in different directions until only Marick and Vinir were left. The young man made a great business of polishing the silver head of his dagger on a sleeve.

Vinir smiled. "I told you it wasn't a toy."

"True," Marick replied. "Though it's still a very good toy, just more dangerous than one you'd give a child."

"You're not a child anymore," Vinir said. "Not the way you and Son-neen act."

"Hmmm," Marick said. "And what about poor Chal-lat? Any letters from him – or to him?"

"No," Vinir said. "And why 'poor' Chal-lat?"

Marick turned the demon's silver face to regard the bane. "Poor, because the man's desperately in love with you, but you only have eyes for demons."

Vinir frowned at her friend. "We all have to have eyes for our enemies, don't we, if we want to win. Besides, how can it matter what we feel about one person right now, in such dangerous times? It's the same with Salick and Garet; why make plans when you don't know if they'll ever come true?"

Marick slapped the side of his head. "Why am I the wise one now?" he said. "Heaven shield us. Because we need hope, fool! Your hope is to see Chal-lat again, mine is to write an even more brilliant play." He slipped the dagger back into its sheath and twirled his cane. "Now, maybe all that hope will fall under a demon's claws, but Vinir, think of this: what if it doesn't? What do you want to happen if, by some mad miracle, we survive?"

He patted her on the cheek, reaching up to do so, and went off, whistling. Vinir watched him until he disappeared into the morning crowds. She sighed and walked back to the banehall, deep in thought and occasionally bumping into other people.

CHAPTER II

PREPARATIONS

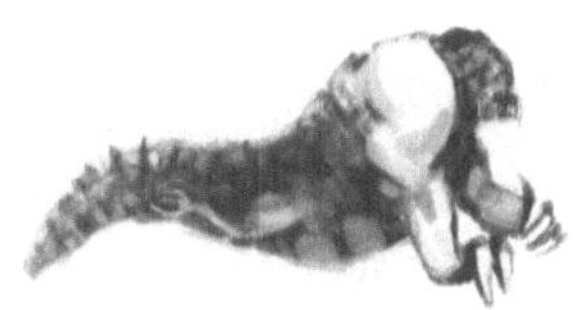

"No, no, no," Bixa said. She took the pike from the masked man and held it under her good arm, point forward. With a grunt of effort, she buried it's point in a sandbag tied between two posts. She left it there and turned to the man.

"Point straight and push even after it goes in," she said. "If I can do this one-handed, you can do it with two. Now, try again."

She went down the line to the next trainee, a woman of middle age not yet given a mask. She watched as the pike went in.

"Shoulders down," she said, and moved on.

At the end of the line, she looked at Cirta and shook her head. The lieutenant, having his own troubles with archers who had never held a bow, shrugged.

Bixa turned and began to work her way back along the line of grunting, thrusting recruits.

"No, no, no."

A voice behind her coughed, and she turned to see Dorict standing there with a bow and handful of arrows.

The bane looked over the grunting, sweating volunteers. "They're not much worse than young Black Sashes," he said. "But new skills always take time. I came to practise my archery, since Yala says I shoot worse than any child of her well."

Cirta waved him over, but before he left, the bane looked at Bixa and said, "Advice, if you'll take it. Get some iron hoops about this wide." He held his laden hands about a foot apart. "And set them rolling across the line. Then have them practise low thrusts to catch the rings."

He turned away, but called over his shoulder, "That's one way we train to kill Rat demons and Shriekers."

Bixa waited until he was gone then called Blellat over. "Get me ten, no, twenty of those rings. This lot will never take down a big demon, so we might as well set them on the small ones."

Blellat went off to find a cooper, and Bixa looked over to where Dorict stood in line, waiting for a chance at the straw targets.

"Claws," she said to the air. "I should have thought of that myself. You there, shift your grip back, unless you want to be in kissing range of the beast. Try again . . . No, no, no!"

DASANAT WORKED THE FORGE HERSELF, letting the others rest. She would rouse them soon enough, for only ten days were left before the equinox. The master mechanical eyed the bright colour of the bar and removed it when it reached the necessary shade. The trip hammer rose and fell as the gears turned – thanks to a draft horse turning a shaft in the stable yard. Spark power was more convenient, but every available spark jar, and any others that could be made in such a short time, were reserved for the new arrow-throwers Trax had demanded from the mechanicals.

The bar lengthened under the hammer strikes. Dasanat teased it out to a flat stave, curving its length until it was strong enough to brace the wooden arms of the thrower. She set it aside for the tempering crew. They would heat and cool it until it was flexible enough to survive drawing and releasing a shaft every seven heartbeats. The wooden bow stave took most of the strain, but the metal fittings were necessary to keep the whole thing from breaking apart.

After wiping her brow, she looked around the great hall. Two hundred and more grey-clad mechanicals were rising of their own accord, ready to labour again in the heat and smoke. While she watched, they rolled up straw palates and blankets, stretched and took up their tools. Dasanat sighed. These men and women had been working with little rest ever since the traitor Tarock had set the date for their doom. If they did survive, the people in this room could claim the victory as much as any bane or guard.

It wasn't supposed to be this way. When they defeated the demons at the Battle of the Bridge, there had been a moment when anything seemed possible. Then the banes sent out to find the demons came back with their frightening tales, and that moment had passed. All her energies and wit had since been bent towards not only the survival of her son and husband, but the survival of all the sons and husbands and mothers and daughters who lived within the walls of her city. Her grand plans for spark-powered barges, soaring bags of hot air that could lift a person higher than the city walls, even a machine to send messages over a great distance all fell to the side.

She picked up a hammer and went to one of the ladders

leading to the loft. With some effort and a bit of luck, she could knock a few more holes in the roof above the forges. That might keep her workers from choking on the fumes. And that might help more arrow-throwers get made, which could save all of them. She began the weary climb, thinking of how wonderful the world would be if the demons would just let her get on with more important work.

CHAPTER 12
THE ENEMY APPEARS

Morning in the Maze was not as active as it was outside the low walls that separated that slum from the rest of the Fifth Ward. In the ward proper, children called to each other and laughed as they went about their chores. Men and women shouldered tools and made their way to the fields or workshops, and an increasing number now went to the guards' barracks to practise with pikes and bows.

Inside the Maze, most of the residents were barely cracking open a single eye to look upon the dawn and curse. It was some time before the tavern men and women stirred enough to stretch, scratch, and make their way slowly towards their own disreputable work. Their children were already up, still seeing each day as an adventure to be enjoyed rather than a burden to be endured. For the adults, the hangovers suffered most days made endurance the only possible choice.

The dregs of the city lived here: swindlers and thieves, women and men fallen into begging by circumstance or inclination, and not a few of Marick's actors. Not the good actors, but those who spent more time moving scenery than spouting lines. It was a closed society, seldom visited by the rest of Shirath, save for those seeking low fun or secret deeds.

Hanal opened his shop earlier than usual, woken by someone shaking the cot he slept on at the back of his business. When he opened his eyes, there was no one there, but he couldn't find sleep again and so got up, stretching, scratching, and cursing. After all that was done, he pushed open his door for the day's business. It took some strength to do that, for it was a substantial barrier, heavily planked and double barred on the inside. It had to be, for Hanal knew his neighbours as well as he knew himself and judged them by his own greed. Using that as a measure, he would have made his door of iron, if that was possible. He began laying out old clothes and cracked dishes on the counter. Each piece had its own special place and had rested there for years, since the shopkeeper's real trade was in stolen goods that came in the back of the shop through an even thicker door.

Something scratched at those planks now, and Hanal grumbled his way back, past his cot, wondering why any self-respecting thief would be up so early selling his loot. He threw the first bolt and stepped back when the door shuddered.

"Keep your hands in your pockets and off my door!" Hanal shouted and yanked back the last bolt. "I'll clout you if . . ."

The reason for a clouting went unspoken, for the door banged in, sending the man falling back against the counter. Chipped dishes flew off to become shards, and dusty clothes fluttered down to hide the ruin. Hanal looked up from where he lay amid the wreckage, shaking his head and peering at the figure that stood in the shadow of the opening. It held something in one hand, a long something, which it raised as it walked forward.

"Yonan, is that you?" Hanal said, and began to stand up, but the figure's arm came down, again and again, and the shopkeeper lay there unmoving while the figure continued its rampage, breaking anything still breakable and beating even the walls of the dingy shop.

Hanal's neighbours, roused by the tumult, approached cautiously, expecting an early morning drunken rage – not uncommon in the Maze – but what they found sent them screaming out of their walled enclave to seek safety in the rest of the ward. There, gibbering about a monster that walked on two feet and bore a bloody club, they met a party of banes running from both the inner gate and the small hall of the ward.

The one leading the party from the Palace Plaza was dark-skinned and so instantly recognizable.

"Garet!" cried a woman. "Hanal's been killed by a demon. It used a club and smashed the man to jelly!"

The bane frowned at this and looked at the young man who stood beside him. "Dorict, take half our force and find out where this Hanal lived. Watch and surround that part of the Maze. Take a guide."

The younger bane nodded and grabbed the protesting woman.

"I'll not go back there," she screeched. "You can't make me!"

"You want to see that monster killed, don't you?" Dorict asked, dragging her towards the gate leading into the Maze. "Or would you rather we left it to wander in your alleys?"

Garet didn't listen to the rest of the argument. He turned to Chitoroth, a Gold in charge of the Fifth Ward small hall. "Chitoroth," he said, "send a runner to the Sixth to make sure the demon doesn't scale the wall and escape into that ward, then take the rest of your banes to the north wall of the Maze and watch for the beast. We'll keep an eye on the east and south walls. When more banes or guards arrive, I'll take them in and find Dorict."

"Right," Chitoroth said, waving a listening Black Sash into a run. "How did you get here so fast?" he asked Garet.

"Lord Andarack's set up signals above the gates that can be seen from the palace and the hall," he said, and pointed to where the bane manning the machine above the Fifth Ward gates had raised a red flag on a very tall pole. "The flag means either a demon has been sighted or his shaking detector started moving. Now go!"

Chitoroth ran off to the north, followed by the six banes under his command: two Greens, three Blues, and a Black Sash.

Salick came running up with Bixa and Yala behind her. The bane's long legs outdistanced the others and she soon skidded to a stop beside Garet.

"It worked then? They saw one and raised a banner?"

Garet shook his head. "I think it was the shaking detector, since the demon was first seen in the Maze."

Bixa spat. "The worst place in the world, especially for demon hunting. We should have torn it down long ago."

Yala used Garet's back to scale the Maze's short wall. The sandwalker stood on top of it, bow in hand and looking out over the low buildings and narrow alleys. After a moment, she pointed to the north-west.

"Dorict is there," she called out. "He is fighting a poison wind."

At that, Garet, Salick, and Bixa ran for the gate and charged in the general direction of Yala's still pointing finger. They soon lost sight of her, but then heard the shouts and curses of the battle. Coming around a corner, they found Dorict and his companions surrounding a demon that was frighteningly familiar to the banes who had seen the Itaalk's valley.

"Claws," Salick said. "A Human demon, and it does have a weapon."

The club she spoke of was a rough branch fitted with spikes that jutted out at odd angles. It was an ungainly tool, but the demon swung it again and again at the surrounding banes. Swung it but hit nothing, for long training made this prey very hard to catch. Dorict stepped in and struck the bony shoulder of the beast, and the club dropped. He raised his bronze-bound staff for a killing blow but stayed his hand when Garet shouted.

"No! Take it alive. We need to know more about them."

That was easier ordered then done, for the beast leaped at Dorict, snapping at his throat. Chitoroth, coming with his team from behind, tackled the demon and then the rest of the banes piled on, bane upon bane until the creature could not move a single clawed finger. Rope was found and added to the loops of Garet's weapon, pinioning the limbs of the demon. Dorict went off to find a cart while Garet steeled himself for a closer examination of their enemy.

As expected, since the demon had spread no fear as it approached, he found silkstone plates fixed to its skull with small iron nails. Unlike others of its kind, it wore a cuirass and kilt of boiled leather, giving it some protection from blades. Its face was no longer even vaguely human, but bore a fully toothed beak, eyes as black as a starless night, and a helmet-like crest that stretched from just above the stone plates to the back of its head.

Even trapped, it snarled and snapped at its captors, and

Garet stood back, hoping Dorict would return soon so they could cart this creature off to Andarack and Banerict for study.

"Storm and sun!" Yala said, having joined them in time to add her strength to the others. "You say these were human once?"

"Yes," he replied. "We think it's the dragon egg they put in the skull that changes them so."

The young woman cocked her head and looked at the bane. "It is not their choice then, to be this?"

Garet started to answer, then stopped. He looked at the demon, trying to see the human within, if any still existed. Was there something about the eyes? No, he couldn't let himself weaken now, not with a thousand and more of these things approaching Shirath.

"No, it wasn't their choice," he said. "But that doesn't matter, does it? They're controlled by our enemies. And even if the Itaalk let them go, the jewel would still drive them to kill and kill again. I'm sorry, Yala, but that is the truth."

The sandwalker nodded. "A sad truth then. They are slaves forever. Why do you not kill it then?" She raised her bow, but Garet held up a restraining hand.

"Salick and I are the only ones who've seen them, until today. And that was only briefly. It may be that they have some flaw, some weakness that we can use against them. Lord Andarack and the banehall's physician, Banerict, will examine this one. Perhaps we can find something."

Dorict returned with the cart and reported that a tunnel came out behind the dead man's shop. Even now, his neighbours were filling it in with whatever stone or rubble they could find. Two Greens stayed to supervise the work, and the rest of the banes covered the struggling demon with a blanket and took it through the narrow ways of the Maze, though the Fifth Ward, and into the Palace Plaza. Yala walked beside the cart the whole time.

"Tell me, Garet," she said, as they approached the inner gate of Andarack's ward, "do you think they will hurt this one?"

"I don't know," Garet said, but knew that was a lie. He felt Yala's eyes on him, and guessed she knew it too.

"I'm sorry, Yala," he said, after several more steps, each feeling worse than the last. "I think they will hurt it, not out of hatred, but because they must to know what it is."

"And the slave inside?" she asked. He expression was calm, but there was a tension in her voice, a sign of an internal argument that had something to do with the twitching thing in the cart.

Garet paused while the ward gate was opened. When they started again, he answered. "There may not be a human mind still inside the demon, and if there is, maybe they would want to die rather than be a monster."

Yala turned on him, her mouth a tight line and her eyes narrowed. "No, town man. If I were inside, I would fight, fight until I was free or dead. Would you? I think you will say yes, but you say no for this one here."

"We have no choice . . ." Garet began, but Yala cut him off with one slim, dark hand.

"This – yes, this – I was told all my years. I was told the same when Dorict and Marick came to my well. If I had listened, Marick would be dead and maybe Dorict too. I threw everything to the wind to make a choice. Have you ever done this?"

She crossed her arms over the bowstring lying diagonally across her chest. "Do not speak to me of no choices, Garet of Shirath," she said, and turned away.

He watched her stride away until Dorict tapped his arm with his staff. "She's a good person," he said, "and knows a lot about difficult choices, but she isn't a bane."

Garet kept his eyes on the sandwalker's red cloak, worn safely within the walls, as the young woman went through the gate and back into the Palace Plaza. He passed a hand over his hair and turned to the other bane. "And we are banes. Claws, I don't know, Dorict. Maybe it would have been kinder to kill it in the Maze!"

Dorict shook his head. "Maybe, but it wouldn't be kinder to the people we swore to protect. We really do need to learn about these new demons. And as for hurting it, Banerict will be there. Do you really expect him to allow Andarack or anyone else to torture the beast, even if the king commands it?"

Garet shook his head. Banerict might seem like a gentle old man, but his principles were deeply held, and Garet had seen him confront hallmasters and make them back down when those principles were challenged.

"Come on," Dorict said, and motioned for Chitoroth and the others to keep pulling the cart.

Lord Andarack checked the restraints one more time, then checked them again. Even with the silkstone plate blocking the demon fear, the creature was terrifying, even more so because he knew it had once been a man.

Or perhaps a woman, for the creature was sexless, squeezed down to the basics of muscle and bone. Banerict was examining the clawed fingers, carefully, with a lamp and one of his host's magnifying lenses. "The claws have replaced the nails, not grown from them," he said. "Like those bony crests have replaced the hair."

A rather flustered assistant made notes, standing as far away from the table as she could while still being able to hear the two men.

Banerict continued, "The skin is tough, like any other demon you've had me study, Lord Andarack, but thinner than a beast this size usually sports. Hmm, I wonder if that is because this one was made from a human and not an animal. We do have a thinner skin than, say, a bull or a bear."

"A weak point then," Andarack said. He shivered a bit, for this cellar room was deep enough to take a chill from the surrounding earth. "And perhaps that is why they wear that boiled-leather armour. Still, this could make them more vulnerable to sandwalker arrows, especially if they use the new needle-points and their poison."

The physician used a pair of tongs to pull open the creature's beak, then jumped back when it snapped shut.

"Claws! I've never had a patient do that," he said.

Andarack summoned a watching bane, and together they used metal bars to open the mouth.

"Don't hurt it," Banerict warned, and looked within. "The tongue is not as forked or thin as those of other demons," he said, and waited while the trembling steward wrote down his words. "But it would be difficult to use in speech, I deem."

He motioned them to let the beak snap shut and turned to Lord Andarack.

"What now?" he asked. "And don't ask me to cut the poor beast open just so you can see how it's put together."

"Why not?" a voice asked, and they turned to see the king standing in the doorway of the cellar room. "I assure you, Banerict, that it would have no qualms about slicing you from top to bottom."

The physician regarded the king as he might an infected wound. "And that is why I am a physician and this is a demon, sire," he said. "Do not ask me to change places with a beast."

Trax laughed a bit, though his eyes were still hard. "Would it help, Lord Andarack, to cut the beast open while still living, or should we kill it first?"

Andarack shook his head. "Neither, I think. Banerict and I have spoken of this already. We want to remove the demon jewel – the dragon egg – and see if the process of, er, *demonfication* can be reversed."

Trax thought for a moment, then shrugged. "Do it then, but if it doesn't, know that my guards will kill the beast."

Andarack and Banerict looked at each other, then at the two armed men who followed the king into the room. The physician turned from them to the steward.

"My tools, please," he said. And the woman came a bit nearer to hand over the satchel the physician required.

Banerict laid out a set of knives, tongs, and probes on a cloth and picked up a blade that shone keen in the lamplight.

"I wish we were doing this in the sun," he said, "And I wish we had some way to dull the pain, but without more knowledge of the beast, well, we might kill it outright."

He set a silkstone mask over his head and nodded for the bane to put blocks on the table and strap leather belts across them to hold the demon's head still. The others in the room, even the nervous steward, likewise put on stone helmets, for the first thing Banerict needed to do was remove the silkstone patch set just above the hidden jewel.

While Lord Andarack gagged the beast and pulled the

restraining straps tight, Banerict used a set of gripping tongs to free the nails holding the stone plate. When he removed it, fear flooded the room. The physician waited until the blunted terror could be managed, then, holding the knife as gently as a writing brush, he made a careful cut across the demon's forehead. A slow trickle of blood appeared, then increased as the cut deepened. At last the knife clicked against something hard, and Banerict had the green-faced bane use hooked probes to pull back the skin, revealing the demon jewel, almost absorbed into the skull with but a small circle of black surface remaining visible.

"It's too deep to just cut free. I'll need the chisel and hammer."

That was too much for the bane, who went out into the hallway to vomit. Andarack took over, looking none too well himself. The king watched as Banerict chipped away at the surrounding bone, carefully freeing the stone and finally holding it in his bloody fingers. He placed it in a silk-stone box and closed the lid. Taking off his helmet, he carefully examined the resulting wound.

"There's bone still beneath it," he said, holding the lamp low over the table. "So the brain is not exposed, thank Heaven! I'll clean and close the wound. Then we can see what effect removing it had."

Trax moved forward to look into the demon's staring eyes. The mouth worked around the leather gag, and the needle teeth worried at it ceaselessly. "It is still a demon," he said. "We should kill it now."

"No," Andarack said, feeling safe enough in his own expertise and his own house to deny the king this particular demand. "The change may be gradual rather than sudden. Banerict and I will stay here, watching, until we know."

Trax looked at the older man, calculating the cost of forcing his will on a very popular lord. "Very well," he said, "but I will return tomorrow morning. Unless this thing is human again and on our side, I will have it put down."

The bane came back in, sheepish, but stopped at the obvious tension in the room.

"Should I get the hallmaster?" he asked.

"No, bane," Trax said. "The protection of this city rests first with me, not the banehall. Andarack, I will be back after first light."

The bane ducked his head as the king and his guards left. He looked at Lord Andarack, who shrugged and told the young man, "Perhaps you should tell the hallmaster." He frowned. "What was your name again?"

"Aralon, sir. But what should I tell him?"

Banerict slammed his hand down on the side table, making the bright tools jump. "Tell him that thanks to the king's anger, we have but one night to learn the true nature of our enemy, and that if he wishes to help, he can come as quickly as he can and help us keep watch."

Aralon fairly ran from the room, and Andarack looked over at the physician. "Branet won't be able to stop the king if he really means to kill this . . . patient of yours," the ward lord said.

"I know, I know," Banerict replied, and leaned over the demon, whose eyes had closed, though the thin chest still rose and fell. "Claws, Andarack, I'm beginning to like this idea of burning down the city." He looked at the closed door and the steward edging towards it along the wall.

"Maybe we can build the next one without a king."

CHAPTER 13
A MEAL SHARED

"So, Trax didn't have to kill it?" Vinir asked.

She handed a plate of food to Salick then filled one for Garet as well. The cooks had left, all save one, and he had put pots full of stew and loaves of fresh bread out on the dining hall table nearest the kitchen rather than try to do the job of a dozen all by himself.

"Not much meat today," Vinir observed as she passed the young man his plate.

"Trax had the guards gather up all the butchered meat in the city," Dorict said. "Half went south with those flee-ing. He's saving the other half for his trap."

Salick looked at him, frowning. "Does it really draw them in, the smell of burning meat?"

Vinir answered for him. "The sandwalkers say it does. They use it to lure their 'poison winds' to be poisoned."

Dalesta, one of Tarix's Greens who had joined them along with her friend Chetorth, shuddered.

"Is one meat better than another?" Chetorth asked. "I mean, maybe they could take all the mutton and leave us the beef for a decent lunch."

He had meant it as a joke but saw that Vinir and Dorict didn't take it as such.

Dalesta hit his arm.

"What?" he said. "I just meant . . ."

"It's not your fault," Vinir said. "We didn't say this before, but it was Marick's amputated leg they burned to bring the demon in."

Chetorth, who'd lost two fingers and half his toes in the Battle of the Bridge, paled. He cupped his injured hand in his good one, and Dalesta put her own hands over both.

"That's horrible!" she said.

"What's horrible?" a new voice asked, and they turned to see Marick accompanied by Son-neen coming up to their table.

When he saw the shocked faces of the people around the table, he threw up his hands. "Not my plays, I hope?"

Son-neen snorted and sat down beside Salick.

"No," Dorict said, then let out an explosive breath. "Phew. We were talking about what the sandwalkers did with your leg. Sorry."

Marick laughed at that, easily it seemed, and that lightened the mood at the table.

"That is horrible, especially if you talk about it while you're eating!"

Salick wasn't ready to laugh. "How can you, I mean, I've seen you talking with Yala and Ke. How can you forgive them for nearly killing you?"

Marick accepted a plate from Vinir and passed it to Son-neen before taking one for himself. He sat down across from Salick.

"It took me a while, I'll admit. But lying strapped to a sled gave me lots of time to think. I realized that Yala had given up everything to save my life. So, even if her people owed me a leg, I owed her everything else. I don't even blame the other sandwalkers, well, not much. They were afraid, and think how many stupid, cruel things we've done because we're afraid of demons? Don't we take children from their families to fight those monsters? And how many times have the hall and palace squabbled over who is more powerful just because they fear losing power?"

"Often enough," Vinir said. "I think our hallmaster is in one of those squabbles even now." She brought more food for Marick and Son-neen.

"Hah!" Marick said. "Trax does need some managing these days. My point is that banes, sandwalkers . . . anyone can make a bad choice because of their fear. Let's hope we have better reasons to choose, whatever they might be."

"Duty," Salick immediately replied. Garet took her hand and smiled.

"Hard work," said Son-neen, listing the prime virtue of the City of Fountains.

"Learning," said Dorict, thinking of the books he had read there.

"Beauty," said Vinir remembering the art she had seen and made in that same city.

"Not giving up," Dalesta said, and Chetorth nodded in agreement.

Garet remained silent until Salick nudged him with her elbow.

"Those are all good ways to guide your choices," he said. "But I think they just tell you what kind of person you already are."

Marick looked at him, head slightly tilted. "And what if you know that you're bad? I thought I was, for a while."

Garet shrugged and spread his hands on the table. "Then you have to be honest about what that means, to you and to those around you. Once you know that, then it's a real choice, not a lie you tell yourself."

"Hmm," Marick said. "I came to find out about the demon you caught but got a lesson instead."

"And a free meal," Garet observed. "As for the demon, it died in the early morning, before the sun rose yesterday. Banerict said the heart just slowed and stopped. Claws, I wonder if we could have done more."

Vinir dropped her spoon back onto her plate. "What is there to wonder at? I hate to say it, because they were once human, but we have to kill demons."

"Do we?" Dorict said. "I'm all for being certain, especially when it comes to my own skin, but what if we could use the Itaalk staffs to control those jewels, force them to turn those demons back into human beings?"

"Can that be done? Did they try it?" Marick asked. He waved away Vinir's offer of seconds, though Son-neen was happy to accept.

"No," Garet said. "Trax wouldn't let them use the one staff we have for fear they would drain its power, if it works like a spark container, which we don't even know."

"The clawed fool," Salick said.

"I wonder who Trax thinks he is?" Dalesta said, more to herself than the others.

Chetorth looked at her. "The king, I'd guess, but what do you mean?"

She blushed a bit at the sudden attention but managed an answer. "I just wonder if he's changed so much because he's made up his mind about who he needs to be to win. And maybe he hasn't thought about the consequences of that for everyone else, like Garet – sorry, Master Garet – said."

"No masters at this table," Vinir said, and sat down with her own plate. "And maybe not ever again, if we win."

"And especially if we lose," Marick said.

"And no desert for pessimists," Vinir replied, wagging her finger at the young man.

The talk turned to other things: Vinir's letter to Challat, the odd uniforms of the Illick and Akalit banes, the most recent dire pronouncements from the city's chief astrologer, Mistress Alanick, and whether or not Lord Kirel was still in Kaela's good graces. The near-empty hall echoed to their laughter, and so they found some ease in companionship and gossip, as people do in desperate times.

CHAPTER 14

THE GATES BESIEGED

irst, the leader the Masks, rode up to Blellat and gave him a mocking bow from the saddle.

The lieutenant regarded the squat man, who to his mind looked like a lump of clay sitting on a guard's horse.

Sad we had to lend these fools good mounts. Even sadder that so few of our recruits can ride a hundred feet without falling off and breaking something.

The Mask, who had been a Duellist before that group had been forcibly disbanded, stepped down easily and rubbed his bottom. "Haven't ridden this much since I escorted Traders going to the Midlands. Pity you don't have guards that can sit a horse, isn't it, Blellat?"

The lieutenant ignored the insult and pointed to the nearest patrol, a mix of guards and Masks coming back from the fringes of the orchards. "It's a bigger pity you don't have enough Masks to make much of a difference, isn't it, Dirst? Well, considering how many died on the bridge or got put on work chains when they wouldn't swear loyalty to the king, it's no wonder."

He grinned at the other man's expression and waved a hand. "Enough pleasant conversation. The spring equinox is only two days away, and we still don't have all the citizens in the northern half of the city moved. Bixa wants to pull two of your patrols and use them to hurry the laggards along. We'll bring out foot patrols of the new recruits into the fields to free up your lot."

Dirst stuck out his chin. "Why us? Isn't herding the citizens your job?"

Blellat gave the man his best guard-training look. "The captain's using the resources the best way she can. Besides, the people like us. You, on the other hand, well, one look at your ugly faces and anyone left in the city will run across the bridges faster than the wind." He would have gone on – this particular Mask always needed some taking down – but a glance at the city walls made him stop.

"Look," he said, and Dirst turned to look in the same direction.

"Red flags," Blellat said, shading his eyes. "Three of them I can see from here, claw it all. We'd better withdraw the nearest patrols to the walls and give assistance if it means more tunnels."

Dirst began to answer, but a tremor fluttered across his face. He grabbed the helmet from his saddle horn and thrust his head inside. Blellat, having seen the effectiveness of the sandwalker's silkstone-filled scarves, had no helmet. He reached over his shoulder and pulled up a hood, similarly loaded with thin slices of the protective stone. Tugging it over his head and down, it reached all the way to his lower lip. He tied it off under his chin and looked through the eyeholes. With a raised hand, he signalled the patrols within sight to dismount, something they were doing anyway as their horses began to buck and run for the city walls.

"The fear's not coming from the city," Dirst said, watching his horse gallop towards the gates. He turned to face the orchards. So did the lieutenant.

The rows of apple and pear trees were pushed aside by at least five huge demons. Blellat saw they were well-armoured Tunnellers, and many others just as large followed. With the Mask behind him, he ran towards the walls. If they could regroup at one of the gates, beneath an arrow-thrower, they stood a chance of holding off even such massive beasts until reinforcements arrived.

If this is the main attack, they're two days early, curse them. Dasanat's crews haven't finished preparing the buildings, and they're still setting up the dart machines and the new throwers.

His lungs began to burn and he heard a grunt behind him. Dirst had tripped, and Blellat cursed everyone and everything he could think of as he dashed back and helped the man to his feet. An arm around his shoulders, he dragged him until they came to the half-open gate. Other guards and a few Masks waited for them, and more were coming. So were the demons.

Then a very comforting sound came to Blellat ears, the *chk-chk-chk-twang* of the repeating bow above the gate. Some of the demons fell, but the thick crests of the Tunnellers, grown back over their bodies and across their blind faces, defied the chattering machine's shafts. Other demons crowded beneath the bigger beasts, using their protection to get nearer the gate.

"Inside, everyone!" Blellat yelled, and was the last one through the gap, dragging Dirst with him. The Mask collapsed inside, holding his ankle.

"Claw it all," he shouted. "You almost got me killed."

"You're welcome," Blellat said, and helped throw the great wooden bar across the gates.

He grabbed a trainee guard, a frightened looking boy of perhaps sixteen years.

"Go get Bixa," he yelled. "Tell her we need sandwalker archers and their poison. Nothing else is going to stop those beasts. Go!"

The boy ran off, and Blellat heard his name called out. He turned to see his fellow lieutenant, Cirta, run up with a dozen more guards and several banes.

"Is this it?" the younger man asked. He paused to catch his breath, the air whistling though the helmet's breathing holes.

"Could be," Blellat said. "If it is we're all clawed, since we're not ready. Take your people to the right. I'll take the left and we'll attack them from the sides when they break through the gates."

Cirta looked appalled. "That's your plan?"

Blellat went off to line up his men flanking the gate avenue, shouting over his shoulder as he ran, "Yes. That and my hope the sandwalkers get here before we're smashed to pieces."

The right side of the gate bowed, creaking in an alarming manner. The pressure eased, then returned and increased. The left panel began to split, and the wooden bar bent like a bowstave. A jagged line appeared across the face of the beam. That crack widened, splintered, and the bar broke apart.

The gates pushed open, and two Tunnellers, beast that could knock down a house without straining themselves, shouldered their way into the city.

Then stopped.

Cirta looked across at Blellat, who was looking at the monsters.

The beasts shook their massive heads, hooted in some kind of pain or confusion, then reared and began to claw at the gate panels. The wood ripped like it was one of Sonneen's paper demons. The beasts moved frantically, and the others that followed did the same, ignoring the men and women waiting to fight them and instead attacking the gates themselves.

Blellat shook himself and yelled, "We need those gates! Take them down!"

They hacked and stabbed the demons without any retaliation. Blellat swung his sword at a Basher's leg, and the big beast went down, its tendons cut, but it ignored its tormentor to continue clawing at the gate. The nearest Tunneller had almost wrenched the top hinge out of the stone, and Blellat climbed over the Basher to drive his sword against the thick skin of its belly. It was no use. He barely scratched the leathery hide and had to jump to one side as the gate came loose at the top and the Tunneller dropped its front legs to the ground.

Blellat got out of the way but the Basher didn't, and its back broke under sudden weight of the falling beams. Another large beast, a Bull demon by its crests, took the Basher's place, fighting to wreck the gates while the guards fought to save them.

Slim arrows fletched in red flew over Blellat's head. The Bull demon fell back, knocking others down in the process. There was another tremor in the fog of fear, and the big demons left the gate, turning towards the fields again. More arrows followed, and the arrow-thrower above began to spit out bigger shafts as the beasts left the protection of the walls.

Blellat saw a crawling, nameless thing collapse in its slow flight, three arrows sticking out of its back. Then one of the Tunnellers paused and fell like a landslide.

Poison! The sandwalkers or the arrow-thrower must have it – or both. We might win this day yet.

Blellat passed a twitching bulk and jumped aside to dodge the swing of a clawed arm sticking out from under it. The remaining demons were joined by ones coming from other gates, and he spared a thought for how much damage the beasts had done.

Claw them all. The signal flags were part of a diversion, beasts digging under the walls just to draw off the banes in the small halls and the ward guards. This was what they wanted, the gates destroyed to make the main attack easier. Too clever, and I can guess who suggested it to them, curse her.

A sandwalker flew past him, firing arrow after arrow as she ran.

"Don't let any live!" he called after her, then realized she might not even speak his language.

Another Tunneller collapsed, and Blellat, without breaking stride, climbed the slope of its back to leap off its shoulder and come down on a smaller – slightly smaller – demon with all his weight behind the sword point. The Bull demon fell, its spine cut through, and the guard dragged his blade free to resume running.

The last demon, another Basher, made it to the orchards before the poison of a dozen arrows brought it down. The fear diminished, then faded away to nothing, proving the rumour true that the sandwalker's potion dissolved demon jewels as well as demon bones.

The woman who had passed him was standing by the beast, eyeing it with some concern.

"Is it dead?" Blellat asked.

The woman answered, speaking slowly. "I do not see. I do not know? This is the first one, first poison wind I see."

He whacked the mountain of flesh with his sword and was pleased at the lack of response. "Dead," he said. "Listen, I need you and all the sandwalkers you can gather."

"Need?" she asked. The eyes peering at him through the gap in her scarf were suspicious.

"Need," Blellat said, and saw a familiar young woman running up with Brada and a dozen other sandwalkers.

"Are these all the demons?" Yala asked.

"Maybe," he said. "But we have to go north as fast as we can. Whoever controlled these demons must still be near. We still have a chance to catch them."

Brada translated his words to the others and a quick consultation occurred among them.

Yala shook her head. "The king will not like this." She lifted the corner of her red cloak, for the women had come running upon Bixa's call and had not had time to disguise themselves.

Blellat had to make a decision, one that might ruin his career and send him back to gate tending in the dark nights before dawn.

Claws, this should be Bixa deciding what to do, not me. I should have listened to my father and made shoes. I'd have been good at that.

He set his shoulders and tried to look decisive. "I know, but this is more important. If this was done by who I think, well, we have to catch her and whoever is with her. Will you help me?"

By now the sandwalkers numbered two dozen and had been joined by several guards and even Dirst, leaning on a bloodied spear and cursing his way across the field.

Yala regarded the lieutenant for a moment and then

nodded. She spoke to the others, a quick rattle of instruction, and the sandwalkers fanned out, disappearing into the orchards in but a few heartbeats.

Blellat shook his head and turned to the others. "Well, don't just stand there, follow them. Do you want them to have all the glory, you clawed fools?"

He led them after the sandwalkers, knowing that if they found who was responsible, he would receive a great deal of praise. This was something he didn't really want, since it usually led to more responsibility.

That's how I came to be a clawed lieutenant, by being too fierce at the Battle of the Bridge. On the other hand, if we don't find her, I might as well keep going until a demon eats me because Bixa won't leave anything more of me than a Shrieker would.

They were coming out of the last stand of fruit trees when he heard a whistle far ahead, a signal soon answered by others. He began to run faster.

CHAPTER 15

PARTINGS

"It's not fair," Allifur pointed out, again.

Maroster picked her up and put her on the back of the wagon beside Corfin.

"Too bad," the big man said. He handed the girl the shield made specially for her shortened arm and dumped a sack of food beside them.

"We won't go!" Corfin said. He frowned as fiercely as he could at Maroster, but the ex-Mask ignored the scorching. "We fought at the Battle of the Bridge, just like you," the boy said. "And we killed a dozen demons on our own."

"Only five," Allifur corrected. "But we really can fight."

Her hair hung down over her face – a sure sign of dismay – and Maroster brushed it back with one sausage-like finger.

"Don't fret," he told them. "If you're really lucky, the demons will kill all of us who stay, and then they'll chase after your lot."

Corfin looked hopeful but Allifur shook her head, letting the hair fall back. "Don't die," she said, and sniffled when he brushed the lock aside again.

The driver chirped to his horses and the wagon set off, the two small banes waving to their friend until the curve of the wall hid them from view. Maroster stood there for a long time, breathing in the air and thinking about what led him to this foolishness. He'd near adopted those two – or been adopted by them. If it wasn't for worrying about them, he might have run off by now to Old Torrick or Illick, found a new employer and a barrel of good wine. He certainly wouldn't be staying here to join Bixa's guards and face even more demons than he had on that clawed bridge. Heaven probably hated him – with good reason, he admitted – to make him so stupid. He gave one last look to where Allifur and Corfin had disappeared.

Let no demon follow them, not one. We'll stop them here. If I have to tear down this whole city on their heads, I'll do it. Claws, I'm beginning to sound like Shirin, or that clawed fool Trax!

The first of the night birds began its melancholy song. Maroster shouldered his axe and turned back to the city walls. It would be a quieter place now, for thousands had already left, heading south, away from the approaching demons. He went back through the gate and straight to the nearest empty tavern to see if they had forgotten any skins of wine in their panic to escape. It was two days to the equinox, and he intended to spend at least one of them drunk.

CHAPTER 16

THE TRAITOR RETURNS

"Why did you put silkstone rooms up there?" Trax demanded. "Those roofs will be held by banes, and the stone could have made more masks!"

He slammed the table with an open hand, making everyone jump except the person he confronted.

"It's simple if you think it through," Dasanat answered, unfazed by the king's display of temper. "Demons can emit through their jewels, but can they sense it too? You'll agree, I think, most communication goes both ways. I can speak a word, and you hear it; you can pound the table, and I hear it."

She paused to consider her next words, oblivious to Trax's glare. "I have wondered about this for some time. We always assumed they smelled out their prey, but we have no proof of that. What if, instead, they follow their prey's fear to the source? This may or may not be so, but to be safe, we need to shield the banes on those roofs so they aren't found and killed before they can complete their tasks."

"But after is fine, I suppose," Branet said under his breath.

Trax glared at him with bloodshot eyes but quickly switched back to Dasanat. "Do you know for a fact that these rooms are necessary?"

Dasanat looked at him in mild surprise. "Have you not been listening? I surmise it."

Trax's fingers curled into fists. "And I surmise, Mechanical, that a woman who shows such small respect for her king should fear for her own life. At least your husband has better manners."

Branet rose from his chair at this. "Claws and teeth, be silent, Trax! If Andarack were here, you'd get the same *surmise* from him. You told us to make everything ready for your mad plan, and we have. These silkstone rooms – boxes, more like – are part of that. Dasanat speaks truth and fact – Heaven's shield, she can't do anything else, and you know it. If you want respect, stop drinking and earn it!"

Dasanat looked wide-eyed at the hallmaster and laid a restraining hand on his arm.

The king's own hand went to his side, where his sword might be, but this was the palace and he was surrounded by guards, though not within this room.

"You dare? You dare tell me how to rule? Do you think to replace me, Branet, like your old Hallmaster Adrix once did, or control me like Mandarack tried? Remember that I am the king of Shirath, and everyone in this city will show me the respect I deserve."

Branet, a man of some temper himself, struggled to control his urge to rush at the king and give him the beating his actions over the last days truly deserved. Instead, he took Dasanat's arm and led the shaken woman to the door. Before opening it, he turned back to the king and said,

"Trax, or Your Majesty, if you wish, we are all at wit's end, but it's better if we're not at each other's throats as well. You were a wiser king once, and may be so again, but if you threaten the hall or friends like this good mechanical again, I will call the lords to have you removed from the throne. By Heaven's dome, I swear it!"

The door slammed behind him and rang again when Trax's wine cup smashed against it.

The king glared at the two stewards awaiting orders.

"Don't just stand there. Clean it up! And get me Bixa right away."

The stewards left more quickly than their dignity usually allowed, one to follow the king's orders and the other, he feared, to alert whoever paid him the most.

"I am surrounded by traitors," he muttered, and searched the table for another glass.

In the plaza, just outside the palace doors, Dasanat looked up at the hallmaster.

"I just said what was needed, but you're angry, and so is Trax. Why?"

Branet guided her farther away from the guards and said, "He's drinking all day and night, which is part of it, I'm sure. The other part is that our king is half mad. Maybe more than half by now. I should never have let him train with a demon jewel! Listen, don't expect any reason from him, Dasanat. Perhaps you should pass any messages for the palace through the hall from now on. It will be more . . . efficient."

The mechanical nodded at that and began walking towards the Eighth Ward gates, not noticing Branet was accompanying her. When she did, he smiled and said, "After the attack at the Third, Fourth, and Fifth Ward gates earlier today, we have to be careful on this side of the river. In fact, Dasanat, I'm going to help you get whatever you need and then take you to join your husband at the bane-hall until this business is all over."

Dasanat shook her head. "The new arrow-throwers and the dart machines are already in place, but I need to stay with my workers."

Branet sighed. "Your workers are already across the bridges, or should be. They – and you – will be needed there and . . . Wait, who is that coming to the palace?"

Dasanat studied the man in the lead. "Blellat, by the shape and walk, and he has several guards with him, and a prisoner. It could be important. Should we turn back?"

The hallmaster considered. "If it is important, Bixa will send word, even if Trax doesn't. No, Lady Dasanat, at the moment, you are the most important person in Shirath."

At that, the master mechanical looked fairly alarmed, but she allowed herself to be led away to her house, where several anxious mechanicals had lingered to make sure she would be persuaded to move to the relative safety of the banehall.

It wasn't Bixa who came into the Shouting Room first, but Blellat, accompanied by three guards and a figure cloaked and hooded so that their identity was hidden.

Trax looked up and frowned.

"What, has Bixa turned on me too?" he asked, and at Blellat's look of confusion, he waved the complaint away with one hand.

"What is it, Lieutenant, and who is this?"

Blellat pulled back the captive's hood. "Someone we've wanted for a long time, Your Majesty," he said.

Trax smiled. "Well, well. The night improves. How good to see you again, Lord Tiralsh."

The woman glared back at the king, her once finely dressed silver hair hanging in limp ringlets to her shoulders, and her face devoid of powder or rouge. Instead of a silk gown, she wore a simple pair of pants over riding boots, and a wool coat that looked to need washing.

"You look a bit ragged, Tiralsh," Trax said, and sat down facing the woman. "Not your usual elegant self."

He swirled the wine in his glass, looking down into the red liquid before he raised his eyes and smiled at her again.

"Don't your friends treat you well? Hmm? Is that why you've returned, to beg forgiveness and resume your duties as a ward lord?"

Blellat shoved the woman into a chair and stood at attention to report. "Caught her in the tree fields, sire. She had help, I'm sure of that, but they were too quick."

Trax kept his eyes on the woman as he answered. "A pity, but I heard about your defence of the gates, Lieutenant. Well done, well done indeed. You are proving most useful, more so than some others in the guards."

With his eyes on Tiralsh, he didn't see the brief grimace on Blellat's face. The man swallowed before continuing. "I'm sorry, Your Majesty, I used the sandwalkers to chase her, so whoever did escape might know they're here."

Trax stood suddenly and shook his head. "No, no. Don't fret, man. There was always that risk, but this is worth it. I have captured the traitor Tiralsh. Did you know, my gracious lord, that we have your son in the cellars below us? And your pawn Gost as well, along with sundry traitors you no doubt paid to help you in your work. Sadly, your lackey, Trest, died before he could kill me or my queen."

Tiralsh looked up at Trax, a mixture of hate and fear on her face.

"Do you think capturing me matters?" she said. "You're still trapped by my allies, and they only listen to what I say."

Trax laughed. "Do they? A prisoner says little that can be heard, Tiralsh, and the dead say nothing at all. And, as a point of fact, I believe you err when you call them 'allies.' I think 'masters' is more accurate. They sent you here, didn't they? Under what threats, I wonder? Destroy the gates, make it easier for us to take the city or you'll end up in a demon's belly? Poor Lord Tiralsh, I fear you are stuck between pike points and claws, and neither is likely to spare you."

Bixa came in then, staring at the prisoner.

"Claws! Good work, Blellat," she said and glared down at the woman. "The whole city will rejoice when they learn you're chained up in a cell, Tiralsh," she said. "You killed many of our guards on the night you ran."

Trax drained his wine and poured another glass.

"A cell? Oh, Bixa, I think we can do better than that."

CHAPTER 17

FINAL ARRANGEMENTS

"It's very small," Chetorth told the leader of the team of mechanicals preparing the building, well, *his* building, for the attack. He stuck his head into the little room and withdrew it when a grey-clad woman pulled him back.

"Don't get in the way," she said. "We still have another two buildings in this ward to prepare – and the room's small because it's made of silkstone, and we have only so much of that, though if the sandwalkers hadn't helped, we wouldn't even have this much. Cheer up, friend, you don't have to stay in it for long, do you?"

Chetorth held up his arms in surrender, and the woman caught her breath at the sight of his maimed hand.

"Sorry," she said. "For a moment, I forgot you were a bane. We're run half to death these days, and well, I'm sorry."

The bane grinned. "Don't be! I'm just nervous, that's why I'm fussing so much. At least let me carry something. I have one-and-a-half hands to lend you."

The woman, not much older than himself, snorted and shook her head, her blond braids swinging back and forth.

"Not likely, no more than you'd let me fight a demon for you! If you want to help, you can climb up to the top of that tank and see how full it is."

Chetorth did as he was told, scaling the attached ladder to look inside. Such large tanks dotted every roof in Shirath, ready to douse a fire that might destroy a building or an entire ward. Now, their purpose had been reversed. The smell hit him before he reached the top, something even worse than the pine tar brewed by the city's loggers. He looked down into the barrel-like structure and saw it half full of a viscous black liquid.

"Half," he shouted down, and the woman waved back.

"That's enough for this building," she said, and called over to her partner. "Done yet?"

A man paused in chopping a hole in the roof and stuck his head in it to look down into the building. After a moment, he pulled back out and waved at the woman. While he collected their tools, the woman came over to where Chetorth had climbed down the ladder. She showed him the heavy mallet in her hand and laid it beside the water tank.

"A few good hits with this and you can free the plug," she said, then laid a hand on his shoulder. "Don't wait too long after that to make your escape."

"I won't," Chetorth said, and smiled down at her. He didn't state the obvious problems with that plan, but he thought of them. And from her worried sisterly look, so did she.

∼

"You won't get away with this, Trax," the woman said. She twisted but the two Masks holding her were much bigger than she. After straining against them with no result, she stood straighter and glared at the king.

Trax regarded her, his face uncanny in its calm, though his eyes seemed much too bright under the glare of the lamps. He signalled the two men and they followed him, pulling their prisoner out into the corridor and down to a lower level crammed with barrels and crates. Thick pillars held up the roof, and the ones in the centre of the room bore captives chained to the stone.

"Mother!" one said, a young man, unshaven and unkempt. He lunged against his restraints, but barely moved, so strongly was he bound.

The woman saw him and sneered. "Fool! Your betrayal led to this. Had you held your tongue, the Itaalk would have taken the city and we would have been spared."

The man lowered his head and mumbled, "I had to. You don't know what they threatened to do to me."

The look of contempt didn't leave the woman's face. "Was it any worse than what they plan to do now?"

The Masks bound her to a last pillar, and she mocked the king as they fixed the chains to rings driven into the stone. "Oh, My Glorious Majesty, do you think this will save your miserable life? The demons will still come, an army of them. I've seen them, Trax. No city, not even Solantor, could stand against them. They will destroy you, your precious queen, and the squalling brat you thought would follow you."

Trax said nothing, but another stepped forward to speak, a squat, limping man holding a Duellist's rapier in one hand.

"Squawk all you want, Tiralsh," Dirst said. "Your time's come."

He smiled and lifted the sword. "But in honour of you being a lord and all, we'll leave you to go last."

He stepped up to the young man and placed the point of his blade over the prisoner's heart.

CHAPTER 18
A LOYAL CAPTAIN

The lights in the Palace Plaza were few. The temple's three domes were completely dark, the priests gone south with the refugees or waiting in the southern half of the city until their services were needed. The market was deserted, as it would normally be at this time of night, but Garet knew there would be no resuming of trade when the sun came up in just a few short hours. In the palace itself, only a few lamps still burned: those above the door, and a single light on the third floor. Between the temple and that building, the rough wall around the guard's barracks hid any other illumination, but within, the bane found enough lit torches to make his way to the captain's office.

Garet came up to the door where he was stopped by Blellat, who guarded the entrance.

"Hold up," the man said. "The captain's not in a mood for guests tonight."

The bane bit back a sharp reply when he saw the worry on the man's face. "I got a message from Shula that there was trouble and I should talk to Bixa," he said. "What happened?"

"Let him in!" a voice, Bixa's, called from inside. "I hope he brought more wine!"

Garet looked at Blellat, who shrugged. "Go ahead," he said. "I'll get the wine."

A lamp hung over a table. Bixa sat on one side and Maroster, the big ex-Mask who had fought so fiercely at the Battle of the Bridge, slouched opposite. The giant turned his cup over and sighed when only a drop fell onto the table. Bixa shook the wineskin and found it just as dry. She peered at Garet.

"Wine?" she asked.

Maroster looked up hopefully.

"Blellat's getting some," the bane said, and pulled up a third stool to sit at the foot of the table.

"Good old Blellat," Bixa said. She put her good arm around Garet's shoulders, almost falling off her own seat in the process. "Caught Tiralsh. He'll make a good captain, mark my words."

"Not as good as . . . you," Maroster slurred.

Bixa pointed a finger near the man. "I like you. You know what's right, or you do now. Didn't used to! Anyway, the way you spoke to him . . . brave!"

"You too," Maroster said. "Told him to go claw himself."

Blellat returned and put a pair of wineskins on the table. He gave Garet a sour look and went back outside.

"What happened?" Garet asked. Getting no response, he sighed and poured wine into both their cups.

Bixa waited until the wine was poured before she answered. "There! What happened? Our good king decided that there was a chance we wouldn't survive the coming battle. That's what."

"Good chance," Maroster added. He threw back his cup and inhaled the contents.

"That's right," Bixa said. "Very good. So, he decided another thing. He decided that if we died, he didn't want Tiralsh and Tar . . . Tarock, and who was the other?"

"Gost," Maroster burped out.

It took some time for Bixa to stop laughing and continue. "Old Gost! That's right. A few others too. Minor players, as Marick would say. The king said they shouldn't survive if we didn't. But" – she spread her hands – "but who'd kill them if we were all dead?"

"Nobody, that's who," Maroster shouted, then laid his head on his arms and closed his eyes.

"Nobody," Bixa agreed. "So, he told me to . . ." She made a slashing motion with her good hand that skidded along the wine-wet table. "Cut off their heads."

"No!" Garet said, he pushed back from the table, but Bixa grabbed his shoulder.

"He did," she said, and the bane saw tears in her eyes. "He did! I said, 'No, Your Majesty King Trax, I won't,' but he said I had to."

Garet swallowed. "Did you?" he asked. "Did you kill them?"

Bixa, her cheeks wet, shook her head. "No, Garet, no, no, no. Hate Tiralsh. Hate Gost. Couldn't do it."

She poured more wine and shoved it towards the bane. "Yelled at me to get out. Me, who's stood by him all this time! Called in other guards to do it. They wouldn't 'cause I wouldn't. Good women and men. All of them."

"So, he couldn't get anyone to do it?" Garet said, hoping that was true but fearing it wasn't.

Bixa wagged a finger at him. "Trax is very, very, very stubborn. He called in Maroster here. Heard he was a cruel, murdering piece of scum." She patted the snoring man on top of his head. "No offence. But even he said no! And he told the king some very rude things. Hah! Very rude. But he found someone, oh yes. Dirst, that ex-Duellist scummery murder . . . murderer. 'Happy to,' he said, claw him. Claw them all!"

She raised her cup and stood at an angle. "And Heaven shield the king," she said and downed the wine. "Because I won't. Not anymore."

"The clawed king," Maroster grunted, perhaps in his sleep.

Garet helped Bixa back into her chair. "We need you, Bixa," he said. "The attack has to be tomorrow now that the northern gates are down, and all those little lizards the sandwalkers carry are afraid of something big in the north. Please, you can't quit now. None of us can, no matter what Trax has done."

The guard captain looked deep into her empty cup. "Last time, Garet. After this, I'll go south, see that land Vinir and the others did. Fight slavers or learn to . . . paint. Don't know. Can't stay here."

"South," Maroster agreed, then resumed snoring.

"Still, we all might die," Bixa added, filling her cup again. "The king said so, and His Majesty's never wrong, is he?"

CHAPTER 19

THE KING'S RAGE

"Is it true?"

Trax turned to see Lysere standing in the door of the Shouting Room. She seemed remote, stern, carved from marble rather than made of flesh.

"It was necessary," Trax said, and turned back to his maps and models.

"It was not!" Lysere said and came towards her husband. "This is not who you are, husband!"

She stopped when he held out a palm, not looking at her but speaking to her nonetheless.

"Is that so?" he said, and his voice was mocking in its tone. "I suppose you're right, in a way. The Trax you knew is gone, Lysere, and just as well, for that Trax was a weak fool. He couldn't even close a silkstone box, no matter how hard he tried."

The queen stared at her husband's back. The muscles of his shoulder were as tight as a twisted wire.

"That was an unfair test," she said. "And Branet should never have allowed it. No one who isn't a bane or protected by silkstone can approach a demon jewel. You didn't fail, my love, no more than if you'd set yourself to leap the city walls. And you will not fail the city."

The king turned now, and Lysere saw that his fists were clenched at his sides.

"Oh, but it was a fair test, for it fairly showed me that I was – what should I say – oh yes, inadequate. I had to destroy monsters, and I wasn't one, nor was I a freak like the banes."

Lysere recoiled. "Branet is your friend," she said. "And you think him a freak?"

"Yes, but a useful one," Trax said, and smiled, though no warmth reached his eyes. "My most beautiful queen, a king has no friends. But he has many enemies, though fewer tonight. Those that remain are monsters and require monstrous deeds to destroy them."

"My dear," Lysere began, but Trax cut her off.

"No, you seek the old Trax, but he's been justly banished. The fool couldn't have shut that box in a thousand years. The new Trax, myself, I mean, would just kill the man who held it." He paused to look down at the city model, now minus the miniature palace and three of its gates.

His next words were spoken to that model, not the queen. "The old Trax would have tried to save all of Shirath, probably by taking that traitor Bixa's advice and meeting the enemy in the fields. Idiot! I know what the demons and their clawed masters want. I see their weaknesses because we are now so alike. They want destruction, fire, and blood, and I will feed it to them, so much that it chokes them!"

He looked back up at his astonished queen and said, "Now, since you refuse to follow our daughter to the Far South, go find some safe place in which to hide."

Lysere said nothing. She turned and left the room, signalling a steward to follow her.

"Send word to Branet and Bixa that I need to see them," she said, and gave the woman at her side a meaningful look. "And don't trouble the king about it."

The steward looked back at the Shouting Room door and then to the queen. She nodded and said, "Since His Majesty is occupied with affairs of state, I can't imagine there would be any need to inform him of such a . . . hmm, private matter?"

"Thank you, Elessa," Lysere said, and went to a smaller reception room to wait for the two she had summoned. While she sat there, surrounded by brocade curtains and dainty statuary, she thought about fear, the terror that had seeped into the walls of the city for six hundred years, fear she had felt all too often, fear that pulsed through the halls of this palace – and through the mind of her husband.

He is fear-mad. The Trax I know – knew – would not kill prisoners. Just last year, he tried to save Shirin from Branet's wrath, but now . . . For our daughter's sake, Heaven, please let him come back to his senses.

She looked down at her hands. Her fingers clenched a silk handkerchief and would have rent it if the cloth had been any weaker.

And if he can't come back, then let me have the strength to do what I must, for our daughter's sake, and the sake of all within these walls.

CHAPTER 20

THE BANEHALL AWAKE

It was halfway through the night and dawn was not even a promise in the sky, yet the corridors of the banehall echoed to the sound of many feet. Those that moved within the hall did not run, for that would have signalled panic, but neither did they tarry, for this was the day they had feared for six hundred years, the day when the demons might win.

Banes of all ranks, except for the Black Sashes, who had been sent south with the majority of ordinary citizens, went back and forth purposefully, bearing messages, taking weapons to be sharpened and resharpened, or checking the maps and lists laid out in the dining hall to find their appointed places. On the top floors, some might have been sleeping, saving their strength for the battle all expected to come this day, but it was more likely that they lay awake in their beds, staring into the darkness and waiting for the call.

Dorict had not bothered trying to close his eyes, not since a message had sent his roommate, Garet, running towards the guard barracks in the Palace Plaza. He moved among the tables in the kitchen, helping the one stubborn remaining cook to prepare pot after pot of porridge and to take racks of bread from the ovens out into the kitchen yard to let cool in the night air.

"There, Insall," Dorict said, wiping his hands on a borrowed apron. "The bread's out and the porridge is ready to serve. Time for you to go south."

The man picked up a butchering knife and used it to tap the crown of a silkstone helmet lying atop the sacks of flour stacked by the door.

"Nobody," he said, ringing the mask again for emphasis, "nobody tells me what to do in my own kitchen. Not banes and not clawed demons."

He put the blade on top of the helmet and went back to his cooking.

Dorict opened his mouth to argue, but a hand pulled him back and he was in the dining hall before he could turn and see Marick standing there, tottering a bit on his walking stick.

"Don't bother arguing," the ex-bane said. "Two years ago, Insall wouldn't have dared say the word, now he's ready to chop demons into sausage. And you too, if you try to stop him!"

Three Green Sashes, wiping sleep from their eyes, came through the room, picked up bowls and spoons from a sideboard, and continued into the kitchen. Marick watched them go, waiting until they were out of earshot before he continued speaking. "It wouldn't make a difference if he did listen. Trax has ordered the southern gates shut. The rumour is he doesn't want people running when the Itaalk come, in case the demons follow them and find the rest of our people."

Dorict shook his head. "A hard order to give," he said.

Marick's face was twisted into a frown. He sat down at a nearby table and motioned Dorict close enough to hear him whisper, "It's not the only one. Trax had Tiralsh, her son, Tarock, Gost, and the rest of their lot killed this past night! I had that from Kaela, who got a note from Shula. I guess Garet got one too, for he was at the barracks not long ago."

Dorict sat back, his mouth open. "Claws, the man really is fear-mad, isn't he? Well, that explains where Branet went in such a hurry not so long after Garet left." He put his head in his hands. "You'd think we had enough to face without a murderous king."

Marick waved over a Green and spoke to her for a moment. The young woman nodded and soon came back with bowls of porridge and a plate of bread on a tray.

"Eat," Marick said. "We'll both need our strength today."

Dorict pulled a bowl closer and found a spoon on the table nearby. He wiped it on his sleeve and began to eat, slowly, mechanically, and not with any of the enthusiasm he usually felt for breakfast. "Did any of your informants tell you what the hallmaster and the lords intend to do about it?" he asked, then paused, spoon hovering over the bowl, waiting for an answer.

Marick shook his head. "They'll do nothing, of course." At his friend's astonished look, he continued, "Taking Trax off the throne would only panic people. I doubt even Branet would try to remove him, though he must be ready to throw Trax from the city walls by now! No, my friend, the king is our leader for better or worse, Heaven shield us, at least until the battle is over and Lysere can take his place."

"Lysere?" Dorict asked, the spoon moving again.

Marick nodded. "Yes, Lysere. She has more wit than

Trax and a better heart. Two souls to his one, as a sand-walker would say."

Dorict nodded. "Speaking of them, I must go and wish Yala and her people luck before the dawn. They have a hard part in this plan, at least they'll think so. Will you stay in the hall?"

Marick drew back in mock outrage. "What, and miss the greatest drama yet to be staged in Shirath's history? No, I'm for this side of the river, ready to push the beasts back if they break through. You?

"The same," Dorict said, his eyes narrowing. "I can't imagine anyone mad enough to put you with the guards and citizens held in reserve. You assigned yourself there, didn't you?"

"No," Marick said. "Here comes my commander now."

Dorict looked up to see Master Tarix come into the room, followed by Masters Relict and Taron. The two men went over to scan the lists set out on the masters' tables while Tarix came to where the two young men sat. She dropped a sharpened shield on the table between them and collapsed into a chair.

"Claws and teeth, this is a long night! I suppose you've heard all the news from the palace? Well, it's nothing we can fix until we find out if we're alive or dead." She eyed the smaller of the two. "Now, Marick, remember that you're weaker on the left and must use more twist of your shoulders and hips to strike. Also, if you're knocked to the ground, that fancy dagger might be more useful than a shield."

"Yes, Master," Marick said, sounding like the Blue Sash student he had once been, a bane who had worshipped every word his training master said. "I'll kill at least ten demons in honour of your teaching."

Tarix put a hand on his shoulder and looked into his eyes. "Stay alive, Marick. That's enough honour for me. Oh, and wear this, would you, for my sake? It might bring you some luck."

She draped a green sash around his neck, and Dorict grinned at his friend's blushing face. However, any hope that embarrassment or humility would silence Marick was soon dashed.

"Master!" the young man said. "I thank you for this, most sincerely, but don't you think a red sash would give me even more luck?"

CHAPTER 21
THE END OF THE WORLD

"Try looking like an idiot," Bixa said, and groaned a bit as her head rattled inside her silkstone helmet.

Blellat tried to ignore his commander, but Bixa kept talking.

"We're supposed to be walking into an ambush," she growled, "so act like you're stupid."

"Fighting with a hangover," Blellat said, adjusting his much lighter hood. "Now that's stupid."

The palace guards' other officer, Cirta, produced a sickly smile, visible through the breathing slit of his own mask.

"What's wrong with you?" Blellat demanded. "You weren't drinking up all the wine in Shirath over the past two days like our captain here, were you?"

"No," he said. "I'm just a tiny bit worried about marching out with two hundred guards to fight a thousand demons."

"One hundred and ninety-four guards," Blellat corrected, and spat on the ground.

A scout came running back through the ranks of trees to stop in front of Bixa.

"They're coming, Captain," he said in a properly respectful shout.

"Ohhh," Bixa said. She straightened carefully and drew her sword.

"Blellat, on the left. Cirta, on the right. Be ready to wheel if they concentrate on any one point. Remember, we have to put up a good fight and *then* retreat. But not before they believe fighting them here was our plan all along."

She held her sword above her head and called out to the line of guards.

"Arrows on strings, pikes forward, and swords loose in the scabbards," she shouted, silently cursing Trax, her drinking partner Maroster, and whoever in this demon-haunted land had first fermented wine.

Despite what they expected and had prepared for with silkstone masks, sandwalker scarves and hoods like Blellat's, there was no fear lashing at them as they dressed their lines. Instead, a rage rose ahead of them, a towering anger that built until the newly leafed trees seemed to tremble with it.

Bixa felt a great desire to charge forward, screaming, but pushed that emotion away and glared back into position any who advanced beyond her.

They're trying to draw us out, break our lines, and run us down in their first charge.

Distant howls and yelps sounded, became louder, closer, and then she could see the first of the demons break the cover of the forest and race towards them. Like the one Garet captured, its weapon was crude, an iron blade tied to a rough handle. Bixa readied for the beast, but a dozen arrows hit it before it could get within striking distance of her.

Oh well, there'll be plenty more chances today.

And soon enough, there were.

TARON BROUGHT up his forces a hundred yards behind Bixa's. If all went well, they would make a stand here and let the fleeing guards pass through their ranks. Then they must close up and fall back by degrees, to slow the demons and make them bunch up and lose any of the discipline imposed upon them by the Itaalk and their staffs. After that, the defenders were supposed to split into smaller groups and pull back through different gates to shelter behind the next line of defenders. Three of those gates hung open, proof of Tiralsh's final treachery. The other two, leading to the Second and Seventh Wards, were in one piece but left half open and barricaded to make it seem like they too were damaged. With luck, a quality much-prized in Shirath, the demons would invade in a mob, unprepared for the welcome that awaited them.

The arrow-throwers on the outer walls sang over and over again, and Taron hoped they were getting as many Itaalk as were within range. The weakest point of their plan was that the demon masters might sense a trap and keep the beasts from chasing them into the city.

A horn sounded and the guards, much reduced, ran headlong through their lines, knocking over some in their desperation to escape. At Taron's command, the banes re-formed and their archers shot from the wings, trying to pile up attackers on the bodies of those they had killed. It slowed the beasts down – for a moment – and then the demons were upon them. Taron took a clawed hand from its wrist with a backhand slash of his shield, the sharpened edge serving as both weapon and defence. The demon, undeterred, reached for his face with the other hand, but a bane to his left pushed it back with a trident. The points failed to pierce the leather shirt the once-human beasts all wore, but the second thrust took it in the neck, the central prong of the trident producing a fountain of blood.

"Step back!" Taron shouted.

He was becoming hopeful, or at least as hopeful as a bane could be when facing hundreds of squalling, shrieking demons armed with rough weapons that they swung with a horrible strength. Banes fell under those bitter iron blades, but it was working. They split as agreed into several groups. Taron's own team, feigning panic, drew dozens after them, around the curve of the city walls and towards the Second and Third Wards. By retreating through different gates, the Itaalk might not suspect a single trap like the one they met last time between the Clawed Walls.

Around Taron, more of his companions fell, yet the banemaster couldn't stop to mourn men and women he'd known for years, some since he was a Black Sash himself. He barely had time to note their faces before another demon crawled over the last one's corpse to try and kill him.

Strike and step back. Strike and step back. Pull the wounded with you, if they didn't vanish under a wave of claws and clubs.

They were still fifty yards from the gate when the number of demons doubled, then tripled.

Where are they coming from? Did the other banes already fall?

The push was too much now, and Taron waved the

surviving defenders back into the Fourth Ward gates, much short of their goal. They stumbled over the small bridge made famous by last year's battle with a smaller demon army, one they had hoped was as big as they would ever face.

How wrong we were.

Taron grabbed a bleeding Green and threw him towards a Gold, Chitoroth, who had but one working arm and no weapon.

"Take him in. All of you get back behind the next line," he cried, and scooped the Green's shield from the ground to slip over his other hand. Now both of Taron's arm were covered from elbow to fist with ovals of steel, wickedly pointed and the front third sharpened as keenly as a sand-walker's shovel.

Two slashes cleared the nearest demons from before him, and he backed away to the far end of the bridge's planks, shields held out like a praying mantis confronting a nest of snakes.

The others need time, and this is a very good place to kill some demons.

He had very little hope for his own chances, but Tarix had been right when she spoke up in Trax's council so many days ago; it was a bane's duty, and luck, perhaps, to die for his city's sake under a monster's claws. Beyond the massed attackers, he saw the robes of an Itaalk, his staff held over the backs of the pushing demons.

This is the time. I didn't die on this bridge last year, but I suppose Heaven was only waiting for today.

He made an abortive gesture to stroke his small, precise beard and then remembered his arms were encased by sharp steel. He smiled, and a calm settled over him. The cries of the wounded, the waves of demon anger, even the fear of his own death, all fell away. He was where he was supposed to be, doing what he was supposed to be doing, and everything else would take care of itself.

He regarded the demons and saw confusion in the wrinkling of their mottled brows and the squinting of their night-black eyes. He walked forward, calmly, as if he were walking the corridors of his beloved banehall. There was a polite smile on his face as if he were about to greet an old friend.

The demons felt his approach as much as saw it. There was a terrible power surrounding this man, and they tumbled back against each other to escape it.

The bane was almost at the centre of the bridge when the Itaalk raised his staff and ground out a mental command: *Kill!*

As the demons snapped back to radiating anger and surged forward, Taron lifted both arms straight out from his sides. As the first monster came close, he began to spin.

THE REASON for the demon reinforcements to the wings of their attack was forever unknown to Taron, but quite understandable to Branet and the other three hallmasters waiting in the next line. The demons in the centre of the attack were being drawn to the wings to make room for new enemies to move in. Well-ordered groups of men, not demons, marched into the space the Itaalk were creating with their staffs. Long spears swayed above their ranks, and colourful banners hung from many of them.

"The Dragon Brigades, I think," Branet growled. "By Garet's description, anyway, and we know they're allies of the Itaalk."

"I don't like those spears," Maroster said. He hefted his axe. He was here because Ward Five's gate was considered the most important of them all, especially if the monsters came straight on, following Bixa's first wave of guards. The second wave, led by banemasters – those who were still fit enough to fight and run, that is – were meant to draw the demons in through several gates. Once in the wards, others of the hall stood ready to fire the buildings and destroy the larger part of the invading army.

Or so the plan had been.

"These aren't demons who can't tell a trap from a meal," Chon said. She blinked her one eye and pointed at the approaching line of spears now lowered so that their points faced the waiting banes. "If they get close to the gates, they might see our planned retreats for what they are."

Branet nodded. He turned to the others.

"I have one idea, but no one will like it much."

"What's that?" Sicarth asked, rather nervously. He grasped his own spear, a needle-pointed weapon with a crescent crossbar – a traditional weapon of Illick's banehall – with both hands.

"Keep the remnants of the second line with us," Branet said. "Add anyone we can from the first line and bring up all our archers."

He raised his own axe, not as big as Maroster's but still quite terrifying. "Then we destroy these clawed pieces of scum who would march with demons against our cities. Anybody who survives retreats into the wards like we intended."

"That's a plan?" Chon asked, then laughed. She pulled a round shield off her back and swept a knife from its sheath.

The shield bore a braced spike in its centre, and the knife looked like it could chop iron.

"You're right, I don't like it," Sicarth said, and grinned.

"It'll do," Corix said. The Old Torrick hallmaster, barely arrived in the city with another thirty banes, flexed the metal fingers of her spiked gloves. Bands of metal ran down her arms and shone in the morning sun.

Branet barked out orders. The banes and remaining guards formed a column that could pass quickly through the gate. A horn signalled the second line to finish its retreat and join them. Facing them, the Dragon Brigades quick-marched forward, spears at the ready and banners flying.

The Shirath hallmaster waved his forces forward, and they charged, Maroster running with them. The huge man shook his masked head as he ran.

Why all the talk? This was the only thing we could do.

He smiled a bit at that and chose his first man to kill.

"WHAT IS HE DOING?" Tarix demanded. She sighted along the length of the arrow, using the iron rings provided for that purpose. From atop the Sixth Ward's outer wall, she had a grand view of the battle, but could not yet see the difference between the demons already attacking and the Dragon Brigades forming up in the newly cleared centre of the fray.

"Distance viewer," she said, and one of the Masks assigned to guard them, Abenth, handed her the tube. After a moment's use, Tarix lowered it and swore.

"Claws and teeth," she said. "Those are men with spears, not demons!"

"Itaalk?" Teelol, the arrow-thrower's other protector,

asked. This woman was an ex-Duellist, one of those who joined the Masks after their failed rebellion of two years past. That history had not taught her humility, as her next remark showed. "Should have put us Duellists out there," she said, positively smirking at the thought. "We'd have cleaned them up in a heartbeat."

Riga, one of Tarix's students, snorted. "Huh! Swords against those lances?" she asked. "Do me a favour and watch the wall so we can get to work, will you?"

Teelol glared but went back to her post, scanning the outer wall for any demons trying to claw their way up the rough stone. Lines of spiked balls and chains were ready to drop on a monster that tried, and the woman swore she could pierce the eye of any beast who got past such defences.

Tarix told Riga to use the distance viewer and keep an eye out for staff-wielding demon masters. They were the target of choice, but she thought they could spare a few shafts for those spearmen who moved forward as a thicket of steel points while Branet and his forces charged out to meet them.

The bane reached down and threw the switch that connected the spark jars. The hum was comforting, or unsettling, she couldn't decide which. She shook her head to clear it of demon-cast anger and made a quick request of Heaven that she wouldn't forget Dasanat's instructions. The bane raised the back ring until its notch rested against a red line, the same colour as the painted stones the spearmen neared.

Was this anger cast for you, demon allies? Do the Itaalk bring it instead of fear so you can more easily kill us?

"Claw you all," she whispered, and pulled the firing lever.

GARET RACED AHEAD on the left of the banes' line. Not because he was anxious to be the first to confront those spears, but because he needed room for what he planned next.

His sword was still sheathed, the length of it bouncing against his thigh, but his hands held the coiled length of his rope-hammer. With each step, he let out more line, whirling the spiked ball beside his body and hoping Salick was keeping a safe distance.

The anger faded now, perhaps blunted by the distance to the Itaalk, who had withdrawn with their grotesque fighters to the wings. It didn't matter, Garet had rage enough on his own.

These are the men who took the people from Lakeside Town. They were innocent, just trying to live and not too proud to shelter strangers when the dragon came and burned their homes. Then, these pieces of scum handed them over to the Itaalk to be turned into demons. They were their own people, and they still did that. I remember that banner on the carts near the Itaalk valley, the crossed spears thrust through a dragon. I remember the men with those long lances. Now I'm going to make sure they remember me.

The spears were indeed long, and wickedly sharp, forming both a defence and a moving attack as the brigades marched forward. Nearing that steel hedge, the bane stopped and waited until the spear points were but feet away. He could see the anticipation in the eyes of the enemy and the mocking smile on the one directly in front of him. A last whirl of the line, and he flung the spiked ball straight at that smile.

I've already killed one man with this weapon. Heaven shield me, for I'm adding to that count today.

And he did, for the weight took the grinning spearman in the face and broke his neck as well. Then Salick was beside him, the prongs of her trident trapping and pushing aside several spears. Into the breach they made, banes rushed in bearing axes, spears, hammers, and, Garet was heartened to see, an iron-bound baker's paddle, the traditional weapon of the first hallmaster, Banfreat the Baker. Tarix's student Ratal swung with a will, scattering spearmen and leaving but a few for Kesla, who struck the survivors down with her flail.

There were too many friends around him now to use his rope-hammer, so he dropped it to the ground and pulled out the sword Trax had given him when he was still a king's agent. The heavy blade, given speed by a strong twist of his wrist and body, cracked a spear shaft and knocked it from the hands of a scowling bearded man. A backslash opened his throat. The man dropped at his feet, but Garet found himself unburdened by any remorse. These men had made the demons possible, and he cut and stabbed with no guilt.

Another man ran past him towards Salick but fell when Garet slashed his leg. He buried the tip of his sword in the man's chest and ripped it out, scattering blood onto an already crimson ground. Arrows flew over his head and sometimes beside it. He spun to look for another foe and caught Salick's fierce expression as she pulled her trident from a spearman's belly. They saw each other, knew the shared reason for their fury, and nodded before running to where Ratal and Kesla fought back-to-back against many men.

In the hacking and screaming, it was impossible to know who was winning.

King Trax stood on the wall above the south end of Shirath's central bridge. Dasanat knelt beside him, giving the dart machine a last inspection. Unlike the arrow-throwers, which worked on the same principle as an ordinary bow but used a spark-driven device to quickly pull back the string and drop a spear-length arrow down in preparation for firing, the dart-thrower shot a vast number of much smaller missiles all at once. They were not meant to kill, though that might have been the happy outcome of a direct hit. They were instead meant to deliver the sandwalkers' poison, a bone and demon jewel dissolving liquid that the desert dwellers had used for centuries to protect them from "poison winds," demons, in fact, that had blundered past the five cities built along the River Ar to attack their wells.

The second difference was the force that shot these darts at their targets. Instead of a bow stave, or a hundred of them, for that was how many darts flew each time the machine was fired, the tubes holding the darts were connected to a great steel cylinder that stored air. That air was first pressed tight within by a pump driven by the cranking of a dozen fit mechanicals. Then the air was released by opening a valve that sent it racing into the tubes, catching the cupped and feathered tails of the darts and sending them arching over the defenders to land – in theory – among the attackers.

In theory, for the testing Dasanat wanted had been postponed by the probable end of the world. She was not pleased. "Aiming is still unreliable. I would use these as a last resort, Trax," she said, never having the time to remember terms like "Your Majesty."

The king stopped looking through a distance viewer

towards the smoke rising from the Third and Fifth Wards. He turned to the mechanical and bestowed a smile upon her that was almost a sneer. "And at what 'resort' did you think we are now, Dasanat?"

He turned back to his vigil. "Make them ready," he ordered. "With any luck – which I think Heaven owes me – Branet will draw the remaining demons into the Palace Plaza. After they retreat across the river to the Banehall Plaza, we'll use your toys to slaughter them on the bridges first, then we'll attack with all our remaining forces and kill those we can't push back to burn in the wards."

He laughed as another section of the city, the Sixth, sent smoke pouring up into the sky.

BRANET WAS LEANING on his axe, panting and wondering if it was age or despair that was shortening his breath. A spearman ran at him, and the hallmaster raised his weapon and angled it to push the shaft out of line, then, as he had twenty times today already, he slid the blade along the wood, slicing into the attacker's hand before pushing it deep into the Northerner's chest.

"Watch out!" a deep voice called, and Branet dropped, letting a lance pass over him, the banner of bloody, crossed spears brushing his neck. He twisted, trying to fling his axe out to ward his back, but it was not needed. The body of a man flew past, blood spraying from a severed spine.

Maroster helped him up. The spears closed around them. "Getting too old for this?" he asked. "You seemed fit enough when we fought in Gost's warehouse."

"I must have been, since I recall beating you there," Branet growled. He put his back to the only man in Shirath who topped him in height and faced his half of a ring of spears.

Maroster grunted.

A shrill cry came from Branet's left, and Bixa came barrelling into the circle, cutting down two in passing. She fetched up against Maroster, and the two defenders became three.

Then four, as another attacker fell at their feet, his face a ruin thanks to Corix's spiked gloves. The Old Torrick hallmaster was bleeding from a pierced shoulder but set herself at Branet's side, stone-straight, arms cocked for another strike.

Maroster picked up that last body in one hand and flung it at the men nearest him. They went down like wheat beneath the blade of a scythe.

"This way," he shouted, and charged the gap, his axe swinging and the others following. He broke through, but before the surviving spearmen could turn, he whirled and charged back *into* the circle and out through the other side. If he took any wounds, he didn't seem to notice. The others followed in his wake, striking the nearest foes and widening the gaps Maroster made in his fury. By the third pass, the enemy was scattering and the banes were in pursuit.

Across the battlefield, the brigades pushed – and were held – by the line of Shirath's defenders. For all Branet knew they might even have been winning, though it was impossible to tell in the chaos of battle. If over the roar he had heard the rustle of red cloaks flying across the furrows of the spring fields, or if he had noted the quick music of plucked bowstrings, a sound signalling the arrival of the greatest archers the city of Shirath had ever seen, the hallmaster might have been more confident. Branet's first real hint of victory against the enemy was in the screams of the remaining spearmen.

A rain of arrows fell among them, finding easy purchase in bodies that bore no armour. Even the demons had better protection than the fine clothing of the brigades, whose members were the richest men by far in the North. They wore no armour because they poisoned their dragon prey before killing it as easily as a farmer kills a bleating sheep. The Itaalk, having spies in Shirath, might have warned them to better prepare, but they did not mean to have the brigades survive. This was to be the end of all humanity in the lands both north and south of the forest. Only the Itaalk were to remain alive.

It wasn't long before the demon masters, seeing the collapse of the brigades, sent their demons to attack from both sides. The banes re-formed and retreated, slowing the attackers until the sandwalkers ran out of arrows and had to wield their sharpened shovels. Many a desert woman lost her life in those fields, killed beside banes and palace guards, but the demons fell even faster.

"Back into the wards," Branet yelled, words that carried over the sound of battle as only a hallmaster's voice could. He couldn't see their own forces on the right or left, led by Masters Taron and Relict. Those parts of the second line were meant to pull any demons they could into the other wards. He hoped they were safe.

As agreed, the Akalit banes made for the Fourth Ward, smashing through a handful of demons they found milling around the body of an Itaalk and taking his fallen staff; the Illick banes made for the Sixth, finding no enemies waiting for them but having plenty on their heels. Branet backed his fighters into the Fifth and began a long, brutal retreat through that ward, drawing the beasts after him.

CHAPTER 22

FIRE AND STEEL

"I wish you were somewhere else," Chetorth said, then held up both hands – the wounded and the whole – as Dalesta bristled. "I only mean that you would be safer on the bridges."

He then became very interested in the ties of his padded clothing.

I hope this can protect me from the fire like the mechanicals said. And what was I thinking to say that to Dalesta? She isn't any stupider than I am to be here, ready to set a building on fire while we're standing on top of it.

He felt a small hand on his chin, and his head was lifted to see Dalesta looking at him, smiling.

"You're sweet to say it, but if you do it again . . ." She lifted the hook end of her weapon suggestively.

Chetorth shook his head, eyeing the edge of the curved blade, serrated like a saw to cut deep and fixed to a two-foot-long haft, and all that attached to a long line that ended in a bronze ring. It was a difficult weapon, but one that he knew she could wield effectively.

"All right!" he said. "We're in this together then. Can you hear anything?"

Dalesta shook her head, her hair flipping over her shoulders and distracting Chetorth from the matter at hand.

"Pay attention!" she commanded and pushed him with her free hand.

He didn't travel very far, for the dimensions of their shelter were little bigger than a closet. His back bumped against the silkstone of the little room tucked against the side of a water tank on a tenement roof in the middle of the Fourth Ward. He knew there were many other such rooms across the northern wards, each with a pair of banes ready to put the king's mad plan into action when the time came.

He pressed an ear to the stone. Was that more than a spring wind howling? Chetorth knew they were unlikely to hear the banes passing, but a thousand demons should have made enough noise to be noticed. He looked at Dalesta and nodded. She opened the stone-faced door a crack and shut it in the face of an overwhelming emotion – anger. The rage that had poured through the crack almost set them at each other's throats. They looked at each other, remembering it was a demon-spawned emotion, and pushed the anger down, holding it at bay in the same way they smothered demon fear.

"Well," whispered Dalesta. "If we can take that without killing each other, maybe we really can get married someday."

Chetorth covered his mouth with a two-fingered hand to conceal his laughter. They had to stay hidden until the demons were all inside the wards. This tiny room was supposed to help them do that, masking their own emotions in case the demons could receive fear as well as send it. They waited for the signal. Until then, all they could do was wait, pressed against each other.

Sometime later – though who can mark time when it's passed in an embrace – a loud horn sounded, piercing even the stone walls of their hiding place. The demons were inside the ward. The two broke apart and smiled guiltily at each other. They steeled themselves and cracked the door again. The hate was worse, but they were ready for it now and used it to smother their own fears as they crept out to look down a gutter hole cut into the edge of the roof.

Five storeys below, the street was full of demons, two-legged brutes that swung crude clubs and axes at everything they saw, even the bodies of their wounded and dead. A stench of burning meat clogged the watchers' throats and Dalesta covered a coughing fit with her hand. Chetorth pulled her back before they drew the beasts' attention.

"Claws, I hope that smell helps bring them in like Yala said it would. Right, get the torch ready," he said, and she nodded, fumbling one-handed for her flint-striker while still covering her mouth with the other.

Chetorth crawled across to the water tank and used the mallet the mechanical had left there to knock lose the bottom plug. It was hard work, lying on his side and swinging at the thing, but he got it free after a dozen hits. Black liquid flowed out, slower than water but still filling the sandbag trenches that guided the oil to holes cut into the roof. There were more holes cut in each floor below, letting the flammable liquid drip throughout the building.

He looked back to Dalesta and saw her hunched over, holding a torch that sputtered and sparked before it caught. Unhappily, he saw what was behind her too.

"Demons!" he shouted, and Dalesta looked over her shoulder to see claws and beaked faces appear over the top of the roof's guarding walls. Like all the flat roofs of Shirath, its space was cut into smaller sections by ten-foot-high walls, pierced here and there by gates, all meant to trap demons so that banes could hunt them more easily.

Unfortunately, such walls could also trap the hunters. Dalesta flung the torch beneath the tank, now nearly empty of its contents, and ran after Chetorth to the nearest place of refuge, a door that led to stairs going down into the building. When the banes tried to pull it open, they found it nailed shut. They looked around, trying to find another escape route. There was a ladder laid on the roof they might have used, but the demons were scrabbling over it even now.

"The other stairs!" Chetorth shouted, and the two ran to them just ahead of their pursuers.

Dalesta pushed him inside and slammed the door closed, setting a wooden brace under the bar to secure it.

"Overrun," she gasped, and her words were confirmed by a sudden slamming against the door. The planks shook but did not break.

They looked around. The banes stood on a landing above a steep staircase. Smoke curled up from below. A red glow barred their escape and they heard something crash as part of the building's interior collapsed. There was no running that way, and the two flinched as the door shuddered again under the demon's assault.

Chetorth hefted his blade, wishing he could exchange it for his arrow-thrower and sweep the roof clear of the monsters. Maybe the banes perched on the ward walls would run out of Itaalk to kill and start on the demons pounding on this door, though he knew they couldn't count on such Heaven-sent luck.

The young man coughed a bit at the tendrils of smoke

reaching up for them, knowing that it would incapacitate Dalesta first but himself soon after. There was no use trying to rush past it down and out onto the street, even if the demons were gone; the stairs at the next landing were blocked with a jumble of furniture, meant to trap demons in the burning building. The banes on this side of the ward were supposed to flee through the roof gates to the ward's interior wall and climb a set of makeshift steps to the top. The demons had been supposed to stay in the street and be burned up, not cut off their only practical escape.

He looked at Dalesta. She was wrapping her left arm in the rope of her weapon, twisting it around and around until her forearm was covered and the ring at the end of the thick line was held firmly in her hand.

"Cut please," she said, holding out the bit of line still loose between the serrated hook and her arm.

Chetorth obliged, grinning at her resourcefulness.

"I wish I had a shield to hold onto," he said, and helped her tuck the loose end into the coils so that the improvised armour would stay fixed to her arm.

Dalesta looked into his eyes and said, "I'm your shield. And you're mine. Right?"

"Until the end," Chetorth said.

They stood there for a dozen heartbeats, ignoring the creatures scrabbling for their blood just outside the door.

Chetorth touched his sword to Dalesta's razor-sharp pike-hook, and the ring of it sounded pure and fierce over the clawing of the wood and the crackle of the flames. She kicked the brace free and they shouldered open the door. The anger that poured in upon them was taken, matched, and doubled in return. Their steel flashed red in the flames, and the cries of rage came from more than just demon throats.

THE BRIDGE BATTLE

Lord Kirel looked at his fellow lords hiding behind the market stalls. Koret of the Third stood beside him, a pike in her hands and an overlarge chainmail shirt on her back. Bereth of the Second and Sabat of the Fifteenth were just beyond, armed and armoured like the rest. All of them wore silkstone helmets.

Across the Palace Plaza, hidden behind cloth blinds, were more lords and their ward guards. All waited for the demons to drive the defenders back into the space between them.

Kirel scratched under his mask but didn't remove it. They could already feel the emotions cast by the horde of demons approaching their position. This time, it wasn't the fear they had trained for, using demon jewels and Lord Andarack's little boxes, but anger, a rage so hot that they could hardly keep themselves from running towards the gates and throwing themselves on the enemy.

"Easy," Kirel said, waving a hand at his shifting guards. The only one who seemed calm was the new captain, Cruster. The woman's eyes looked out of her mask with little interest. She leaned against her pike and peered around the corner of the baker's stall where they hid.

"Nothing yet," she said. "But the noise is louder."

It was. A distant clamour came on the wind, and more than that, the smell of smoke. Kirel let some of the tension fall from his shoulders. That meant the beginning of the king's plan was actually working. The teams with the arrow-throwers on the outside walls – if they still lived – were supposed to drop oil on onto the ground behind the gates and fire it as soon as the demons flooded into the wards. The inner ward gates of the First and Eighth, behind the lords and their troops, were spiked and sealed, protecting them from a surprise attack. Cruster raised her hand, fingers folded in a hard fist, and Kirel drew his sword. His thoughts seemed to fly everywhere.

No pike for me. A lord wields a sword, like my father. Though, with no masks back then, he never had a chance to use it against demons. A lucky man indeed. I wish he were here.

He looked to Koret and the others. The anger still washed over them, seeping through the thin stone, but now it was cancelled by an internal dread, a nervous anticipation of what would happen when the woman dropped her hand. Kirel felt that confusion of emotions more than some. He knew he had a chance to redeem himself here, as his wife had in her efforts against Tiralsh's spies. It would be good to regain his fellow lords' respect. He swallowed, remembering Shula's message about the executions. He might have joined his uncle in death, had it not been for his wife's cunning.

Cruster lowered her fist as the noise increased.

"Ready," she said. "They're almost here."

Kirel touched his blade to the stone of his mask.

I am ready. Ready to be worthy of my lordship, of my city, and most especially of Kaela's regard, Heaven shield me.

Palace guards ran past them, making for the bridge. Others followed, banes and a handful of Masks, some helping wounded comrades. The last groups came in organized ranks, led by Branet and the other hallmasters, stepping backwards and holding out a fierce array of pikes and other weapons that the demons tried to reach beyond to tear soft flesh.

Kirel charged out at Cruster's side. Across the plaza, the other waiting defenders did the same. The plaza seemed wider than it had ever been before, so that they must run forever, but it was really only a short time before they changed places with the retreating men and women, letting them fall back to the bridges while their own forces took the brunt of the demons' hate.

Now the surging anger was welcome, and Kirel let it flow down his arm and into the bright length of his sword. He cleaved the head from a demon that squeezed between the pikes. Kicking the body back, he shouted out, "For Shirath! For Shirath! Hold them all!"

The call was taken up across the plaza, while the ward guards and their lords held the line, letting those demons who escaped the fire in the wards bunch up and become perfect targets for the remaining arrow-throwers.

Kirel hacked and thrust until he felt his arm would drop off, but he held his place until the bell rang behind them.

"Step back!" he shouted. "But keep the line!"

The defenders who were left took a step backwards towards the bridge gates.

"Again!" Kirel cried, and so, step by step, his diminished forces retreated towards safety. At the eastern gate, he waved the wounded in first, and was the last one through, backing over the bridge while throngs of thin, beaked horrors scrambled after him, striking at him with their clubs and blades. He was bleeding from a dozen small wounds by the time he reached the halfway point. Lord Andarack shouted at him to run faster, and he turned to flee. A few demons followed close behind, but fire arrows struck near his heels and the oil-soaked timbers caught immediately.

The beasts that survived that roasting were feathered by arrows from the palace guard, now re-formed and waiting just within the gates of the Banehall Plaza. Kirel stumbled into Andarack's arms and was pulled to safety.

"Kirel," the older man said. "Well done! This bridge is gone, and the west one is aflame. We hold the centre for a counter-attack when the fire in the northern wards has completed its work."

Kirel looked to that centre span. All the remaining arrow-throwers and Dasanat's dart machines were pouring their fire onto the bridge. He saw a robed man, not a demon, go down near the northern gate and felt the demons' massed anger turn immediately to fear. The change didn't seem to stop the attacks: if anything, they were redoubled as the creatures howled out their terror and hunger, pushing into the waves of death that struck them down from above.

"Heaven shield us," Kirel murmured.

"Not likely," Cruster said, and he turned to see the broad-shouldered woman squatting on the ground, resharpening the point of her pike on a paving stone.

When she saw his masked regard, she bent her head and said, "Sorry, my lord. I only meant that if Heaven did shield us, why would we have to do all this?"

Kirel had no reply to such wisdom. A quick glance

towards Heaven brought no comforting answer either, but it did show the figure of the king, standing on the wall high above the centre gate, looking down on the destruction and death below. The lord of the Thirteenth Ward couldn't be sure – he didn't have the sharpness of Kaela's eyes – but he could have sworn Trax was laughing.

CHAPTER 24
A RAIN OF ARROWS

Not all the demons came through the gates in the northern wards. Some clawed their way up the city's walls to where banes and Masks fired arrow-throwers and poured oil onto the fires below. Many of those beasts fell to the Masks who guarded the archers or were swept off the walls by the spiked balls and chains prepared for such an attack. Those that did reach the top struck wherever they saw a life to rend.

Tarix's post was soon besieged. Her team shot their last arrows into the faces of the demons charging them and fled, moving as fast as they could along the top of the wall towards the river. Teelol, a Mask, proved her skill by clearing the way of those beasts who gained the wall ahead of them. Her thrusts were as precise as a surgeon's probe, and they were soon standing alongside a few other survivors above the Eighth Ward. That section of the city was still safe, blocked off at the inner and outer gates to protect the backs of Lord Kirel and the others now retreating below them in the plaza. From the river wall, they looked down upon the bridges, the milling, howling army of demons, still hundreds strong, pushing to cross the defences and tear apart the southern half of the city.

Cannel, a Gold from Akalit who had trained with Tarix on the arrow-throwers, spat over the edge of the heights.

"By Boreth," he said, which Tarix had early on decided was a curse of some kind in his city, "we're stuck here until they counter-attack from the south."

He lifted his hammer, a blunt mass of iron that looked like it could knock down a house.

"I want to get in the fight!"

The Mask laughed and pointed the way they had come.

"Heaven's luck," she said, and flicked the blood from her blade. "The fight's come to you."

More demons had mounted the wall, and they came, some running on the top, some crawling just below its edge. Tarix tapped the shaft of her trident against her knee brace. She moved up to stand beside Teelol, for Cannel's hammer was best left for any beasts who snuck by them, not that a seven-foot-wide path gave much scope for sneaking.

"You any good with that?" the woman demanded.

Tarix could see narrowed eyes behind the slits of the mask.

Two years ago, these arrogant sword-wielders were the enemy we all feared. Now we stand side-by-side while the world burns. Heaven has a sense of humour that escapes me at times like this.

The thought *times like this* made her laugh, softly at first, then a chuckle that carried over the howling of the approaching demons. At the puzzled look in the Mask's eyes, she spared a quick hand to lay on the young woman's shoulder.

"Listen, my friend. Let's keep a tally, and we'll see who's the better demon slayer."

No more could be said, for it was time to start counting.

WHILE MOST OF the demons burned in the wards or rioted in the Palace Plaza, a few, no more than two hundred, ran howling around both ends of the walls, looking for easier prey. The doors of the two wards nearest the river were barred with iron bolts and great spikes, so while some stopped and clawed their way up the wall, the rest continued loping towards the nearby river. There, at both corners of the river wall, they found targets for their malice, barges full of women, cloaked and hooded. Some stood still while others waved their arms and cried out in exaggerated terror.

The demons did not notice that the barges were anchored to the far shore so that they stayed unmoving in the swift current, nor did they see the bows and quivers of arrows hidden at the women's feet.

When the beasts had all gathered howling on the bank, watchers on the southern walls blew their horns and the women pulled back their hoods to reveal faces wound about with thick cloth, leaving only their eyes showing. They stopped screaming and waving their hands. Silent now, they reached down and lifted strung bows, set shafts to the strings and fired volley after volley into the masses gathered on the northern bank. The points of the arrows were needle sharp, and each bore a green sheen from the poison that covered it.

The demons fell, some tumbling into the water. Even dying, they tried to reach their tormentors but were swept away in the current. The southern bank had even more archers, and more targets, as they shot those creatures who had managed to keep their malformed heads above water. Others simply drowned.

Yala marked her target and led it by enough to make up for the swiftness of the river. She let the string slip through her fingers and watched the arrow bury its venomous point deep in a thrashing body.

"Not bad," Breda said, and fired two quick shots in succession, both at the same target, and both hitting it.

Before Yala could beat her with three arrows, Ke called to them from the next barge. "Hey! We brave deep water to fight these demons like no sandwalker ever! This is no game. Make each arrow count so these town folk will remember us!"

Yala and Breda exchanged a glance and knew each had a smile hidden under the folds of their silkstone-laden cloth.

"Yes, Grandmother," they both said, in a wonderful harmony nearly spoiled by the dying cries of demons.

Ke smiled, then pointed upriver. "These women and men are good fighters. Look, their king leads them across the bridge."

CHAPTER 25

THE RIVER WALL

"Seven," Teelol said. She wavered a bit, but Tarix pulled her back from the edge of the wall.

"Easy there," the bane said, and backed up over the bodies of the demons they had slain.

"How many?" the woman demanded.

Tarix shrugged. "Not seven," she said, and no more.

Cannel, the Akalit bane, helped guide Teelol to where Riga had fixed the rope she carried to a spike driven into the top of the wall.

"Lower her down," Tarix said, and passed the woman over. The Mask looked with some surprise at the blood on the bane's hands, then down to where her own tunic was shredded over one hip. She was still frowning when she disappeared from view.

"What about any demons down there?" Cannel asked. He peered over the wall, one hand on the rope.

"It looks like the sandwalkers took care of them," Riga said, and slid over the edge, letting herself down, hand over hand.

The other Mask, Abenth, went next, then the Illick

bane, Cannel. Tarix took one last look from this height before following. Five wards were ablaze and burning pieces of debris were drifting down into the Palace Plaza, setting pools of waiting oil alight. The fire would soon spread to the last two barricaded wards, completing the destruction of this half of Shirath.

"Tarix," Riga called up from far below, and the bane-master tossed her trident down. Gripping the rope tightly, she followed the others down to the riverbank. Once there, she found the sandwalkers had cut the barges free and pulled themselves on submerged ropes across the river to join the other defenders.

"Ah, Tarix. We have beaten both demons and deep water. Have we won?" Ke asked. Yala stood beside her and a bemused Brada towered over them both.

The bane had no answer to that. They went towards the bridge gates, stepping on and over dead demons. The sandwalkers recovered spent shafts, and the banes killed any beasts still clinging to life.

"This is butcher's work," Riga said.

Tarix nodded. She had no answer for that either, nor needed one. The truth spoke for itself.

CHAPTER 26
BATTLE'S END

It was not a march across the bridge, nor a charge, but a stumble. The decking was choked with demon bodies, here and there mixed with the corpses of fallen defenders. Marick saw Lord Bereth, a close-mouthed man, now silent forever, his broken sword lying beside him. He almost fell then, but Dorict heaved him up and carried him forward until they reached better footing inside the Palace Plaza gate.

"Maybe I should have stayed in the hall," Marick said, getting his cane untangled from his legs. "I'm little use to anyone here."

The temple was aflame, its blue domes blackened and cracked, while the palace roof was even now crumbling into the gutted remnants of that once-magnificent building. The wards beyond the plaza were covered in a smothering smoke.

Dorict pointed to where groups of banes, guards, and Masks fought the remaining demons.

"You're still of use to them," Dorict said. "And to me. Come on, time to play the hero again."

The bane raised his staff and launched himself into the battle, aiding a harried group of Masks trying to hold back screaming death. The defenders began to push the demons back from the bridge gates, reducing their number while taking wounds of their own.

Marick muttered to himself, "Twist your shoulders and hips, bane," and pulled the green sash straight before hobbling after his friend. When he reached the fight, he found that Tarix's instructions were as wise as when he had first heard them as a Black Sash.

SOMETHING CHANGED when the last group of Shirath's forces crossed the central bridge and fell on the beasts still in the Palace Plaza. The demons all at once stopped attacking and tried to flee. It was too late, for there was no place for them to go. Fire raged to the north and steel marched from the south. A cordon of defenders, reinforced by many surviving sandwalkers and Tarix's small group of survivors, pushed the remaining beasts back until the demons were hacked down against the blood-soaked walls of the wards. With no hope of escape, the last of the demons in the plaza fell fighting, but fall they did.

Branet called all the banes to him. They stood amid blood and shattered bodies, panting and clutching at their wounds.

"It's not over," the hallmaster shouted over the crackle of flames and the screams of the clawed. "We have to go into the wards and search for the banes who lit the fires and those who were with us on the retreat. Some might have survived, if Heaven shielded them. Teams of ten, senior sashes to lead. We'll let others patrol the plaza and make sure all these demons are dead."

He drew a shaking hand over his forehead, smudging the soot but not clearing it. Spotting a Gold nearby, a young man with one arm bound to his chest, he waved at him to approach. "Claws, so many jewels will be hard to take!" he said and drew the bane close enough to hear him speak over the sound of screams and roaring flames. "Chitoroth, there're silkstone chests in the guardhouses near the Centre Bridge. Take anyone who can walk but is too wounded to search. Dig out as many jewels as you can and seal them away. Then, maybe, we can think again."

Fear-struck or not, the banes moved to their tasks, some leaning on others' shoulders, some stumbling on their own. Guards and Masks, such as were left, took up their places around the plaza. In the wards, the searching banes found hundreds of burned demons, and sadly, many bodies wearing the same uniforms as themselves, though so charred as to be almost unrecognizable. Branet knew who had been assigned to each ward, and he took it upon himself to name each one as they were carried on stretchers back into the Palace Plaza.

"Kistlan and Wultan from the Third. This one came from the Seventh, it must be Anteth, she was the taller of the two. And little Bors too; they fought together to the end. Who are these? Gollain and Scabral, claw it all. Claw Heaven too for these deaths. Good banes all! Do you hear me? Good banes all!"

This last he shouted at the smoke-tainted sky, and not a bane around him, nor any of the priests moving among the bodies, chided him for his blasphemy.

More were brought, and Branet continued his sad accounting.

Tarix was deep in the Fourth Ward, separated from the other banes who had followed her in. Once inside the gates, they had split up to search more quickly, for any bane who survived was likely in danger of dying from their wounds or suffocating under the smoking rubble.

But there was still hope, for the flames were fading now for lack of fuel, though walls still tottered and fell, and roofs still folded down into the buildings they were meant to protect. Among the demons, she found an Itaalk dead in the rubble, a long arrow through his neck. She took the staff from his hand and found the heartstone still blazing. Remembering how she had used such a jewel to control demons on the forest road, she broke off the head and thrust it through her belt. That done, she leaned on her trident a moment before setting off again. With each step, she winced at the pain lancing through her knee.

Garet swung his sword backhanded, knocking aside the feeble attack of a wounded demon. He held the club down while Salick pierced the beast above its thick leather cuirass. The demon fell, and she withdrew her trident, grunting at the effort of pulling the barbs back through the tough skin.

The fear coming from it trembled, and for a moment, in the surrender of the beast to death, Garet swore he could see some peace in the relaxation of its muscles and the slow fading of life in its eyes.

"Garet, demons don't die like that," Salick said between

heaving breaths. "Not so . . . gently. I think, no, I believe there's still a human mind inside these beasts."

She looked sickened by her own words, and Garet felt his stomach heave as well. To be trapped so, and perhaps to know what held you. It was a horrible thought.

"No bodies here," he said, tearing his eyes away from the dead demon and looking over the rubble-strewn streets. "Human, I mean. Claws, Salick, I feel the same way. It's one thing when they're swinging an axe at you, but killing them when they're wounded and helpless? We could try to tie them up or something, but we can't do it alone. Where did Ratal and Kesla get to?"

"Still searching," Salick said, leaning on her trident and looking down at the dead demon.

Garet tried to find his bearings, turning in a slow circle. "Chetorth and Dalesta must have been further down. I can hardly recognize the ward, though I've been through it dozens of times."

Salick nodded. "Hundreds of times for me, and I can only tell where we are by our distance from the outer and inner walls! Come on, let's find the others and see if they've had more luck in this ruin your mad king made."

Garet paused for a moment, and Salick looked at him, eyebrow raised.

He shrugged. "Sorry. I'm truly worried about Trax. I haven't seen him since he led the charge across the bridge. I know he's been cruel, but even so, I hope he's safe."

Salick shook her head. "I'd worry more about those around him, with his temper the way it is. Listen, I wouldn't fret too much. Bixa will keep him out of trouble."

～

THE CAPTAIN TRIED to focus on what the king was saying, but two days of drinking and a clout from a spear shaft made concentration difficult. She looked to Maroster, but the big man just shook his helmeted head and spat blood from a cut lip through the breathing hole and onto the cracked stones. Bixa blinked and looked back at the king.

"Kill them," Trax said. His voice sounded hollow coming from behind the gold-chased mask. The king held his sword in one hand, the bright blade hidden in a veil of blood. The other hand clutched a demon's head, the beak gaping, the eyes dull grey in death. Between the king and Master Tarix stood two figures, one bearing a staff and the other holding a bright dagger.

"Stay where you are, Trax," Marick said, "or I swear my next play will be called *The Gutting of the King*."

Dorict growled in agreement.

A dozen living demons cowered under the staff Tarix held. The red jewel gleamed and pulsed as she concentrated on one thought: *Surrender*.

"I won't kill them," she said, spitting out the words through clenched teeth. "They might be changed back." Sweat stood out on her forehead, and her eyes stayed fixed on the crouching demons.

Garet and Salick came running up, stumbling over corpses and charred beams.

"Trax, no!" Garet shouted.

Salick glared at the king. "Where are your guards, Trax?" she asked.

"My minders, you mean," he said and laughed, spittle forming at the corners of his mouth. "I slipped away to deliver a little justice," he said, and raised the demon head to show them his meaning. "The same kind that Tiralsh and the others received."

"Listen Trax, they were human once," Garet said, holding out his hands to calm the raging man. "If Tarix can keep them helpless, we can bind them, lock them in Tiralsh's silkstone cell. Maybe with the staff, Banerict—"

"Kill them!" Trax screamed. "Maroster, I command you!"

Maroster stood to the side, supporting Bixa. The captain's brow was slick with blood. The huge man shook his head as the banes looked their question at him.

"I was bringing Bixa back to the physicians when we came across this fool bothering these banes," he said, hooking a thumb at Dorict, Marick, and the still-concentrating Tarix.

"Says he wants every demon killed," Maroster said. "Even if they're captured. Even if they're already dying."

The giant shrugged and set Bixa down on a block of fallen stone.

"I've killed enough today, so I said no. So did she," he said, pointing to Bixa, who wobbled as she sat.

"Did I?" Bixa asked. She shook her head again and grabbed her helmet. "Ow! Good for me."

"You will obey your king," Trax said, swinging towards them, sword raised. The bloody head fell at his feet.

Maroster lifted his axe, a truly fearsome weight of sharpened steel. "No," he said. "I won't. I'm tired of following a fool's orders. You're no better than Gost now. Put down that sword before you hurt yourself." He lifted the axe high. "Or I hurt you."

Trax was speechless for a moment, then charged the bigger man, swinging his sword for a cleaving blow to Maroster's neck. The axe, which his opponent wielded one-handed as if it were a Duellist's rapier, knocked the blade aside. When the king stumbled, sent off-balance by the fury of his attack, Maroster calmly clouted him on the side of the masked face with his free fist. Trax, the king of Shirath – or what was left of it – fell to the ground like a polled ox.

The giant glanced down at the king then back at Bixa. "Still want to go south?" he asked.

Bixa nodded, trying to focus on the improbable scene before her.

"Then I'm going with you. I doubt His Clawed Majesty will ever forget the gentle tap I gave him. Now, I'll get you to the physicians, or the priests will have you for the fire."

He put the guard captain over one shoulder and strode off through the wreckage, making for the bridges and the help beyond. Garet and Salick looked at each other and hurried over, Garet to the king and Salick to the still-concentrating master holding the staff tightly in both hands. Marick and Dorict turned to guard against the still-quiet demons.

"Not easy," Tarix grunted. "Let me try something."

She took a deep breath and frowned again. The demons stirred, some trying to rise, then they all dropped back, black eyes closed and clawed hands limp at their sides.

Salick blinked and forced away the thoughts of sleep that the heartstone was pouring into her. With Dorict, she searched the ruins for something to bind the demons, and they came back with a collection of rope, cloth, and netting. Garet, his concern for the king's life allayed, came to help, and soon all thirteen once-human demons were secured. Tarix collapsed to her hands and knees as soon as it was done, the staff fragment falling from her grip. Marick held her while she trembled. She blinked several times and rubbed her temples.

"Oh! I'll never complain about controlling a room full of Black Sashes again, though I suppose I won't have to anymore, will I? I didn't find any of our banes but came on these beasts, if beasts they are, digging their way out of a blocked alley. How's Trax?"

"Unconscious," Garet replied. "Maroster was gentle – for Maroster, that is."

"I wonder what Allifur and Corfin will think of their friend now?" Marick asked as he helped Tarix to her feet.

The older bane smiled. "They'll applaud him for doing what was right, and so will I. Proof that some folk learn from their mistakes."

Garet looked down at Trax. "And some are destroyed by them."

A clamour rose from the bound demons. Without the control of the staff, they were crying out and struggling against their restraints, but Salick and Garet had been thorough; they were truly caught.

"What do we do with them?" Salick asked. "I have to agree with Maroster, Heaven shield me, I've killed enough today, and it doesn't seem right to slay them if they're bound, even though the wounded ones I killed seem almost … glad to die."

Tarix looked down at the beasts with a mix of disgust and sympathy. "They were human once," the older bane said. "Maybe they can be again, though, thank Heaven, that will be Banerict's job, not mine."

"It didn't work with the one we captured in the Maze," Dorict said. "That one only lasted half a night after they cut out its jewel."

Marick picked up the broken top of the bone-white staff from the ground and examined the red stone set in its tip. "Perhaps we have to … turn off the jewel," he said, "just like Dasanat turns off one of her spark jars. Maybe this clawed thing can help us do that." He handed the staff to Tarix.

She took it and tucked it back into her belt. "If we've captured any Itaalk, and I hope we have, they might know. For now, round up some banes and take these ones directly to the banehall, to Banerict, put silkstone helmets on them and cover them up so no one sees. I guess many will be as unforgiving as Trax. Go, I'll take this staff along and see if we can save anymore."

"What about him?" Salick asked, pointing to the king, and her look was one of pure disgust, with no sympathy added.

"I'll stay with him," Garet said, shaking his head. "It would be easy to hate him, but he's really another victim of the Itaalk, as much as these demons are." He took off his purple vest, folded it, and put it under Trax's head. "And we know there are lots of ways to be clawed."

Tarix nodded and moved off. Salick made to follow but stopped beside the bound demons.

"Garet," she said, raising her voice over the hoots of the beasts. "Come here."

The bane did as he was told and stood beside her.

"What? Do we need more bindings?" he asked, then grimaced for he was nearly shouting to be heard over the yowling of their captives. "Or gags?"

Salick didn't respond at first. She knelt beside one of the beasts and stared at its beaked face. "I think this is . . . no, I can't really tell."

Garet came over to stand beside her, mindful of the writhing limbs of the demon. He kicked aside a crude copy of an axe. The iron blade was thin-hammered into a bitter edge rather than sharpened on a stone, but the bloodstains showed it was keen enough to kill. He squatted down, and after a long and thoughtful inspection, shrugged. "Maybe, but they're all so changed, I can't say for sure. If it's her, well. Leave it for now."

Salick stood again. After a last look at the creature now staring back up at her, its twitching momentarily stilled, she ran off after Tarix. Garet went back to mind the king. He saw some banes coming up the rubble-choked road and waved to them.

"They won't like this," he muttered.

CHAPTER 27
THE TOLL OF WAR

Banerict looked up as Garet opened the tent flap and came inside. The physician stepped carefully around the scores of wounded lying on pallets made ready in the days before the battle. He motioned the bane to follow him outside.

The stars were dim beyond the torches of a tent city that had grown to cover the Banehall Plaza. Full of displaced families and exhausted fighters, the shelters spread out over the playing fields, the gardens, and any spaces left between. The wounded were kept in shelters nearest the hall so that Banerict could have easy access to his medical supplies.

"Are there more survivors?" he asked, running a hand over his face. It had been a day since the battle and much more than that since the physician had slept.

The man looked exhausted, and Garet led him over to the steps so that he could sit for a moment.

"Yes," the bane said. "More lived than we expected. Some banes and Masks on the walls survived by using ropes to either climb down the outside of the wall or by dodging the fire as it went from ward to ward."

"I don't suppose you know if Dalesta . . ." Banerict said and stopped. He had treated the young woman's breathing problems ever since she had entered the hall.

Garet smiled, the expression feeling odd after so much grief. "Yes, your favourite patient is alive, and Chetorth too. You'll find them coming on stretchers to you soon enough."

At Banerict's expression, both relieved and anxious, Garet hurried to explain.

"They were in the Fourth Ward on a tenement roof when the demons flooded in. They did their jobs, lighting the oil to fire the building, but then they were cut off, or so Dalesta said before she began coughing too much to speak. I fear the smoke has been hard on her lungs."

"They were never strong," Banerict said, and Garet could see his eyes stare into the distance as he mentally prepared a treatment for the girl.

"But she is," Garet said, sitting down beside the older man and groaning a bit as he did so. "Strong, I mean. Both of them are. We found them laid out like a king and queen from one of Marick's plays, surrounded by the bodies of their enemies! I wish Vinir had been there to make a drawing of it! The physician who first saw to them said they were singed, but their padded clothing kept them from the worst of it." Garet stopped to breathe out a long sigh and added, "Well, she also said that Chetorth will likely lose the hand he'd already injured in the Battle of the Bridge."

"Another demon bite?" Banerict asked, letting out a sigh of his own, for he had never grown used to treating the same banes over and over again for different injuries.

Garet grinned, a fierce flash of white teeth in his soot-stained face. "I suppose so. When we found him, it was jammed down a demon's throat. The two of them must have killed a half-dozen of the beasts before the building they were on collapsed. I think they rode that roof down like a sled on the Northern ice."

"Dalesta broke her leg," he added, as an afterthought.

Banerict rose again, slowly, and ascended the steps. "More splints and burn ointment," he muttered. "I'm glad we prepared so much of it."

Garet watched him go.

I'm glad there are so many still to use them on. What now, sleep or back to searching the rubble?

Guilt won out over exhaustion. He stood and looked at the front doors of the hall, behind which lay food, comfort, and a bed he hadn't seen for two days, not since Bixa summoned him the night before the battle. He shook himself, slapped his cheeks until his eyes widened, and set off between the tents, ignoring the moans coming from within the canvas shelters.

There was still work to be done, and, Heaven willing, more living men and women to drag back into the light.

LYSERE LOOKED from the cradle where her daughter slept to the bed where her husband tossed and turned. A great purple bruise stretched from his ear to his jaw, but she knew his main wounds were not of the body. Garet and a guard she did not know had brought him back on a cart, unconscious and without any explanation, save that the king was unwell and should be kept here until a physician could examine him.

Trax clutched the blankets, tearing at them, and she wiped his forehead with a wet cloth, murmuring to him until he relaxed into a deeper sleep. A hand touched her shoulder, and she turned to see Lady Kaela standing there with a cup of tea. The queen smiled and took the cup, moving away from the bed so that they could talk without disturbing either sleeper.

"Thank you," Lysere said, and sipped the bracing mixture, hoping it would keep her going for the rest of the night.

Kaela shook her head. "You amaze me, Lysere. When was the last time you slept? Go now. Rest, and I will keep watch."

At Lysere's raised brow, Kaela hid a smile behind one delicate hand.

"Don't fret! I'll not try to steal him from you, though I might have once. No, Kirel has grown on me, now that he's out of Gost's shadow. He was very brave in the plaza, Branet says."

"So I heard," Lysere replied. She made to put the cup down on a nearby table but missed and almost dropped it. Kaela caught it just in time and put it safely on the marble top. She took the queen by the elbow and gently but firmly led her to the door.

"You are guests in my house, so you must let me take care of you! Now, go to my chamber and rest. I'll stay here until the physician comes, and of course I'll watch Noella. She took the trip to the Far South and back very well, I'd say. Better than my own Dael, who cried at every bump of the cartwheels, according to his nurse."

Thus chattering, Kaela got the queen out the door and into the charge of a steward who led her away.

She closed the door to the chamber, a room of some opulence that had once been occupied by her husband's uncle, Gost. She went first to check the sleeping child, then to stand over the man who had ordered Gost's death. She looked at his sunken eyes, his bruised cheek, and the shadows that spoke of many wakeful nights.

"Oh, Trax," she said softly. "I know you like to joke that you fear me, but if you break that poor woman's heart, I will poison your wine. I swear it by Heaven's dome."

She sank into the chair beside the bed, dropping all pretense for a moment to reveal her own exhaustion.

"She really is too good for you, fool," she whispered. "You should have married a hard-hearted schemer like me."

CHAPTER 28

THE NEW SHOUTING ROOM

Only five of the Itaalk still lived after Cirta and Blellat, leading whoever could still fight, chased Shirath's remaining attackers out into fields. Once they came within arrow range, it was easy to kill the demons still among them. But not the Itaalk. Bixa had been very definite about that, speaking to her lieutenants from her awkward position over Maroster's shoulder.

"I will skin the man who kills any one of those pieces of scum," she growled, trying to focus her blurred vision on the two who looked like four, or maybe eight. "Claws! We'll need someone to guide us back into their forest, so be gentle with them."

"How gentle?" Cirta asked. He was scowling at the thought, for few of the fighters he'd led in the second wave had survived their retreat through the Seventh Ward.

Blellat put a hand on the younger man's shoulder. "Easy," he said. "I guess the captain means she wants them talking and walking, or at least talking, is that right?"

But Bixa was unconscious again, and thus unable to make her wishes any clearer.

When it was done, all the captives could talk and three could still walk, or at least hobble, when they were returned to Shirath. Lord Sabat of the Fifteenth Ward had a deep cellar room suitable for wine or prisoners, and they spent a night and a day there, waiting to learn their fate.

IN THE NEW SHOUTING ROOM, formerly the audience hall of Lord Kirel and Lady Kaela, several survivors argued what that fate might be.

"Kill them!" Kirel said. He chopped the edge of his hand down onto the table for emphasis. His wife nodded and added, "Then take Tarix's road up to that valley Master Salick told us of and kill the rest."

Garet looked at Salick, who seemed almost ready to agree.

Before either could speak, Lord Andarack stood up. The lord of the Eighth Ward, which was now a smoking ruin, shook his head. "No," he said. "What kind of luck would Heaven give us in return for such a massacre? And tell me, Lord Kirel, who. . . no, *what* would you be when you returned to your family? Don't become another Trax, Heaven shield him!"

His wife, Dasanat, took his hand in a rare public show of affection. "Well said, husband. I think we need to talk to those we captured. To end this war, we must know why they fear us."

Queen Lysere leaned forward in her carved and cushioned chair. "Isn't it enough to know why *we* fear them?" she asked.

"Is it?" Tarix demanded, her voice rising. "Is it enough to kill a whole people?" The bane looked around the table and stood with her husband's help, for her brace was so bent it left her leg unable to straighten. She leaned on a crutch and shook her head. "No, we'd be demons ourselves. There are things we must do. Kill any that attack the city, yes. Go north and seize all those dragon eggs and silkstone boxes, yes, though we might need the help of the other cities. But I agree with Dasanat and Andarack on this. Talk first. Bring an Itaalk here. Question them."

Dasanat nodded. "See, Tarix has some sense. You can't design anything, even a peace, without information. Besides, I lost my home two days ago and the work of a dozen years, so whatever comes of that, I want it to be well-made."

The master mechanical paused to look at Kirel and Kaela. "If that means we must kill all the Itaalk," she said, "I need to know there is no better solution. My dreams are bad enough as it is."

At that last observation, the table fell silent. No one in Shirath escaped nightmares, most born from brushes with demon fear and, for the people in this room, brushes with demon claws.

Chon, the hallmaster from Illick, agreed. "Dreams! I don't know if I ever dare sleep again, but your master mechanical is right. My banes will not kill Itaalk children to stop some future war, and I think I can speak for Hallmasters Corix and Sicarth in this as well, may Heaven heal them quickly! Talk to these Itaalk and make some kind of peace."

Cirta stood up, uncertain, but Lysere nodded for the young guard to speak.

"Can we talk to them?" he said. "I mean, do we know their tongue?"

"I do," Garet said. "Or at least enough of the Northern dialect to understand basic things."

Lysere stood up, and those still sitting followed suit.

"Master Garet, go with Lord Andarack, please, and bring one of those . . . one of our guests to explain to us why we should spare their lives." She turned and left the room.

Salick sighed. "She's gentler than Trax, at least on the outside, but there's steel underneath all that lace."

Kaela laughed and tapped the bane on the arm with a folded fan. "That's why we wear the lace, my dear, to hide the steel."

THE OLDEST OF the Itaalk was too wounded to serve, but he pointed at a slightly younger man, who then stood, his white robe filthy with blood and soot.

"Come," Garet said in the tongue of the Itaalk's Northern cousins and was understood, it seemed, for the man stepped forward to be bound at the wrists by Blellat.

"Let's throw a cloak over him," the guard lieutenant suggested. "So we don't all get beaten to death by angry citizens when they see who he is."

Lord Sabat did better than that, lending them his carriage, blinds drawn, to take them from the Fifteenth Ward to Lord Kirel's house in the Thirteenth.

"Will you come with us, Lord Sabat?" Cirta asked.

"I would," the man said, "but I'm too busy finding space for a ward's worth of people added to my own."

He escorted them to the door and no farther.

Blellat waited until they were in the carriage to comment. "Probably doesn't want to be seen with us. Come to think of it, neither do I."

THE GROUP CONFRONTING the prisoner was large but carefully selected: the queen; Lords Andarack, Kirel, and Cheemon; Banerict and Dasanat for their respective schools; Relict, Tarix, Garet, and Salick, for Shirath's banes; the two other hallmasters, Chon and Sicarth, the latter just released from the physicians' care; Ke, Yala, and two other sandwalkers; Son-neen for the City of Fountains; Marick; Lady Kaela; the historian to record it all; and finally, a rather despondent Blellat for the guards.

"How is Bixa's head?" Garet asked him.

Blellat snorted in return. "Hmmph! It would be better if she didn't keep dipping it in wine. Then she could be here and I could go back to the barracks and sleep for a week!"

The bane shook his head. Bixa's retreat from responsibility had much to do with the cruel demands of the king. Garet had hoped that, with the king forced to his bed, Bixa might have returned.

"Tell her we could still use her counsel," he said, and turned to the other banes.

Salick nodded to the guard as he walked past, summoned by one of the lords to check yet again the bindings of the prisoner.

"Poor Blellat looks so unhappy," she said. "With Bixa hiding, he's doing a job he never wanted."

"So am I!" Garet replied. "This diplomacy is beyond my skill. Fillar didn't teach me words like 'treaty' or 'compromise.'"

He checked to see that his notebook, which held lists of sea Itaalk words among a hundred other observations he had made in the Far North, was still safely in his vest pocket.

"I wish he were here to help me," he said.

Salick smiled at the memory of the man, a farm labourer born to a sea Itaalk mother. The poor holding where he worked – more as a partner to the farm family than a servant – had sheltered both her and Garet while they made a sled to take them even farther north for a fateful meeting with Garet's father. Those days of preparation had been a peaceful time, especially compared to what had happened since.

"Fillar was a good man, and he is kin to these people," she said. "Just like you are and just like Yala and her folk are, so maybe they can listen to reason even if you do mangle it in the telling."

"So kind of you," he replied, and took her hand.

Lysere caught Garet's eye and nodded. Setting his shoulders, he took a chair facing the Itaalk and looked him in his eyes.

Now we fight by other means.

He took a deep breath and began. "Why do you send . . . beasts like men to kill us?" Garet asked, remembering that there was no word in the sea Itaalk tongue for demon.

The man looked at him, bound wrists on his lap. Garet repeated his question.

"Men kill like beasts," the prisoner finally said. "You send men to kill us. We send *skororlisanba* back."

It seemed the forest Itaalk did have a word for demons, which was no surprise to the bane. He wrote it down and then reported the answer to those sitting around Kirel's table.

"Tell him we don't want to fight his people, but we will destroy them all if they don't make peace with us," Cheemon said, then quickly looked to the queen for approval. Garet did the same and repeated the words – as best he could – when Lysere nodded.

The Itaalk's eyes shifted from one to the other and took his time in answering. "Why should we trust you who kill us such a long time before?"

Garet reddened. "Or at least, that's what I think he said."

Ke grunted and struck the bane lightly on the shoulder with one gnarled fist. "Close, boy, close. I can hear some of his words, though others fly past me. He says why should they trust killers from long ago."

Garet caught a slight alarm in the eyes of the prisoner. Ke turned to him and spoke in her own tongue, so rapidly that Garet caught but a few phrases. The Itaalk answered, briefly, then Ke spoke again, bringing forth a longer answer from the bound man.

The old sandwalker twisted to look at the queen.

"He does not know much about sandwalkers," Ke said, "even though we were the same people once. He says we should help the Itaalk kill all of you."

She chuckled then, and even Yala smiled at the thought.

Then Ke's voice lost all its customary humour. "I told him that his people must first answer for the poison winds, then we would talk about how we are long-ago sisters and brothers."

Yala was watching the Itaalk's face as the others spoke. While the ward lords and Lysere thanked Ke for her friendship, the sandwalker caught Garet's eyes and raised an eyebrow. The bane frowned, then nodded. Facing the Itaalk again, he spoke directly to the man.

"Considering what you've done to their wells, I don't think you can ever turn them against us, no matter what kinship you claim. Besides, they saw how you treated your other friends, the Dragon Brigades. We value our allies, but you send them to their deaths without any support or rescue."

The others in the room looked at him, for he had spoken in the common tongue of the South, not in broken Itaalk. The prisoner's face was impassive, but Garet saw a drop of sweat forming on his forehead.

"Master Garet?" Lysere asked.

Whatever else the queen would have said was lost in Lord Andarack's sudden laughter.

"Hah! Yes, of course. Well done, Garet – and Yala too, if I read that look right. How else would the Itaalk instruct spies like Tiralsh if some couldn't speak our language?"

Even if the prisoner couldn't understand every shout and curse raining down on him, he must have realized his position had changed dramatically. After the tumult had lessened, he leaned forward and spoke in the Southern tongue.

"I do understand your words. All who come south do. So let us speak it, for it is much better than listening to this one chew words he doesn't understand."

Garet would have bristled at this, but the logical part of him had to agree with the smirking man.

"Very well," the queen said. She leaned forward. "I should ask your name, but I don't care to know. As long as you can speak for your people, you have a purpose here, though only one, and that is to help us decide whether there shall be peace or a final war between our people."

The prisoner's smirk widened. He leaned back and raised his bound hands as if they held something. "I can speak for them, else I would not have wielded a staff. Of the ten highest, I am sixth," he said, and looked around the room, his dark eyes cold. "Your words of peace and war have no meaning. I know I am to die." He dropped his arms. "So, let it be. But you will die too, in time. How many are left of your fighters, your banes? A hundred, a few hundred? How many will be left when we return next time with another army? Remember, we can make as many of the *skororlisanba*, the demons, as we need."

The smile disappeared from his face, and a look of real hate took its place. "It is too late to *decide*. You were supposed to stay in your cities. If you did, we might have let you live, but now you become arrogant. You think you can come again into the trees. We will destroy you, you and the other cities. I swear this on the great tree, on the temple's pillars, on the heartstone."

Lysere rose then and walked forward until she stood over the man. When she spoke, her voice was ice and her eyes a green fire. "Think on this then, you cannot make demons without dragon eggs," she said, and nodded at the shock that showed in the Itaalk's eyes.

"Oh yes, we know how you make these monsters, and what part the Dragon Brigades play in it, or should I say played? I don't think a single man of them survived. Am I wrong, Banerict?"

The physician, who had stood along with all the others when the queen did, bowed his grey head. "No, my queen, you are not wrong, though I wish you were."

Lysere looked back at the prisoner. "You may think you can find more allies in the cold North, new partners who will collect the eggs for you and take more slaves to twist to your perverse means, but I doubt it, for we will spread the news far and wide of how the brigades died! And know this, neither will slaves come to your valley from the Far South, demon-maker. That trade is already wiped out."

She bowed her head to the sandwalkers. "May the wind always blow in your favour, sisters," she said, much to Ke's delight. The queen then turned to Son-neen and added, "We must thank the towers that rule the City of Fountains as well, for they have redoubled their efforts to destroy those who think that selling men and women is a legitimate trade."

The smile she bestowed on the girl died as she turned back to the prisoner. "As Master Garet told you, Itaalk, we value our allies. Now they stretch from the deserts of the Far South to the frozen seas of the Far North. Yes, the Far North. I'm told the sea Itaalk will welcome our help in protecting dragons and their clutches, and the rest of the population won't complain when we show them friendship and fair trade instead of the tyranny of your brigades. Think on these things and answer wisely."

Kaela smiled behind a lace-cuffed hand. As Lysere turned back to her seat, she caught the queen's eye and gave her the tiniest nod of approval.

"You cannot," the prisoner said. "We are many. We have many eggs. You cannot find them all. We will hide them and strike you again and again until . . ."

"Until what?" Salick demanded. The young woman stood behind Garet, hands on hips, the scar on her cheek white against her flushed skin. "Until we attack you in force? Until we destroy your secret roads and those horrible caves?" Her voice rose until the man cowered before her rage. "Until we burn your forest to the ground?" Salick cried, and then wrapped her arms around her chest. "Until we have to kill you all?" she added in a smaller voice, and even the most bloodthirsty lord lowered their eyes.

"You cannot," the man whispered.

"Sadly, we can," Lysere said. "You've made us very good at killing. But do we have to? We have faced conflicts before in Shirath, some you had a hand in. We ended them, sometimes with force and sometimes with reason. You have tasted the first, so why not try the second? You despise us. Why? Because we might come north again, like we did six hundred years ago, and defeat you? Make a peace then! We will stay out of your forest, now and forever. You will stop making demons and taking dragon eggs from the Far North."

The man looked sideways at Salick, who stood, breathing heavily. He switched his gaze to Garet but found no mercy in the young man's eyes. The rest of them, sandwalkers, banes, and lords, studied him coldly. Though some would have preferred steel and fire, the offer had been made.

"We cannot trust you," the Itaalk said.

Ke stalked over to the man, now angrier than anyone, including her granddaughter, had ever seen. "Trust?" she growled. "You speak of this when you hurt these people and my own for so long? I will tell you a story of my mother's time. A poison wind, that is one of your *skororlisanba*, came to our well. Our little fear lizards felt it in time, so we made our poison. We had no captives, no one from outside our tribe to feed the poison to the beast. But my mother's sister was born with a bent back. She couldn't walk in the desert, so she begged to serve our well. My mother was sad, but there was no choice – because *you* made this thing that must kill. My mother went with her, helped tie her and pour the poison over her. They burned a dead calf to call the beast in. Three days later, my mother went back. It was forbidden, but she did. She told me there was nothing left of her sister, and the poison wind, your *skororlisanba*, was dead, a sack of skin on the sand."

Ke's hand went to her belt, almost touching the sand shovel that could so easily cut a throat or cleave a skull.

"That woman would have been my aunt, teaching me as I teach Yala, but no, you took her from my well, so I tell you, Itaalk who is no kin of mine, if you do not have peace, I will bring every sandwalker from every well to your forest. We will look behind each tree, under every rock until you are all dead. Your children we will bring back to our wells, to teach them how to be human again, but every woman and man grown will be cut down."

The other sandwalkers stood and shouted, "Hear this! Hear this!"

Yala hugged her grandmother and said, "The wind speaks in you! If I could, I'd make your name shorter still."

Ke snorted at that and sat down again. She nodded to the queen.

"Well," Lysere said, regarding the now freely sweating prisoner. "That makes things clear, doesn't it? Four cities' worth of guards, their banes, and now every sandwalker, all ready to hunt you down, and you have no place to go for more weapons, not if we send forces to sit in the Far North between you and the dragons."

The prisoner made to stand but collapsed back into his seat. He glared at Ke, then Lysere, but said nothing.

"Take him back, Lieutenant Blellat," the queen said. "We will speak again after lunch, when the reality of his situation has become clear."

The guard pulled the Itaalk roughly to his feet.

"If it doesn't become clear," Blellat said, "I can let him loose in the Banehall Plaza among those tents. I'm sure anyone burned out of house and home could explain it to him."

Lysere shook her head. "No," she said. "At least, not yet."

From the look on the prisoner's face, his position was coming into a very sharp focus indeed.

CHAPTER 29
TEARS AND WINE

Branet was not ashamed to weep over the lists of names. He made notations beside them, marking deaths and proclaiming that they were lost in the defence of the city. From time to time, he referred to notes he had made the day before, but for the most part every name was clawed into his memory. When he came to Master Chovan's name, he put down the brush and rubbed his eyes. A knock on the door was a most welcome diversion.

"Come in," he said.

Relict entered, a fresh bandage around his arm and a wine jug, two goblets, and a scroll held awkwardly in the other hand.

"Here," Branet said. "Let me help," and he took the jug and goblets.

"Hah!" Relict said. "I should have known you'd grab that first. Pour us a good measure each before we talk."

"About what?" Branet demanded, but he obeyed Relict's order to fill the cups to the brim. He took a sip and raised a brow. "That is the best wine I've ever had. Where did you find it?"

"I got it in Solantor. Their hallmaster gave it to me. I think it was in compensation for all the time I wasted there. I thought to drink it immediately, to soothe my disappointment, but on a mad whim I put it away until the day we won."

"Have we?" Branet asked. He drained the cup and poured himself another. One more gulp and he pushed the ledger across to his friend.

Relict looked at it and sighed. "I know the count. But what's this? I heard about Taron, of course – what a stand he made! But Chovan too? I thought she survived the crush at the bridge."

Branet set the goblet down. "She did but was wounded badly. Banerict couldn't save her." The hallmaster pointed at the scroll. "What is that? More trouble?"

Relict looked into the red liquid in his cup, swirling it around before answering. "No. And yes." He spread out the scroll, pinning the corners with the jug, the cups, and the book. The page showed a map of the River Ar, with the cities of Shirath, Old Torrick, and the others marked. To the north, amid a few symbolic sketches of trees, was a network of roads, villages, and a pair of parallel lines marked *Demon Valley*."

"That's where they make them?" Branet asked, scowling at the map.

Relict nodded. "Yes. Garet and Salick drew this map, and we've added to it with information gained from our prisoners."

Branet raised an eyebrow at this, and Relict explained. "You've been busy with the wounded and the dead, so maybe you don't know that Cirta and Blellat chased down the Itaalk as they retreated into the forest. They had some demons with them, big brutes, but they didn't stand a chance against a hundred bows. They captured a few of them alive – the Itaalk, I mean – and brought them back. Bixa has them hidden in Lord Sabat's house for now."

Branet shook his head. "Those, those demon masters in our city? Claws and teeth!"

Relict nodded. "Most feel the same. That's why they're moved in closed carriages to the negotiations with the queen and her advisors! You see, since the king is . . . indisposed, we're arranging a peace without him." He then made a face and added, "Just as well. I think our king would rather execute than negotiate these days. And I . . ."

Branet stood up, nearly overturning the jug. Relict caught it and held it to his chest. "Careful! I went through a whole season of failure to get this."

The hallmaster ignored him. He stared at the ceiling for many heartbeats and then dropped back into his chair. Relict poured more wine, and it disappeared down the bigger man's throat.

"Clawed murderers," Branet growled. "Worse than the demons they made! And yet we must treat with them. Oh! It is too much, Relict. It is too much!"

Relict laid a hand on his arm. "Yes," he said. "It is too much. All of this is too much – claws, Taron was bad enough, though he took many demons and one of their masters with him, but Chovan too? I remember her as a Gold when you and I were Black Sashes and ran to her whenever we were in trouble, which was often enough. She'd always laugh and smooth things over for us. Claws, she was more a mother than the one I left behind! Yes, it's much too much. I'd rather choke on the words than talk to the Itaalk, but what else can we do?"

He wiped his eyes, sat back in his chair, and reached for the wine again. "As you guessed, the king, when he briefly wakes, demands the enemies' death by the most horrible means imaginable, but we can't kill every Itaalk in those woods, or maybe we can. But should we, if there's another way?"

Branet shook his head and asked, "Was it true what Garet said, that we started this war six hundred years ago?"

Relict shrugged. "We? Not I, nor you either. As for our many, many great-grandparents past, who can know after all those centuries? No doubt there was fault enough to go around. It seems clear that the Itaalk feared an invasion by our ancestors, and I suppose that makes sense."

"How so?" the hallmaster asked. He swirled the wine in his cup.

"Well, as Dorict tells it, our people moved into the Ar Valley after the Itaalk were weakened from their war with an empire in the Far South, the one that built that sand city our banes found. Our population grew, probably cutting down more and more of the forest border for fields and new towns. My dear wife told us about the ruins of a hill fort deep in the trees, one whose stones bore writing much like ours, so maybe we were invading. Or expanding. Or exploring, claw it all. Who knows?"

He sipped at his wine before continuing. "Ahh, that's good! Now for the Itaalk side of things. Their chief negotiator, who looks as unhappy as I did when you sent me to Solantor, said they tried to fight us but we had better weapons – steel, I think – and were very fierce. So, the invaders – us, I mean – pushed them farther north, and then farther still."

He waited while Branet fetched another jug of wine.

The vintage was not as good but it was still wine, and this was the night for it now that the city was safe.

"He claims they were a peaceful people," Relict said, accepting another cup. "With no way to defend themselves save through their magic."

Branet snorted at the word. "Peaceful? He dared to say that? And magic, what is that, like the tricksters in the marketplace?"

Relict shook his head. "No, because their magic really works. Remember, they could turn animals and people into monsters and even transform those into things even more terrifying, like the demon in the fields who birthed other beasts and Ratal's two-headed brute."

He traced a finger across the paper, going from the boundaries of Shirath to the edge of the map. "The Itaalk's villages once stretched up to the Northern Sea," he said, "so they already knew about the dragons before something split them off from the sea Itaalk. Maybe they learned their magic from looking into the sky lights Salick saw, the ones that give you visions. Maybe they found out how to make demons by accident, but once they did, they possessed a weapon worse than any other."

"And so it began," Branet said. "The war with that southern empire then the war with us."

"Yes," Relict replied. "With hundreds of years in-between! I suppose we were easier to defeat. After they forced us behind our walls, they kept a close watch on us, paying for spies among our people. That explains Tiralsh and her son, Heaven take them – though I don't think they deserve any place in the sky."

Branet nodded. "So, we were right. Their spies knew we planned to build another city. They must have feared we were getting ready to expand into their forest again."

"Not just Shirath," Relict said. "Illick plans to grow, and Akalit will need to soon enough, or so their hallmasters told me when we met last year. The only reason Old Torrick hasn't joined in is because they have the new Midland towns to support and grow into. As for Solantor, well, who knows what they think, but yes, that's why the Itaalk changed their attacks; they were trying to keep us locked up behind our walls."

"Starting with the Caller demon that killed Mandarack," Branet growled. "And ending by the twisting of those poor slaves into demons."

He took a deep breath and sipped his wine this time, looking over the rim of the cup at his old friend. "Tell me then, do these clawed talks go well?"

Relict shrugged. "Well enough. I think we will be able to call a truce, if not a full peace. We stay in the valley and the Midlands, and they keep to the forest and make no more demons. To make sure, the queen is demanding that observers be allowed in both lands. The other hallmasters agree."

"Lysere demands?" Branet asked. "Does she truly rule Shirath now?" He blinked and looked around the shadows of the record room, perhaps realizing how long he had been kept in the hall and infirmary tents nearby.

"As much as anyone," Relict said. "And the lords listen to her, thankfully. Her idea of observers is a good one. Besides," he added, a ghost of a smile on his face, "what else will unemployed banes do if not keep watch on the Itaalk?"

"What does Garet think of the plan?" Branet asked. He stood and stretched before sitting again with a groan. Days of pushing his body to breaking point had consequences.

Relict stretched his good arm, dealing with his own

aches and pains. "I don't know if he's heard the final one," he said. "He and Salick left Lord Kirel's house after the basics were agreed upon. Why do you ask?"

The hallmaster waved at the stacks of paper spread across every available surface in the room. "Few masters remain, and there is much to do to reorganize the patrols. We cannot let down our guard, especially if this peace falls apart or the Itaalk are only pretending to it. At the least, I need him to talk to the priests and make sure our fallen banes receive the honours they deserve, even if the temple is in ashes."

Relict looked extremely pleased with himself, for some reason.

"What?" Branet demanded.

"Oh, nothing," his friend replied. "It's just that, the last time I saw Garet and Salick, they were already looking for a priest."

The raised cups for that long-anticipated event emptied the second jug, and Branet searched the shelves of the record room until he found some more.

"Good," he said, pouring more and sitting back in his chair. "Good for them."

Relict regarded the hallmaster, who was looking at a scene somewhere beyond the walls of the room. "That happy news aside, do you think it's a good idea to send banes north?" Relict finally asked.

Branet focused his attention on the man in front of him and nodded. "I do, if only so I can see those demon caves for myself and watch every single dragon egg smashed to bits."

Relict smiled. "And I'll stand beside you to see such a wonder, if I can escape Lysere's plans for Tarix and me."

"Plans?"

"She wants us to work with the other halls and the

mechanicals to design a new city on the site of the ruins of Terrich. Dasanat is practically swooning over the chance to make something other than a weapon, and Lysere has promised her a very large workshop if she takes over the project."

"Then what are you and Tarix needed for?" Branet asked. He felt a twinge of unease. With so many of his companions gone, Relict and Tarix were a last reminder of how certain his life had once been.

"Us? Our job is to remind Dasanat that a city is lived in by people, not machines," Relict said.

"Will this new city have a banehall?" Branet asked.

Relict noted how his friend's voice had dropped to a near whisper. He leaned across the table and put a hand on the bigger man's shoulder.

"Will Shirath? Lysere listened to Garet on this matter. There will be no hall as such, at least if the peace holds, but both cities will have a school, like this banehall was for us when we were children."

Branet frowned. "A school for what?"

Relict raised his glass and Branet followed suit.

"For whatever is to come, Hallmaster. For whatever is to come."

CHAPTER 30
PARTINGS

Twenty-five days had passed since half the city burned. Temple priests still sent the dead rising as smoke to the sky above, and many people still lay with their wounds, but something like hope had risen among the survivors of that horror. Messengers had been hurrying back and forth along the forest road and the Dying River for two ten-days, fixing the terms for a world without claws in the night.

Of the many hundreds of Human demons who attacked only a few dozen had survived, and they were confined to a floor in the west wing of the banehall. Banerict worked with them, using the staffs now in his possession to coax their bodies back into a more human form. When that was done, if it could be done, he intended to remove the stones set into their skulls. He didn't know – no one knew – if they could bring those poor unfortunates all the way back. It was understood, but not said out loud, that if the physician failed, the banes would have a final, sad duty to complete.

GARET AND SALICK, along with many of their friends, stood in the Banehall Plaza, in the narrow space between the hall's steps and the forest of tents and rough shelters that still occupied the playing fields and gardens. Half the city now held all the surviving citizens and would until the rebuilding was done.

Ke was drawing a wind mandala on the paving, using a stick of charcoal Vinir had provided. She was explaining it to Garet as she filled in each quarter and half-quarter.

"Here is the north, your part," she said, and pointed to the top of the circle. "The wind from there means death in our lands and in yours too, I think."

"That may be changing," Garet said as he copied the symbols into a notebook. "It is kind of you to explain this all to me," he added.

Yala sniffed. "It is not so kind. Tell him, grandmother."

"I have a bet with my friend Das that if we keep filling your head, you will finally stop asking questions," the old woman said, and laughed.

"Das?" Salick asked.

The sandwalker kept chuckling and Yala answered for her.

"Dasanat. Grandmother thinks that such a wise woman shouldn't have a long name." She looked at her feet. "She tries to call me Yal now. I don't like it."

Ke poked her with a bony finger. "That means you deserve it!"

"Well, you'll lose that bet," Marick said. "I've known him long enough to tell you that his head will never be full."

"And so his questions will never end," Dorict added. The two of them were looking over one of Marick's plays. Dorict crossed out passage after passage while his friend groaned.

"The only thing left will be the introduction and the applause!" he protested.

Dorict snorted. "Those are the parts you like best."

Marick waved him away as if Dorict had turned into a bothersome fly. "Pfff! Tell me, Salick, does the king still want your heads?"

The bane, for she still wore the uniform which many had put off, nodded. "Not our heads," she said, "but he doesn't want to see our faces in the city."

Lord Andarack bristled at this. "Without your scouting in the North, we'd have lost this war," he said.

"That may be," Salick replied, "but when he recovered enough to shout, he ordered Garet and me arrested for treason and exiled ten years for our 'crimes.' The same for Bixa, Maroster, and maybe Tarix and these two, but I'm not sure of that. Supposedly, there's a list, but no guard will arrest the people on it. It doesn't much matter; Tarix and Relict are already gone to where Terrich stood to plan the new city, and nobody in their right mind would try to arrest Maroster, if only because that would set Allifur and Corfin on them. As for the king, I hear he's locked in his room now, under Lysere's care."

"Unless he's coming to banish you in person," Marick said, pointing with his remade cane at an ornate coach driving carefully down the narrow avenue between the tents. He shifted his stick to the other hand, the dagger-handle ready to be quickly drawn.

Garet and Salick looked at each other, and with the others took a similarly cautious stance.

The royal carriage, accompanied by mounted guards bearing spears, came rumbling to a stop in front of the banehall steps. A steward leaped down and opened the door, but it was the queen not the king who emerged, carefully, for she was holding her sleeping daughter against one shoulder.

"Greetings, all," she said. "She always falls asleep in the carriage! Oh, don't bother lowering your voices. She nearly slept through the whole journey to the Far South and back!"

Branet came forward and held out his arms to take the little girl, not yet a half-year old, from Lysere. He held her tenderly, smiling down into the baby's sleeping face.

"Ah! This child grows lovelier each day, as do you, my queen."

Lysere laughed. "Oh, Branet, you flatterer! A woman always seems lovelier as a mother, but I thank you for kind words in a bitter time."

"The king won't change his mind about us, will he?" Garet asked. He felt Salick's hand slip into his. A silence fell on the group.

"No," Lysere said, her eyes on them, full of sympathy and a touch of anger. "Though he's forgotten most of his list. I told him ten years was madness, and I would . . . well, I convinced him to reduce it to two years, though you must leave soon. I doubt the guards can pretend you're invisible for much longer."

"True enough," Bixa said. She came down the banehall steps, wearing no uniform, just a regular tunic and pants. Her sword hung at her waist and a pack rested on her shoulders. Blellat, in full guard kit, descended slowly behind her.

"The city guard may be fools and worse, especially under this lout's care," Bixa said, hooking a thumb back at Blellat, "but even he can't ignore you forever."

Her once second-in-command growled in protest. "Bixa! If I'm so bad, why don't you stay? I keep telling you, and everyone else, that I don't want to be captain of the guards. I never did!"

Bixa clapped her good hand on Blellat's shoulder. The other hung limply at her side, and Salick swallowed at a sudden remembrance of Master Mandarack, whose arm had also hung so.

Bixa sniffed. "You'll do well enough. Cirta's ambitious, so he'll nip at your heels – which should keep you diligent. Look, I'm sorry, Blellat, but I've had enough. I can't work in Shirath anymore. It's time to see new lands."

"We're glad of your company," Vinir said. "And your skills as a commander will have some value in the Far South, where they still wage war against the slavers."

"Wonderful," Bixa said. "More blood and fire! Well, at least Maroster and I won't have to wear silkstone boulders on our heads to fight those pieces of scum."

She gave Blellat a last look, half commanding, half commiserating, and the man left, grumbling.

"He'll do a fine job, if only out of spite," she said, and turned back to Vinir. "As for the trip, well, I'm glad to have such experienced guides."

Garet shook his head. "I can't imagine the guards without you, Bixa."

She tilted her head and looked at the young man who was, like Salick, still in uniform.

"It seems you can't imagine the banehall without yourself, Garet, but my mind's made up. It's time for me to leave Trax's service. No offence, Lysere, but the man's not well."

The queen sighed. "No, he is not, but I hope he will be. The lords" – she nodded to Andarack, who stood beside Branet – "have taken up much of the burden of reconstruction and the planning of a new city in concert with our friends in Old Torrick."

Marick whistled. "So it's true. Terrich is to be rebuilt."

"Yes," Lysere said. "The lands around that ruin – when they are cleared and planted – will take the surplus of our city, and some from Illick and Akalit as well, in gratitude for their support in the battle. I wish the king was involved, for it might distract him from . . . other thoughts, but it is Dasanat and some newly unoccupied banes like Masters Relict and Tarix who do most of the work. I'm afraid he just sits and broods. It is only when I bring our daughter to him that he seems like himself again."

At this, she smiled, and with the others looked to the child sleeping in Branet's arms.

Salick reached out and stroked the baby's cheek. "Lysere, you know that I wish you well, and I hope that Trax . . . finds his way back to you both."

The queen embraced the bane, and they stood that way for many heartbeats before breaking off to wipe away tears.

"Men are complex creatures," the queen said. "Remember that, Salick, now that you are wed."

"That's very true," Son-neen said. The girl had been using the time to read a sheaf of papers in her hand. She pointed at Marick. "This one's worse than a scrambled contract."

Marick raised an eyebrow. "Complexity is useful in a writer," he said. "But about our king, I think there's a good chance Trax will recover. Humiliation is painful but not fatal."

Lysere's green eyes narrowed, and Marick raised a defensive hand.

"I mean, now that the crisis is over, he has time to think about what he's done and feel all the smaller for it. Believe me, I know that feeling well. Your Majesty, he did terrible things, but if I can come back, so can he. That's all I meant."

Vinir cuffed the back of his head, gently. "Imp, perhaps you should go talk to him, since you're one of the few standing here who, I think, intends to stay in Shirath."

"Yes, you should," Lysere said, her eyes less angry but still fixed on the young man.

"Hah!" Son-neen said. "Caught again."

The others laughed.

Lysere smiled and took Garet's hand. "Congratulations on your wedding! Both of you. I'd say you're too young, but it does seem a very long time since we met at that banquet. Do you remember how I tricked you into sitting beside Trax?"

Salick smiled. "I believe all he remembers of that evening was your eyes, Lysere."

Garet protested. "No, I'm sure I recall there was a demon of some kind, after the meal, I think."

Bixa slapped him on the back. "Don't bother," she said. "I'd wish you luck, my queen, in all things, but you won't need it. The people will look up to you like they looked up to Trax, and with better reason."

The woman in question took back her baby and raised her eyes to the banehall's imposing façade.

"That may be, Bixa, but, since I was a child, I've looked to this hall to lead us. I promise it will again, in a new way. My child will know it as the greatest school in the Five Cities, perhaps the world. She will come here to learn from people like Dasanat and maybe all of you, in time. It is such a grand new world, my friends. Come back some day and tell us of the wonders you see."

They bowed, and the queen mounted the carriage. The steward climbed back into the box and shook the reins. Within the small space, the carriage managed to turn and wheeled away.

"I really do hope Trax gets better," Salick said, "for her sake, but the clawed fool still exiled us for two years."

"Better than ten," Branet said, frowning. "And Heaven shield Lysere, for she accomplished that much where I failed utterly."

"I hear you threatened to beat sense into Trax," Marick said. "Is it true?"

Branet's scowl deepened. "True or not, you'll put it into one of your wretched plays! Enough. Garet, Salick, what will you do now? Go south with Vinir and the others?"

The two banes looked at each other.

"We've talked about it, of course," Salick said. "Two years or ten, we still have to leave. We were wondering, Hallmaster, if you needed more observers among the Itaalk?"

Branet smiled, then chuckled, then laughed, nearly doubled over with mirth. The man seemed a decade younger when he straightened up.

"Well! It seems upon careful consideration that I do have two more places, especially for the only banes who have been to that clawed valley and seen the caves where demons are made. This treaty with the Itaalk still needs proving, on both sides."

"I'm almost sorry I'm going in the other direction," Vinir said, biting her lip.

Dorict shook his head. "I'm not. There must be more to life than demons, and I want to find it."

Vinir looked uncertain and turned to the hallmaster. "Branet," she said, "you know I'd go with you, but . . ."

Her words were stopped by the raising of a large hand. "I know, and don't worry. If there is a need, I'll send word and have no doubt of your answer. Learn how to make beauty in the City of Fountains, Master Vinir, and bring that back to us, if you will. We have lived with the ugliness of demons and death long enough."

He turned to Garet and Salick. "In any case, we cannot send too many, lest they think we mean to attack them. Yet we cannot send too few, or else we might miss some treachery on their part. We must hunt out all their secrets or risk them launching yet another attack."

He scratched his greying hair and regarded the two banes. "Now that I think of it, with the finer details of the treaty still in the air, I doubt we'll leave for the forest before midsummer. And you two must be out of Shirath very soon. Hmm. I'm sure Tarix and Relict would like your company and help if you chose to stay the next season in Old Torrick."

"Perhaps," Garet said, and a look of understanding based on long talks in the night passed between himself and Salick.

"There may be one or two things to take care of before we join you."

The hallmaster clapped a big hand on each of the bane's shoulders. "Well enough," he said. "I'm glad you offered. I would have asked, but I still held a little hope that Trax would relent and you two could live a normal life here in Shirath."

Garet smiled and shook his head. "Travel to dangerous places, hunting for hidden demons and confronting their masters? I thought that was a normal life."

CHAPTER 31

THE BANEHALL INFIRMARY

The physician had been by to check on her and the others early, making his "morning patrols" as he liked to call them. He moved slowly but had recovered somewhat from the strain of using the staff in such a long, single-minded effort to change them back. Sul remembered how his fingers had shaken, then steadied when he removed the jewel from her forehead. The stone's thunderous voice was finally silent, leaving her alone with her own thoughts. She looked at her fingers. They no longer ended in claws, or nails of any kind, an unfortunate side effect, Banerict said. The same was true for her hair and some of her teeth. The good news, according to the man, was that new teeth were growing back in. The bad news, according to Sul, was that it hurt like dragon fire and made her drool like an ancient.

She looked down from the banehall window. The people gathered on the steps were hugging each other and waving goodbye. One, Salick, looked up and raised a hand. Sul did the same, pressing it to the window. The reflection in the bubbled glass showed a mostly human face, scarred across the forehead but no longer something out of a nightmare. The young woman on the steps turned away, taking the hand of the young man by her side. Her friend was leaving, but she would not be alone. An amazing thing had happened. Once the story of a demon cure had spread throughout the remnants of the city, the people of Shirath had come to visit, to sit with them, bringing small gifts of clothes and food and promising work in the city-to-be.

Some of the others had spoken of going back to the North, now that the brigades were destroyed and the dragons had no reason to bring fire. This morning, Banerict had asked her if she intended to go with them. Sul remembered how she had laughed at the question. "No, I'll stay," she had told him, as always, searching for a way to make words in the changed hollows of her mouth. "This is a city of wonders."

EPILOGUE

The horses pushed through saddle-high grass. There had been a trail here once, packed down by sheep driven to market and by the poorly shod feet of a farmer and his family. At the end of the vanished trail, a cabin stood, flanked by a barn and a few leaning sheds. They all looked neglected, with shingles fallen from roofs and leaves blown in through the open doors.

Salick dismounted beside the cabin and tied her reins to a sapling. She peered inside and cautiously entered, stopping when the floor creaked. Two winters of abandonment and neglect had taken a toll. A table and chairs stood in the middle of the main room. An open door to the left led to a bedroom, though no bed remained. Above that was a loft, buzzing with circling bees. A ladder that might have given access to it was broken to kindling, but the hearth was empty. Ashes lay piled in windrows across the floor.

Garet stepped in behind her and took a deep breath. For his whole childhood, this had been his home. The limits of his world had been these walls and the sheep fields higher on the hill. He closed his eyes and listened. After a moment's silence, he heard his mother's voice singing when he fretted and cried at the mocking in his father's tone.

"Lost in memories?" Salick asked. She walked over to stand beside the table, the same spot she had stood two years ago when Master Mandarack had come to bring Garet to his new home. She put one hand on the back of the chair where he had sat that day, talking to Garet and his mother.

She caught Garet looking at her and smiled.

He went back outside and shaded his eyes to look up to the pastures and the rock where he once sat, dreaming of a life in Shirath. Those dreams had come true, though with more danger, joy, and grief than he could ever have imagined back then.

Garet smiled. He had learned how to throw rocks up there, flashing them past the sheep to control them. That skill had helped him survive his first year as a bane.

"This is all I could find," Salick said, joining him. "But I didn't climbed up into the loft, not with all those bees."

She held out a wooden spoon. Garet took it and looked at the handle, imagining Allia's tiny fist waving her favourite weapon at Garet's bullying brothers. Her fist was not so tiny now. On the way through the Midlands to this farm, they had stopped in Bangt and found his mother, Allaina, and his little sister, Allia, quite happy in their new lives, and happier still to see Garet.

There was much joy in the Midlands. Across that wide space between the North and South Ar, the news of a treaty with the Itaalk had been greeted as a Heaven-sent miracle. Farmers displaced by the sudden appearance of the demons more than two years before now spoke of returning to their abandoned lands and again plowing the deep, black soil that had made them so prosperous.

To Garet's surprise and delight, his mother had remarried. The man was a farmer, of course, and seemed the type of gentle spirit Allaina deserved. He saw no reason to tell her that her first husband still lived, carving beautiful little animals and brooding over his past in the Far North. Some secrets were better kept, and perhaps forgotten.

His sister wept when Garet left again, unsatisfied by his promise to visit again as soon as his duty in the northern forest was done. The only thing that convinced her to let go was Salick's promise that she could call her "sister" now.

"Shall we stay the night here?" Salick asked. She waited while Garet took a last look around.

"No," he said. "Let's go back to Three Roads and stay at the inn. We'll have enough of sleeping rough on the way back to Terrich."

The old ruins of Terrich, soon to be the newest city on the River Ar, was where they were to meet Branet's party and their reluctant Itaalk guides.

"Good," Salick said. "I didn't much like anything about this place when I first saw it."

"What?" Garet said in mock outrage. "Not even me?"

Salick looked at him judiciously. "I'll admit you grew on me, my dear husband," she said, smiling at her own words and mounting her horse.

"Race you to Three Roads," she called over her shoulder, and spurred down the overgrown track.

Garet grinned and climbed on his own horse. It was a spirited mount and had no hesitation in leaving this dreary place behind to chase Salick.

And neither did he.

LIST OF NAMES

Abenth: A Mask assisting in the city's defence.

Adrix: A former hallmaster of Shirath Banehall whose actions led to chaos in the city.

Alanick: A seer and astrologer of the Fifth Ward.

Allaina: Garet's mother, a gentle woman born in the Far North.

Allia: Garet's sister, a fierce child born in the Midlands.

Allifur: A young bane of Shirath Banehall. She and her friend Corfin often find themselves in trouble.

Andarack: A mechanical, lord of the Eighth Ward, Master Mandarack's brother, and married to Master Mechanical Dasanat. He has a newborn son, Mandoran.

Aralon: A Green Sash of Shirath Banehall who looks to Master Tarix.

Arict: A previous records master of Shirath Banehall.

Banerict: A skilled physician who serves in the banehall infirmary.

Banfreat: A baker who became the first Shirath hallmaster six hundred years ago.

Barick: Once the king's butler and now the historian.

Barla: A Sea Itaalk woman who lives with Garet's father on the shores of the Northern Sea.

Bereth: Lord of the Second Ward.

Bixa: Captain of the king's guard, wounded at the Battle of the Bridge.

Blellat: One of Captain Bixa's lieutenants in the king's guard.

Brada: A sandwalker of Old Carving Well. Yala's older sister.

Branet: Hallmaster of Shirath Banehall.

Canarr: A mechanical working with Marick's theatre troupe.

Cannel: A Gold Sash from the city of Akalit, in Shirath to help in the city's defence.

Chal-lat: A student of art from the City of Fountains. Close to Vinir.

Cheemon: Lord of the Fourteenth Ward.

Chetorth: A Gold Sash of Shirath Banehall who looks to Master Taron. He was wounded at the Battle of the Bridge but remains a bane.

Chitoroth: A Gold Sash of Shirath Banehall in charge of the Fifth Ward small hall.

Chon: Hallmaster of Illick Banehall.

Chovan: A master of Shirath Banehall who once taught Tarix.

Cirta: One of Captain Bixa's lieutenants in the king's guard.

Corfin: A young bane of Shirath Banehall and friend of Allifur.

Corix: Hallmaster of Old Torrick Banehall.

Cruster: A guard of the Thirteenth Ward. Her loyalty is to Kaela.

Dalesta: A Green Sash of Shirath Banehall who looks to Master Tarix and is a friend to Chetorth.

Dasanat: The master of all the mechanicals in Shirath. Married to Lord Andarack. She has a newborn son, Mandoran.

Dirst: The new leader of the Masks, a group that once challenged the banehall but are now allied with it against the demons.

Dorict: A Green Sash of Shirath Banehall. He is a friend to Garet, Salick, Vinir, and Marick.

Draneck: Salick's cousin and a Duellist who was demon-killed while trying to murder Garet.

Elessa: A palace steward, loyal to the queen.

Fillar: A man of both Northern and Itaalk heritage who befriended Garet when he and Salick travelled to the North.

Garet: A young man born in the Midlands and taken to Shirath Banehall by Master Mandarack to be a bane. He and Salick are in love.

Gost: A traitor to the city who is imprisoned beneath the palace.

Hanal: A shopkeeper and dealer in stolen goods living in the Fifth Ward's Maze.
He died killing the Caller demon, a fearsome beast who could control others of its kind.

Insall: The chief cook in the banehall.

Isaken: Lord of the First Ward.

Kaela: Wife of Lord Kirel of the Thirteenth Ward. She works with the king's agents to track down any traitors remaining in Shirath.

Ke: A sandwalker of Old Carving Well and Yala's grandmother.

Kesla: A Red Sash of Shirath Banehall. She once looked to Tarix.

Kirel: Lord of the Thirteenth Ward, husband of Kaela, and nephew to the traitor Gost.

Koret: Lord of the Third Ward.
Lord Andarack is his brother.
Lysere: The queen of Shirath. Mother of Noella and wife of
Trax.
Mandarack: A master of Shirath Banehall who trained
Salick, Marick, Dorict, and Garet.
Marick: Once a bane of Shirath, he is now an acclaimed
writer and producer of plays, in partnership with Son-neen.
Maroster: Once a henchman to the traitor Gost, he was
saved by Allifur and Corfin at the Battle of the Bridge and
has since supported the hall and the palace.
Meesa: A lead actor in Marick's theatre troupe.
Ratal: A Gold Sash of Shirath Banehall. He looks to Tarix
and moons over Kesla.
Relict: A master of Shirath Banehall and husband to Tarix.
He is a good friend of Hallmaster Branet and serves as the
hall's chief diplomat.
Riga: A Gold Sash of Shirath Banehall. She looks to Tarix.
Sabat: Lord of the Fifteenth Ward.
Sacourat: She was the Lord of the Fifth Ward until she was
murdered by the traitor Tiralsh.
Salick: A Red Sash of Shirath Banehall. She and Garet are in
love.
Shirin: An ex-Duellist who blamed Garet for the death of
her love, Draneck. She was exiled from the city of Shirath
and died killing a demon. She was acknowledged as a true
bane after her death.
Shoronict: A Duellist killed while attempting to assassi-
nate King Trax.
Shudan: A playwright who helped Marick learn the trade.
Shula: Chief of the king's agents.
Sicarth: Hallmaster of Akalit Banehall.
Son-neen: A determined young woman from the City of

Fountains. Marick is indebted to her, and she means to recover that debt by whatever means necessary.

Staxan: The new Lord of the Twelfth Ward.

Sul: Once a debt-held servant in the North, she was turned into a Human demon.

Tarix: A master in Shirath Banehall and wife to Relict.

Tarock: The son of Lord Tiralsh of the Twelfth Ward and a traitor to the city. He is imprisoned beneath the palace.

Taron: A master of Shirath Banehall. He is a friend to Relict and Tarix. Dalesta once looked to him. Chetorth still does.

Teelol: A Mask assisting in the city's defence.

Tiralsh: Lord of the Twelfth Ward, now fled after attempting to damage its defences.

Toonan: A lead actor in Marick's theatre troupe.

Trax: The king of Shirath.

Trest: A traitor who followed Tiralsh into the northern forest.

Vinir: A Red Sash of Shirath Banehall. She is good friends with Salick, Marick, Garet, and Dorict. She has feelings for Chal-lat, but events have separated the two.

Yala: A sandwalker of Old Carving Well who accompanied Vinir, Dorict, and Marick back to Shirath.

About the Author

Kevin Harkness is a Canadian author who, at a late age, began writing the books he wanted to read. He lives in Vancouver, walks a lot, and occasionally mutters.

https://kevinharkness.ca

www.ingramcontent.com/pod-product-compliance
Lightning Source LLC
Chambersburg PA
CBHW051142190726
48290CB00006B/1953